THE WIFE'S REVENGE

BOOKS BY EMMA TALLON

Anna Davis and Freddie Tyler series

Runaway Girl

Dangerous Girl

Boss Girl

Fierce Girl

Reckless Girl

Fearless Girl

Ruthless Girl

The Drew Family series

Her Revenge

Her Rival

Her Betrayal

Her Payback

Her Fight

Her Enemy

Her Feud

The Capello Family series

A Family Betrayal

Standalone Novels

Snow Going Back

# EMMA TALLON

THE WIFE'S REVENGE

bookouture

Published by Bookouture in 2025

An imprint of Storyfire Ltd.
Carmelite House
50 Victoria Embankment
London EC4Y 0DZ

www.bookouture.com

The authorised representative in the EEA is Hachette Ireland
8 Castlecourt Centre
Dublin 15 D15 XTP3
Ireland
(email: info@hbgi.ie)

Copyright © Emma Tallon, 2025

Emma Tallon has asserted her right to be identified as the author of this work.

All rights reserved. No part of this publication may be reproduced, stored in any retrieval system, or transmitted, in any form or by any means, electronic, mechanical, photocopying, recording or otherwise, without the prior written permission of the publishers.

ISBN: 978-1-80550-182-4
eBook ISBN: 978-1-80550-181-7

This book is a work of fiction. Names, characters, businesses, organisations, places and events other than those clearly in the public domain, are either the product of the author's imagination or are used fictitiously. Any resemblance to actual persons, living or dead, events or locales is entirely coincidental.

*For my babies, Christian & Dolly.
It's all for you. Always.*

ONE

'This is all just completely absurd. It really is. We hooked up once. Just a bit of fun between colleagues, nothing sinister, for God's sake. Then suddenly here I am, bloody enemy number one. Christ, it used to be that girls *liked* men showing them a bit of appreciation. These days you can't even look in their direction without being hauled in for *sexual harassment*.' The man in the seat on the other side of Maria Capello's desk rolled his eyes. 'Clearly she's sore I didn't want to follow up after our little rendezvous. That's all this is. That girl is absolutely begging for attention, every single day. I mean, sorry to be uncouth here, but you can practically see her cheeks, her skirts are that short. Why dress like that if you don't want to be noticed, eh?'

Maria took a deep breath in and exhaled loudly, before replying. 'Mr Campbell, you're not just facing charges of sexual harassment, you're facing charges of *rape* too.' She sifted through the papers in her hand and shook her head. 'What you claim was *a bit of fun*, the complainant attests was several weeks of you touching her inappropriately in the office, followed by you pushing her into the print room one evening, while you were both working late, and forcing yourself on her.'

'Lies,' the man declared, folding his arms over his protruding waistline. 'She was just as up for it as I was. Ask the boys I work with. Dave, or Ian. Go on – they'll tell you. She'd been flirting with me for months.'

'Dave or Ian? They're friends of yours, are they?' Maria asked.

'Yeah. And they'd be happy to stand up in court with character references,' he confirmed.

Maria's bright hazel eyes narrowed as she stared at him across the desk. 'Lot of good that'll do you when they play the CCTV.'

'What?' The man paled, and his eyes widened.

'They have CCTV in the print room, Mr Campbell,' Maria told him, a hard edge to her tone. 'It's right here in the report. So, to put it in as simple terms as I can manage for you' – she leaned forward – 'you're fucked.'

He wetted his lips, panic beginning to show in his expression. 'But, hang on, you can explain that, right? That it ain't what it looks like. Or – or, well, I never gave my permission to be filmed in the office, so that's inadmissible evidence, isn't it?'

'I won't be explaining anything,' Maria answered coldly. She gathered the papers together and shoved them across the desk towards him. 'Take these and get the hell out of my office.'

His jaw dropped open. 'What? But I need a lawyer! I'm trying to hire you, for God's sake!'

'I wouldn't represent you if my life depended on it,' Maria replied.

'But...'

'The answer is no. I don't represent rapists,' she said firmly. Her gaze darkened as she glared at his gaping mouth. 'Now, *fuck off*.'

After staring at her in shock for a couple of seconds, he grabbed the papers and stormed out of the room, muttering insults under his breath.

Maria watched him go, with the distinct feeling she wasn't the first lawyer to turn him down. She detested men like him. Men who thought they were above it all. Who thought they had enough money or power to treat women however they wanted and get away with it. Men who used their natural advantages to rape women who'd said no, like the detestable creature she'd just ejected from the room. It rarely stopped there, though, she knew. Because those men enjoyed the thrill of using their superior strength against those physically weaker than them, far too much. They used it to control women, or to bully and belittle them. Sometimes, if they felt untouchable enough, even to take their lives.

A sour feeling rose from her throat, and she swallowed it down, twisting her chair to face the wall of windows behind her.

It was bad enough knowing that there were men out there like that. That there always would be. But knowing there was one so close to home festered like a sore in her core. Knowing her own brother, Antonio, was capable of what he'd done and that he'd walked away with no consequences whatsoever ate away at her like a cancer. And there was nothing she could do about it.

Perhaps, as a lawyer, she could have. But she was, first and foremost, a Capello. One of the heads of a thriving criminal firm, alongside her other brother, Alex. Which meant that she'd had to protect Antonio. She'd had to allow their men to cover up his messes, to bury the bodies of the girls he'd brutally killed, somewhere they would never be found. And although this had been the final straw for them, and Antonio had been ousted from the firm, he still walked free. He still worked the parts of the business they'd allowed him to take. His life hadn't changed that much. He hadn't paid for what he'd done. And the reality was, he never would.

Not many things got under Maria's skin. She'd been

brought up in the life. Her father had made sure she'd grown a thick shell and could deal with the darker sides of the underworld they thrived in without baulking. But this had got to her. Bad things happened, but knowing it was Antonio, her own blood, who'd done that to innocent women – just because he could – left a weight on her soul.

Running her hands back through her long, dark caramel-streaked hair, Maria stared out across the smoky rooftops of Central London and forced her mind off the subject, pushing the guilt she carried back into the mental box she kept it in. It wouldn't do to dwell on this, not today, she told herself firmly. She purposely moved her attention elsewhere – over the sharp lines of steel and concrete down below her prestigious top-floor office, across the river and over the edge of the city to one of her other, more nefarious enterprises.

The Capello siblings ran a multitude of illegal operations, some well known to the rest of the underworld, some they protected the privacy of fiercely. They printed and laundered money, they provided local protection and kept the peace between warring gangs. They bought and sold a variety of things on the black market. They had run drugs throughout their North London territory until recently. But this part of the business was now solely in Antonio's hands. A grudging parting gift, after they'd gone their separate ways. What the Capellos were most well known for, however, was their problem-solving services. If there was a problem that someone in their world, or sometimes outside of their world, couldn't solve, the Capellos would find a resolution. And they'd do whatever it took to do so.

Maria slipped one slim leg over the other and eased herself back in the chair, deciding to take five minutes for herself before ploughing ahead with the rest of her day. But her moment of relaxation was short-lived, as the shrill ring of her phone shattered the silence. With a tut, she reluctantly swung her chair back around and answered.

'What is it?' she asked.

'Antonio collared Danny last night,' her brother Alex's deep voice rumbled down the phone. 'Sent him back with a message.'

Maria's frown deepened at the mention of their other brother's name. It seemed he would continue to haunt her thoughts today, whether she liked it or not. 'Which is?'

'He wants a sit-down.'

Maria's face darkened, and her lips pressed together in a hard line. 'No.'

'We need to find out what he wants,' Alex urged.

'He wants back *in*, Alex,' Maria shot back. 'That's what he wants.' And that was *never* going to happen.

'We don't know that,' Alex replied.

Maria scoffed.

'Alright, yeah, he does. Of course he does,' Alex continued. 'But we don't know that that's what *this* is about. It could be serious.'

'It could be a waste of our time,' Maria countered.

'Maria.' The word was full of soft reproach and was followed by a heavy silence.

Maria sighed and rubbed her forehead, stressed. Alex was right. They did need to find out what this was all about. Antonio was many things. A liar, an unpredictable liability, a cold and violent man she'd often suspected might actually be a psychopath. A suspicion not helped by his latest antics. But he was also smart, savvy when it came to business and, unfortunately, their brother.

'Fine,' she agreed. 'But we set the place and time. And he comes alone or we walk.'

There was a short silence, and Maria guessed that this was likely because Antonio had also demanded the same terms, and Alex was probably weighing up which of his siblings was going to be the easiest to talk down.

'OK,' Alex said, his tone grim. 'I'll tell him it has to be

tonight. Get it over with. Leave no time for him to plan anything shady. Where do you want to go?'

It was Maria's turn to pause, as she pondered this. 'Gino's. Nine thirty. I'll call Gino, get him to close early.'

'Done,' Alex said quietly. 'But, Maria?'

'Mm?' She frowned into empty space, already not looking forward to this meeting.

'Don't tell Mum,' he warned.

'You don't need to tell me that,' she reminded him. 'The last thing I want to do is bring it all back up for her.'

'Good. I'll see you later,' Alex said. The line went dead.

Maria put the phone down, and her frown deepened as she wondered what Antonio wanted. They had no choice but to go, but Antonio was still Antonio. He'd been cut off for good reason, and he was a man who loved to hold on to a grudge. She knew him better than most people did. She knew him better than he, or Alex, realised. And whatever Alex might think, she knew there would be nothing good to come out of this meeting. Nothing good at all.

TWO

Cat stood in the middle of the large, airy, empty room and turned in a circle, a slow smile warming her face. She took in the big sash windows and the ornate plaster moulding on the lofty ceiling that added to the character of the old property, and saw, in her mind's eye, exactly how she would decorate this room. The cast-iron fireplace needed a bit of love to get it back to its former glory. Perhaps she and her daughter, Orla, could paint it white, to match the windows. She would leave the soft buttery yellow walls as they were and perhaps add some greenery to complement it.

Yes, she decided. *That's exactly what it needs.*

'Mummy!' Orla's excited voice broke through her thoughts. 'Nonna says that big room at the end upstairs is all *mine!*'

Cat's smile widened as her three-year-old's infectious excitement caught hold of her. 'It is!' she confirmed. 'And the bathroom next to it is all yours too.'

Orla squealed and dashed back out to survey the extent of her new domain.

An older woman walked in, chuckling at the young girl's

retreating back. 'She is in her element,' she confirmed. 'Gorgeous girl.'

Sophia wasn't really Orla's nonna, but Sophia had insisted on the title, begging Cat for the privilege after lamenting that her own children hadn't had the decency to give her any grandchildren yet. And as she was the closest thing Orla had to a grandparent these days, Cat had been happy to assent.

Several months before, Cat's father had died, leaving her crushed. He'd been the only blood relative she'd had left in the world. In the aftermath of his death, her soon-to-be-ex-husband, Greg, and his mistress had defrauded Cat out of everything she'd owned, leaving her and Orla on the streets with no money, no home and no one to turn to. But following a chance meeting with Maria, Sophia's daughter, Cat had ended up working for Sophia, while she recovered from a bad fall.

It had been a rocky start between the pair, Sophia too stubbornly independent to want help, and Cat desperate to keep the position that at least paid for their room at a nearby B&B. Over time, though, Sophia had thawed, and the two had formed a great friendship. And when trouble had landed at Cat's door, in the form of Sophia's own son, Antonio, it had been Sophia and her other son, Alex, who'd held her up and seen her through the storm. It had also been Alex who had convinced Greg, through some rather extreme methods, to hand Cat back what was hers. He was the reason she was standing here today, looking around the beautiful new home she'd been able to buy for herself and Orla.

The kindness and support this family had given her when she'd had nothing to give back was something Cat would never forget and could never repay. But she would probably spend the rest of her life trying anyway.

Sophia looked at her watch. 'I need to go. I promised to help Nikki with the flower arrangements for her son's engagement party.'

'Oh, that's nice,' Cat replied, walking her to the door. 'I hope it goes well.'

'Yes, the party is tonight. You should come,' Sophia said, her eyes lighting up at the idea. 'You know she has another son who's single. Very successful, very good to his mother.'

Cat laughed. '*Oh no*,' she declared strongly. 'I've had enough bad luck in that department to put me off for a while.'

There was a short silence, and Cat bit her lip, feeling instantly guilty as Sophia cast her gaze away. She'd been thinking of her ex, Greg, when she said that, but she realised Sophia must be thinking of Antonio.

'I mean, marriage to an arsehole like Greg would put anyone off,' Cat added, pressing home her true meaning.

The corners of Sophia's mouth lifted in a quick smile of acknowledgement. 'I'll see you tomorrow then.' She squeezed Cat's arm and glanced over her shoulder to the stairs, raising her voice a little. 'Goodbye, *bambina*. Be good for your mother.'

'Bye, Nonna!' came the answering shout from somewhere upstairs.

Cat closed the front door behind Sophia and stared after her through the glass side window for a moment. She hated that she was the reason Sophia had cut contact with one of her children. It had been Sophia's own choice that had finalised the break in the family. But this still didn't make Cat feel any better about it.

From what she understood, Antonio had been a problem for his siblings for some time before it all blew up. But when he'd kidnapped Orla and tried to rape Cat, that had been the final straw. There had been others, Alex had told her. Other women who'd ended up in a very bad way. Antonio was sick. Twisted and broken inside. And he was beyond the stage where the family could pull him back into line. When Sophia had turned away from him, had disowned him in shame, Alex and Maria had cut him loose too. They'd given him part of the business and told him to go his separate way. That had been three months ago, and he hadn't come around to the house since. Not once.

Cat knew this because she'd been there nearly every day, still housekeeping for Sophia while her bones were healing from a fall. She didn't need the money, not anymore. After Alex had got everything back from Greg for her, she'd sold her father's company, and the house she'd once called home, and it had made her a fairly rich woman. But she'd sworn to keep helping Sophia until she was capable without her.

Looking down at the keys in her hand, Cat twisted them slowly. Today wasn't a day to think about Antonio. Today was a day to look forward. To celebrate closing on their new home. To enjoy the new life that two men had tried so desperately – and failed spectacularly – to take away from her.

'Orla?' Cat cast her gaze up the stairs. 'The delivery van will be here later with the furniture. How about we pop out and you can choose some new bedding.'

'Oooh, yes!' came the squeal of excitement.

Cat smiled as her daughter ran down the stairs to get her coat. No one would ever take anything away from the two of them again, she silently vowed. No matter what it took, no matter what she had to do, she'd make sure no one would so much as have a chance to pose a threat to them, ever again.

THREE

Alex Capello descended the few concrete stairs down from the busy Camden street and ducked under a low door frame covered in chipped black paint, into the small, dark grubby-looking dive bar below. Inside, there were a few small tables, an assortment of mismatching chairs, and a cloying mixture of damp, BO and stale beer permeating the air. Some rock music Alex wasn't familiar with screeched away in the background, and the bald man behind the bar stared at him with beady eyes as he entered the room.

Alex unbuttoned his light grey suit jacket and swept his gaze around, checking that no one was listening in as he approached the bar.

'Alright, Harry? How's the weather been?' he asked the barman. It was a coded question.

Harry twisted his mouth to one side as he considered. 'It's been alright. We expected a spot of rain so kept the laundry in, but it turned out sunny after all.'

Alex nodded, satisfied. Antonio hadn't tried his luck here since they'd parted ways. That was a good sign. Technically.

Alex had warned everyone at all their usual haunts what might happen. That Antonio was no longer considered part of the family firm. That he still ran the drugs but that he might overstep and try gaining access to some of their other enterprises and boltholes. And if he did, that he was not to be given access. But so far, other than an initial – and not wholly unexpected – raid on their main cash safe, Antonio hadn't stepped a toe out of line. It was quiet. Too quiet.

'I don't want to be disturbed,' Alex said in a low, stern voice as Harry lifted up the bar hatch to let him through.

Harry just nodded and handed him a set of keys.

Alex walked through the back of the bar and down the dark, dingy hallway behind, to a door. Checking over his shoulder, he unlocked this and relocked it behind him, before descending a set of stairs. Flipping the switch at the bottom, Alex waited for the dull lightbulb to come to life, then crossed the crate-filled basement to the wall of shelves at the back. The shelves weren't attached to the wall. Rather, they were a neat row of matching shelving units, butted up against each other and perfectly fitting the space. None were full. There were a few old boxes and some cleaning equipment, but they were empty, for the most part. Scanning the second set of shelves in, from the left, Alex pulled off a couple of heavier boxes. Then, dusting his hands off, he yanked it away from the wall, revealing a hidden door behind.

The keys jangled in his hand as he found the correct one and unlocked this door, then he slipped inside and closed it behind him. He was instantly enveloped in darkness, so pitch-black he couldn't even make out the general shape of the room, but a quick grope to his left revealed a string hanging from above. He yanked it, and a thin strip light flickered to life. Alex took a deep breath in and exhaled loudly as he looked around the small, square space. A desk and one wooden dining chair stood in the middle, nothing else around. At least, that was what it would look like to someone not in the know. Moving to the corner of the room, Alex hunched down and lifted the corner of the cheap grey linoleum covering the floor and rolled it back. Underneath, sunken into the ground, were four six-foot wide, rectangular safes.

He punched in the code to one of them and swung open the heavy lid, propping it up before reaching in and pulling out a smooth black box. Straightening up, Alex placed this on the table and opened it, then he sat down. His eyes raked over the Glock 19 nestled inside, and then over the two magazines and the silencer. He wouldn't need the silencer today. Or, at least, he hoped he wouldn't. Today, he only needed this for show. As a deterrent. And, of course, as a backup, should things go horribly wrong. But he couldn't dwell on that. Always meticulous about the state of his gun, when he had need to use one, Alex took the weapon apart and began cleaning it methodically.

They didn't keep weapons in their homes or in any buildings that were officially linked to them. Only fools put themselves at that kind of risk, and the Capellos were far too seasoned to make such a rookie error. It was how half the criminals trying to climb the ranks of the underworld got put away. It was often too difficult for the police to pin their actual crimes to them, with the need for concrete evidence and with such skilled lawyers around, binding the force with the very laws they fought to uphold. But possession of a deadly weapon, such as a firearm, came with a minimum sentence of five years' jail time. All the police had to do was find one on your property and – boom – your criminal career was over. Or put on hold at least.

Twenty minutes later, Alex tucked the freshly cleaned handgun into his waistband, buttoned up his jacket and locked up, making sure the shelves, and the floor before them, showed no sign of his visit. He jogged back up the stairs and through the hallway, only catching the warning glare in Harry's eyes as he stepped through to the bar.

'There he is,' came a sarcastic sing-song voice he knew all too well. He froze then turned to look into the cold brown eyes he'd known almost his entire life. 'My big brother.'

FOUR

'Well, ain't you gonna say hello?' Antonio asked, unable to help the smirk on his face as Alex tried and failed to hide his shock. 'What's the matter? Cat got your tongue?' He raised an eyebrow suggestively. 'I bet she got a bit more than just your tongue, after that hero act of yours. You fucked her yet?'

A flash of rage crossed Alex's eyes, and it seemed to snap him out of his shock. 'Don't you *dare* speak about Cat, you stupid cunt,' he growled.

Antonio scratched the side of his face as if considering his brother's words. 'Cunt I'll give you. But we both know I ain't stupid.'

'Oh, I beg to differ. I'd say going so far in your sadistic games that you get ousted from your own fucking family makes you pretty damn stupid,' Alex retorted.

Antonio felt a frisson of heat lick up his spine and settle in his chest, and he had to work to keep the nonchalant expression on his face. He sniffed and rested back on the bar stool with a cold smile. 'Well, I guess we'll have to agree to disagree, won't we?'

Alex glanced at Harry, and Harry took the hint, bowing out

and disappearing into the back. There was no one else in the tiny bar, so the brothers were finally alone.

Antonio subtly took in his brother's appearance. It had been a long and torturous three months without Alex. Antonio could live without Maria – they'd never been that close. But Alex was his brother. His wingman. His only true friend in the world. He'd thought Alex understood him. That there was an unspoken agreement between them. A loyalty that meant no matter what they did, or whether the other agreed, that they'd have each other's backs. But it had taken five minutes and a few pretty smiles from some nobody – from their *cleaner* – to take Alex away from him. To make Alex and the rest of his family banish him. Like he meant nothing. And that hurt.

'What do you want, Antonio?' Alex asked, his tone cool and controlled now.

Antonio let a devilish smile sweep across his face and then let out a low chuckle as Alex unbuttoned his jacket to subtly show that he was armed.

'Nice piece. Are we dick swinging now?' Antonio asked, cocking an eyebrow. He unbuttoned his own jacket to show that he was similarly armed and noted the flicker of confusion in his brother's eyes. 'You really think I don't have my own boltholes? I've got plenty you don't know about.'

Alex huffed out a humourless laugh. 'Good for you. Now answer my fucking question.'

Antonio took a moment to compose himself as his anger lashed and strained at the thin leash he had contained it with. Every part of him wanted to explode at Alex. Ask him why he'd betrayed him, why he hadn't backed him up over some stupid woman who meant *nothing*. But he knew that wouldn't get him anywhere. Alex would close up and leave. So he had to play this carefully.

'I apologise for my earlier comment,' he said carefully, holding his hands up in surrender. 'It was just too easy a pun. I couldn't resist.' He smiled, but it wasn't returned. He took in a deep breath and released it heavily through his nose. 'I understand that I went too far with everything, with Cat. And I understand why you felt the need to send me for this little time out.'

It grated like barbed wire across bare skin to utter such ridiculous platitudes, but it seemed nothing less than a good grovel was going to get him back into the family fold. And when it came to self-preservation, there wasn't a lie Antonio wasn't willing to tell.

'But it's time to end this now.' He eyed Alex seriously. 'No one gains from this game going on any longer than it has already. I will extend my apologies to Cat, and I'll smooth things over with Maria. Because we can't go on like this. It's getting ridiculous.'

Alex was silent for a couple of moments, a thoughtful frown knitting his dark brows together. 'Why did you come *here?*' he asked. 'Why *now*, when we had a meeting set for tonight? How did you even know where I was?'

Antonio scratched his forehead with his index finger. 'I had a watch on this place and a couple of others. Keeping tabs on you. Same way you were keeping tabs on me. And I came *now* because you're alone.'

'Because it suited you better without Maria here,' Alex surmised.

Antonio didn't bother to reply. They both knew it to be true.

'Thing is, Antonio,' Alex said, glancing away with a grim expression, 'this is exactly what you always do. We agree one thing between us all – set mutual boundaries and agreements – and then you undermine it all and just do whatever the fuck you want.'

Antonio frowned. This wasn't going the way he'd expected.

'And that wouldn't necessarily be an issue if you had your

own boundaries. If you weren't a complete liability. But you are.' Alex stared at him with a mixture of sorrow and hardness. 'You killed two women for no reason whatsoever. It wasn't a job, it wasn't necessary to protect the family, you just... killed them. Brutally. Violently. And then you hid that from us and forced our men to keep your secrets. To take sides within our own firm.'

Antonio made a small sound of dismissal but managed to keep himself from rolling his eyes. 'Is that what it's about?' he asked. 'Not Cat?'

'It's all of it,' Alex replied. He shook his head and pinched the bridge of his nose. 'You kidnapped a fucking *child*, Antonio. And even if all that hadn't happened, you were already a liability. You'd already pissed off so many people. Fucked up deals, lost us clients – Christ, you nearly caused a war with the fucking *Tylers*.' Alex shook his head again incredulously. 'Even before all this, we were trying to work out what to do with you. But then you went and tipped the scales all by yourself.'

The anger roiling inside Antonio reached boiling point, and he jumped up off the stool, moving towards Alex with fury in his eyes.

'How *dare* you talk about me as if I'm some employee you can sack off,' he roared. 'I'm your fucking *brother*. I'm as much a part of this firm as you are. *You* don't get to decide. *You* don't get to kick me out.'

'Yes, I *do*.' Alex grasped him by the scruff of his shirt and slammed him against the bar, his eyes blazing and his teeth gritted. 'Not alone, no. But it ain't just me, brother. It's all of us. It's Maria – it's even *Mum*. Did you know that? *Mum* was the one to give the order to get you *out*.'

The words hit Antonio like a physical blow to the gut, and shock wiped everything else from his mind. '*What?*' He recoiled, and Alex released him, stepping back. 'You're lying. It was *you*. You and your fucking obsession with Cat. Nothing else.' But even as he tried to convince himself of this, he could see from Alex's face that it was true. He shook his head, his brows furrowing. 'No. *No.*' He pointed a finger in Alex's face. 'You're a *fucking* liar.' His cheeks reddened. 'Mum would never do that to me. I'm blood.'

Alex turned and paced a few steps away, running a hand down his face, the anger having faded to a tired sadness. 'We'll exist in peace with you, Antonio. *Because* you're blood. But you ain't welcome in this firm anymore. Or this family. I thought we'd made that clear.'

'In *peace!*' Antonio grasped the bar stool in between them and threw it across the room. It collided with a set of tables and chairs, sending them clattering to the floor, but he barely noticed as he took a menacing step towards Alex. His eyes flared, and the veins in his temples bulged as he faced his brother with a feeling of pure wrath. 'This isn't peace, it's fucking *dictatorship*. It's *you*,' he seethed, 'freezing me out and telling me to go quietly.'

'Fine,' Alex replied. 'See it however you want. It changes nothing.'

Antonio glared at him, his entire body shaking with a mixture of pent-up emotions. He shook his head slowly, watching all the plans he'd made these last three months crash around his ears.

'You cunt. You two-faced back-stabbing cunt.' He backed away from his brother, knowing he had to leave now or he wouldn't be able to stop himself doing something he'd sorely regret. 'You made a big mistake today, brother. A fucking colossal one.'

Alex just stared back at him, his expression unwavering, and it simply served to madden Antonio even more. Antonio *had* been ready to bury the hatchet. He'd been ready to forgive them all for leaving him in the cold these past months. He'd even been prepared to grovel with apologies. But not now. Not after this. Because if they weren't family anymore, then they were enemies. And Antonio was about to show them just how stupid they'd been, to let themselves become his enemies.

'This could have gone so differently.' He pointed a finger at Alex as he reached the door. 'You just remember that when the shit hits the fan. And it will. That much I promise you.' A cold, manic look skewed his features, and he nodded to his brother, wondering if Alex had any idea what was about to come his way. 'You remember, Alex. *You* chose this.'

FIVE

'What do you mean?' Maria demanded, her face dropping into a furious frown. 'You *are* kidding me?' She sank back in her desk chair and ran a hand through her dark, caramel-streaked hair. 'Right.' Her voice fell flat. 'Well, I guess at least that frees up my evening.' She threw a hand half-heartedly in the air and let it drop down on the desk.

As she listened to Alex's brief account of the interaction with Antonio, she felt a hot ball of anger begin to bubble in her core. How *dare* he spring up on Alex like that? How *dare* he sideline *her* like this? Treating her like she was irrelevant. Unimportant. It was *just* like him. Antonio had always known how to needle her. Maria pinched the bridge of her nose, these thoughts of their younger brother gnawing away at her nerves as always.

'Look, I— Alex, I need to go,' she said shortly. 'It's done with. Forget about it. Nothing's changed. I'll catch you later.'

She put down the phone and heaved out a long, angry breath.

'*Fuck you*, Antonio,' she muttered.

For a few moments, she thrummed her long red nails on the desk, thinking of ways to relax and rid her mind of Antonio completely. Eventually, she decided on reaching out to Cat, to see if she fancied a glass or four of wine. That would definitely take the edge off.

Picking up her phone, she was about to call her when a message pinged up. She frowned. What on earth did *he* want? She opened the text.

We need to talk, Miss Capello. I'm at the Connaught. Come and meet me in the bar.

Maria's eyebrows shot up. Malcolm Ardley was a respected MP and one she had, not too long ago, blackmailed into making sure that the plans for two hundred houses to be built on land too close to one of her less legal ventures didn't go ahead. Not that he knew why she needed that of course. She'd not had to give him any reason after showing him the CCTV video of his passionate rutting with the Secretary of State's wife on the poor man's desk. It had been a simple arrangement. He stopped the build, and Maria didn't leak the tape and destroy his life. But she'd had no need for him since, so why on earth did he want to talk to her now? She texted back.

My diary is full, I'm afraid. Feel free to contact my secretary, who will come back to you with a suitable appointment.

She pressed send and made a mental note to tell Jen, her assistant, to drag her heels if Malcolm did pursue this. Picking up her bag, she went to throw the phone inside then paused as another reply pinged through. She clucked her tongue in annoyance as she opened it. And as the image became clear, her olive skin paled, and she dropped her bag to the floor in shock.

. . .

Fifteen minutes later, Maria entered the Connaught and made her way to the bar, trying to calm her racing heart. She needed to keep a clear head for this. She needed to figure out exactly how bad it was, without giving away her fear. To show fear would be to show weakness, and Maria Capello was anything but weak.

Malcolm sat wedged in the corner of a dark green overstuffed sofa, his protruding belly resting on his thighs as he took a sip of what appeared to be an Old-Fashioned. His beady eyes glinted as he caught sight of her, and his mouth widened in a slow smile.

As Maria walked over, she absently wondered what on earth the Secretary of State's wife, and all the other women he cheated on his wife with, saw in this man. With his thinning blond hair, ruddy complexion and weak chin that was almost swallowed up by the rolls of his neck, he wasn't exactly every girl's dream.

'Miss Capello,' he drawled in a silken voice that reminded her of a snake. 'Do take a seat. What would you like to drink? The cocktails are *very* good here.'

Maria had to work not to clench her jaw as she sat down opposite him. She forced herself to relax into the seat and held his gaze across the table with a cold smile.

'Why did you send that photo to me?' she asked calmly. 'Is it supposed to mean something?'

Malcolm guffawed, as if she'd just shared the funniest joke he'd ever heard. 'Come now, Miss Capello. Let's not play games. I have you by the balls, and you know it.'

Maria studied him and crossed one slim leg over the other, as if settling in. 'I think you and I might be on very different pages, Malcolm,' she told him, using the crisp plummy accent she only put on while at work. Something she'd learned to do back at university, so that her own accent didn't cause her to stick out in the legal world as she climbed the ranks. 'You're going to have to explain in a little more detail.'

'I suspected you for a while, you know,' he told her, clearly in no rush. 'There was something about you. Something... something more cut-throat than the rest of us. And in a room full of lawyers, that's really saying something.'

'I'll take that as a compliment,' she replied.

'Oh, do. Do,' he replied, nodding. 'And it truly is. But you see, I like to understand the people I'm in bed with. So to speak.'

He waggled his bushy eyebrows and gave her a flashy little smile that Maria assumed was supposed to be flirty. It only served to make her feel a little nauseous.

'I was just curious to begin with,' he continued. 'But then after you tried to blackmail me—'

'Succeeded,' Maria interjected. 'I don't like the word *tried*. It implies I wasn't successful, and we both know I was.' She widened her smile, pressing home the reminder of the advantage she had over him. Both then and now.

'Mmm.' Malcolm squinted and cocked his head to the side as though in contemplation. 'Perhaps at first. And, actually, even when I did happen upon this rather juicy secret of yours, I wasn't going to say anything. I figured it was best kept in my back pocket, for a rainy day. Or the promise of a sunny one.'

Maria frowned. 'I'm not following.'

Malcolm stretched his back and took another sip of his drink before replying. 'I quelled that build you so... *kindly* asked me to.' His look was accusing. 'But you see, I've had another interested party approach me with a very, *very* attractive offer, if I arrange it so that *they* can build there. The sort of offer I just can't refuse.'

Maria's stomach tightened. 'Well, you'll just have to find a way to.'

Malcolm shook his head. 'No, I don't think I will. I have

you, Maria Capello.' He pulled a brown file from his briefcase and passed it to her.

She opened it and flicked through the photos inside, trying not to curse. They were all of her. Walking into The Raven's pub, walking out again. Watching as it blew up, her head held high and a hard, satisfied smile on her face where there should have been horror. The last two pictures were of her calmly paying off the homeless man in the alley, with the building burning behind her. It was incredibly damning, even without physical evidence. She snapped the file shut and moved her gaze to meet his.

'You've become real pro at Photoshop, Malcolm. I'll give you that.' She offered him a cold smile.

Malcolm returned it. 'And that might have held up as a defence, had I not got the raw negatives squirrelled away, to prove them real.'

Maria felt her heart plummet. If that was true, she was fucked. She exhaled slowly as she desperately tried to come up with a plan.

'What do you want, Malcolm?' she asked flatly. 'Let's cut through the bullshit, shall we? If you really wanted to use this story you *think* you have, you would have done it already.'

'As astute as always, Maria,' Malcolm chuckled. 'Here's how this is going to go. And *no*, it's not a negotiation. I'm going to lift the red tape I tied so neatly around that land, so that my new friends can build houses. And *you* are going to do nothing. Absolutely nothing.' He smiled and held his hands out, as if pressing home the simpleness of the situation. 'That's it. However...' His tone turned cold. 'If you leak the footage you have of me with my lady friends, or even so much as start a *rumour* about my private affairs, then I'll have you arrested and make *sure* these photos get into all the right hands. Do we understand each other?'

Maria was almost shaking with the mixture of fear, shock and rage his words evoked, but she simply gripped the arm of her chair, staring into his eyes with an unreadable expression.

'That doesn't work for me,' she managed, forcing the words out through gritted teeth.

'Oh, I'm sorry, I must not have made this clear.' Malcolm shifted forward in his seat, his gaze growing colder. 'I don't *care*. What I *do* care about is the financial freedom this deal will afford me, once it has all gone through.'

'From a lovely bolthole in the Cayman Islands, no doubt,' Maria spat.

'Jersey, actually. Not quite so exciting, I know, but...' He shrugged. 'I like London too much to go that far.'

'You have nothing on me, Malcolm,' Maria said strongly. 'It's not a crime to be in the vicinity of a tragic accident.'

'And yet, you're here,' Malcolm countered. He closed his briefcase. 'If you weren't afraid of those pictures coming to light and your personal life being dug into by the authorities, we wouldn't even be having this conversation. So try me.' He held her gaze with one that told her he wasn't messing around. 'Ruin me and see where it gets you. Somehow, I don't think you will.' He stood up and buttoned his suit jacket. 'That's the annoying thing about sweeping dirt under the carpet, Miss Capello. There's always the threat of someone lifting it up. And now I know you like a good sweep...' He paused, a dark glint in his eye. 'Well, you've suddenly become a lot more interesting. I wonder what else I'll find.' He turned and walked away, leaving Maria staring after him with pure hatred and gritted teeth.

Once he'd disappeared from view, she cursed under her breath and dug into her bag for her phone. As she pulled it out, a waiter appeared and left a small silver tray on the table, a folded piece of paper laid on top. Malcolm's drinks bill. Maria almost laughed out loud at his final slap in the face, but things had just become far too serious for her to muster any outward humour right now.

Her mind was reeling, questions racing around her mind as all the implications began to sink in. How on earth had Malcolm got hold of those pictures? Who had taken them? And, most importantly, how on earth was she going to get out of this mess?

SIX

Alex pulled up on his driveway and killed the engine. Pausing for a few moments, he rested his head back and exhaled tiredly. He wondered, for the twentieth time since he'd left the bar, whether he was making the right choice in bringing the gun home. It wasn't a wise thing to do under normal circumstances. The police didn't need much of a reason to search their homes and known premises, and if a weapon like this was found, he'd be facing time. But something in Antonio's eyes had sent a shiver right through him.

Antonio had never quite been like other people, even by their standards. There had always been something more cold, more competitive and more unpredictable about him. He was a little eccentric, a little flamboyant. He liked to put on a show. And this had always been part of his charm. But those who found it charming often never saw the darker side of his personality. Alex was more than familiar with all Antonio's faces, but he'd never looked upon them as an outsider before. He'd never felt his brother could be a threat to *him*, until now. And Antonio's famed unpredictability meant that Alex had no way of knowing what to expect. Antonio might turn up one night to murder them all in their beds. Or he might crash a family party laden with gifts and a gun, trying to force them all to play happy families again. Whatever he eventually decided to do, it just seemed prudent to make sure there was a weapon within easy reach. Risky move or not.

Touching his jacket, where the gun was tucked underneath, Alex got out of the car and made his way into the house. As he opened the door, his eyebrows rose in surprise. For once, instead of the clinical apple smell of their cleaner's surface spray, there was a delicious garlicky aroma in the air. The air was warm, and the lights in the kitchen were on. Realising he'd paused in surprise, Alex closed the door behind him and continued into the kitchen.

Bianca, his wife, was busy pouring a glass of wine, humming along to the tune coming out of the radio behind her. She jumped a little when she saw Alex in the doorway, her wine sloshing over the side of her glass onto the kitchen side.

'Oh, Alex! I didn't hear you come in,' she said with an awkward laugh.

He grinned. 'Clearly. Here...' He walked over to the roll of kitchen paper and tore some off, wiping up the spill as she lifted her glass. 'Something smells good.'

'Yeah, I made us lunch,' Bianca stated proudly. 'You know. Like a good little wife.'

The last part was tinged with sarcasm, but it seemed to be in good humour, so Alex chuckled. 'Lucky me,' he remarked. 'What are we having?'

Bianca had cooked for him a grand total of three times before now. Two of these occasions had been in recent weeks, following the near breakdown and attempted rescue mission of their marriage. The first of the recent dishes had been a ham salad, and the second had been cheese on toast. The smell currently wafting from the oven, however, left him feeling hopeful that Bianca might be venturing into more complex culinary waters.

'Mushroom risotto,' Bianca replied. 'Hence the wine. I read it pairs well.'

Alex nodded, impressed. Perhaps Bianca was finally finding something she was interested in, beyond drinking herself into oblivion and gambling all his money away. Cooking was a great hobby to get into. Lots of scope for creativity. But as he opened the bin to drop the kitchen towel in, Alex's hope faded. The packaging from the ready meal for two sat at the top. He closed the lid and turned back to her, forcing another smile. Maybe tomorrow she'd find something to capture her attention.

Their marriage had been an empty sham for years. At least, that's how Alex felt. They had drifted apart, argued and bickered until any connection they'd had had been destroyed. Bianca spent her time boozing and spending and generally ignoring him, and Alex had buried himself in work. But even though their marriage had made him deeply unhappy, Alex took his responsibility as a husband seriously. When he'd married Bianca, he'd made that commitment for life. Through thick and thin.

For a long time, he'd thought that nothing short of an ultimate betrayal could break their marriage. But eventually all the bad times and all the poison that was slowly eating away at their relationship got too much. Bianca finally pushed him to the brink, showing some truly ugly colours, and Alex had been ready to call it quits. He'd told Bianca he needed space to think and had been working up the courage to tell her it was over. That he was leaving. But at the last moment, Bianca had seemed to wake up. She'd seemed to realise what she was doing to them. She'd stopped fighting him and had said she wanted to try.

It had been hard to stay then. Almost impossible. After all they'd been through – and looking around at the wreckage, he wasn't sure was still salvageable – all he'd wanted was for it to be over. But despite it all, one thing hadn't changed. Him. His values. And so he'd stayed. He'd stood by her and agreed that they would try, together, to make this work. And so far, things weren't terrible. They certainly weren't great, and there were days Alex felt like they were back at square one. But he could see Bianca was trying. And whilst she was trying, he would try, too. Because that was what marriage was. It was a team effort.

Alex's phone chimed, and he pulled it out of his pocket to look at the screen. It was a text from Maria. With a frown, he opened it and scanned the message.

Big problem. Meet at the house ASAP.

'Do you have to be on your phone right now?' Bianca asked. 'I mean, we are supposed to be having lunch together.'

It was one of the things they'd agreed to doing. Lunch together at least once a week. Alex felt a pang of worry at Maria's words but tried to focus on Bianca.

'Mm? Yeah. Sorry. Just... give me a minute,' he replied.

Bianca huffed but didn't protest, so he typed out a quick response.

Will be about an hour but call if urgent.

Alex bit his top lip and slipped the phone back in his pocket.

'So, what did you do this morning?' he asked, taking the wine glass she offered him.

It was the wrong question, he realised, a second later. Bianca froze, her body tensing and her lips pursing.

'Why?' she asked, her tone belligerent now.

Alex stifled a sigh. 'No reason. I'm just showing an interest.'

That's what he was supposed to do, wasn't it? That's what

all the marriage self-help bollocks online said at least. *Show an interest in your wife's day when you get home, as this tells her you care.*

'What, so you can keep tabs on me?' Bianca replied, sounding distinctly prickly.

'No,' Alex replied, annoyed. 'Because I'm interested. If I wanted to keep tabs on you, I'd already fucking know.'

Bianca's eyebrows shot up, and Alex sighed loudly, rubbing his eyes with his thumb and forefinger. 'Look, I ain't trying to argue with you, Bianca. It was just a question.'

This was why it felt so damn impossible, some days, to be with her. He could barely have the simplest conversation without it turning into a full-on fight, and he was tired.

Bianca's expression soured. 'Yeah, sounds like it. Nice one, Alex.' She picked up her wine and stalked past him out of the kitchen. 'Enjoy your lunch.'

'Bianca,' Alex started, holding a hand out towards her. 'Hey. Come on. Let's just have lunch together, OK? Let's not do this today.'

The oven timer pinged, and with one last huff, Bianca slammed the kitchen door.

SEVEN

Streaks of sunshine broke through the leaves of the magnolia bush outside the window and landed on the spread of photographs, now laid out over the square wooden coffee table in Sophia's lounge. Neither Maria nor Alex still lived there – indeed, they'd all moved out into their own places years ago. But this house was still the family home, and the hub for all their business dealings.

Maria sat back on one of the large cream sofas surrounding the coffee table, her eyes glazed as she bit down on one of her long red nails. Alex was on the other sofa, leaning forward as he frowned at all the pictures in turn. Danny and Joe, two of their closest men, were also in the room. Each waiting quietly to find out what was required of them, their faces careful masks of neutrality.

'He claims he has the raw negatives,' Maria said quietly, knowing her brother would be going through the exact same thought processes she'd had not an hour before.

Alex ran a hand down his face. 'Who else would he have shown these to?'

'I can't be sure, but, knowing how he works, I'd wager it's

just him and whoever took the photos. He's too careful to involve anyone unnecessarily,' she replied.

'Who took them?' Alex mused.

Maria shrugged. 'Politicians like him use photographers to do this sort of dirty work all the time. But they always pay top whack for the negs, so they're the only one with the information. Whoever it was, they'd have sold him the lot and moved on to the next job without a thought.'

Alex nodded, but the worry didn't leave his expression.

'What's the plan then, boss?' Danny asked from where he perched on a windowsill across the room.

Both Maria and Alex looked up, but it was Maria he was directing the question to. Maria whose problem this was. She stared back at him for a moment before speaking with quiet determination.

'We need to find the negatives before we make any big moves. Get the others, organise a tag team to follow him. And I mean everywhere. I want to know where he keeps things. I want the layout of his office, eyes on it if we can get a camera in. I want to know his comings and goings, his little habits, who he meets with, what he's working on, who these new people are that want to buy the land.' She sat forward, driving home her point. 'I want him so covered it's like our own personal season of *Big Brother*. If he so much as shits, I want to know where and when, and you need to keep covering all of this until we can work out where he's keeping the raw negs. Or at least make a decently educated guess.'

Danny pushed forward off the ledge. 'On it.'

Joe nodded and followed him out.

'I'll reach out to Bill Hanlon,' Alex said. 'See if I can recruit him to help us out with eyes and ears.'

'Good idea,' Maria replied.

Bill Hanlon was an ally and sought-after freelancer in the murky depths of the London underworld. Once famed for his daring escapades as a bank robber, he now used his considerable tech skills to help steal information. If anyone in their circles needed hidden cameras, listening devices, hacking services or anything else illegal and high-tech, he was the man to go to.

There was a short silence before Alex asked, 'What's the situation if we can't get on top of this?' He turned to look at her. 'What would it take to move it?'

Maria made a sound of derision. 'The whole operation?' She shook her head slowly. 'It's not possible. The workers, the bunkers, sure. With time they could be set up elsewhere maybe. But there's years' worth of intricate set-ups in there. It's bedded in too deep.' She leaned forward on her thighs and dropped her head into her hands.

The venture Malcolm was now threatening to allow houses next to had been her pride and joy for a long time. It was her favourite enterprise, one she'd cultivated all on her own. One that had proved very lucrative over the years. Up until now, it had remained hidden from view. Mainly built underground, it was linked to the world above by entrances hidden by old barns. A small underground village of activity that had taken her years to perfect. No one outside their inner circle knew it existed.

Even the fifteen men and women who worked there were hidden from society. People she'd approached with the offer of working for her, mostly when they were facing the probability of life sentences in prison. It was an unusual perk of her job, having access to such desperate people. And they'd been more than willing to swap a life inside a miserable concrete cell for a secret life in a country commune where they were valued and rewarded for their loyalty. It had been the perfect set-up. Until now.

The only way she'd been able to keep it so under wraps thus far was because it was so remote. With all the supplies required for fifteen people and the operations they were managing, coming in and out, it was too busy not to be noticed by two hundred new neighbours. If this build went ahead, she'd have to shut it down and start again from scratch. Years of hard work all down the drain.

'I don't care what we have to do to fix this, Alex. We just have to,' she said, sounding resolute.

He lifted his eyebrows but didn't disagree with her. He knew what this would cost them as much as she did.

There was a sound by the door, and they both looked over to see their mother, Sophia, enter the lounge. She was drying her hands on a tea towel, which she then folded as she walked over to peer at the photos splayed across the coffee table.

'Well, that's not good,' she observed. She glanced over at Maria. 'Who sent you these?'

'The politician I blackmailed to stop the build near the bunkers,' Maria told her.

Sophia's mouth tightened. 'And what do you plan to do about it?'

'We're on it, Mum,' Alex informed her. 'We'll find the negs, clear up any copies and scrub things clean. Don't worry.'

Sophia sniffed, her expression still pinched, and she lifted an eyebrow at her daughter. 'If he's dug up this much, I doubt taking it away will deter him from looking for more. *No.*' She shook her head. 'You can do better than that. You don't keep your special skills secret for nothing.'

She gave Maria one more long, hard look and then walked back out of the room. Maria stared after her, thinking about it. She was right. Malcolm wouldn't stop here. He'd just keep coming. He'd told her as much in the bar.

Biting her bottom lip, Maria picked up her phone and found Malcolm in her contact list. She hit call and put it to her ear.

'What are you doing?' Alex asked, frowning.

Maria put her finger up to shush him as the call connected. 'Malcolm, hi.' Her professional tone kicked in. 'I've been thinking about our talk earlier, and I've had a possible idea I want to put to you, but first, I just need to check, have you already put the wheels in motion to lift the red tape on that land?'

'Not yet,' came the bored drawl down the line. 'I've been a bit busy and, of course, I wanted to make sure you and I were on the same page first.'

Maria nodded. *Good.* This was good. 'I have a proposal that I think could give us both what we want, and more, but I just need to run a few numbers. See if I can move some things. Could you hold off for one week?'

There was a short pause and then a low groan of reluctance. 'That's a big ask, Miss Capello.'

'One I wouldn't put to you if I didn't think it would be worth our while,' she countered. 'But I do. I really do. You said you wanted complete financial freedom. Well, if I can pull this off, then you won't have to worry about money for the rest of your life.'

Another short pause and then a sigh. 'One week,' he agreed. 'I'll hear you out because I'm curious as to what you could possibly have to offer, but I'm not promising anything. If I don't like what I hear, I lift the red tape as planned.'

'Thank you.' Maria forced the words out in a pleasant tone that was far from her true feelings.

'One week,' he repeated.

'One week,' she confirmed.

And then the line went dead. She chucked her phone back into her bag and turned to face Alex. He held her gaze for a moment and then shook his head.

'If you're thinking what I think you're thinking, then I agree,' he told her.

'What is it you think I'm thinking?' Maria asked.

'You want to take him out, right? I know you're just buying time with that bit of bait you just dangled,' Alex replied.

Maria frowned and tilted her head to one side. 'I don't know. I think it's too risky.'

'It's riskier not to at this point,' Alex argued. 'Like Mum said, he won't stop. He made it clear earlier that he wasn't done.'

Maria rested back into the sofa, running her hand back through her long dark hair. 'He's a high-profile hit. If we do it, it won't just go away. Old Bill will chase this case like hounds at the first smell of blood.'

Alex turned to face her, his gaze hardening. 'Not if there's no blood to be found.'

EIGHT

Perspective was a funny thing, Cat decided, as she stared at a neon pink wooden lamp that had been carved into the shape of a monkey with an oversized black velvet shade covering its face.

'It's a powerful piece, don't you think?' came a woman's voice in a thick Parisian accent.

It needs to be, if it has any hope of getting light out through that shade, Cat thought wryly. Knowing this was not what the saleswoman meant, though, she simply murmured a vague agreement.

'Such a bold statement piece. A piece that really tells people who you are,' the saleswoman enthused.

Cat's brows puckered, and she shot a sidelong glance at the woman. 'Mm,' she murmured again. 'It's, er, *interesting*.'

'And only seven thousand three hundred,' the woman replied.

'*What?*' Cat couldn't help but exclaim.

'I know.' The woman smiled. 'A steal, huh?'

Cat's eyes widened, and she clamped her mouth shut before giving the woman a polite smile and moving on.

'Let me know if you need any more information on any of our pieces,' the woman called.

'Will do,' Cat replied. '*Jesus Christ*,' she muttered under her breath.

Turning back on herself, once the woman had walked away, Cat made her way out of the shop and hurried on down the busy London street. She'd been hoping to buy a few things for her new house while Orla was at pre-school, but that place had definitely not been for her. Even with all the money she now had in her bank, she would never pay those sorts of prices for a damn lamp. Especially one that was so outrageously tacky.

As she turned the corner, she almost collided with someone and sprang back, the automatic apology already on her lips.

'So sorr— Oh! Alex!' She smiled up at him.

'Cat, what are you doing here?' The corner of his mouth quirked up in a return half-smile.

'Well, I thought I'd try some of these swanky furniture places for a few special bits for the house, but...' She trailed off as she glanced back at the shop she'd just departed. 'Well. They're not really what I was expecting.'

Alex followed her gaze. 'Yeah, the shops around here are all super overpriced. What sort of thing are you looking for?'

'Um, I don't know exactly,' Cat replied with a laugh. She pushed her chocolate brown hair back with one hand. 'Was hoping to find a couple of nice bits for Orla's room and some lamps for the lounge. Maybe a statement chair for that alcove bit in the hallway.' She shrugged.

Alex glanced back over his shoulder and scratched the back of his head. 'I know somewhere you might like. A friend sources stock for a load of boutique furniture places in London. Has a warehouse not too far from here actually. He don't usually sell direct to the public, but he's always happy to sell to me. I could give him a call, see if he could let us in to have a look around?'

'Really?' Cat's eyes lit up. 'That would be amazing, but are you sure it's not putting you out? You're on your way somewhere, right?'

Alex shrugged, the material of his perfectly tailored suit briefly crumpling under the movement of his broad shoulders. 'Nothing that can't wait.' He checked his watch. 'I've got time. Come on. I'll drive.'

Fifteen minutes later, they stepped into a large brick warehouse with tall ceilings, full to the brim with the largest array of furniture Cat had ever seen in one place. Nice stuff too, she realised. Not one neon monkey in sight. She pushed her hands down into her pockets and shook off a shiver. It was next to freezing in here, but she didn't care. It was like walking into a treasure trove, and she was only too happy to dive in, cold or not.

'Alright, Leon?' Alex said as a tall man approached.

'Alright, mate,' Leon replied with a crooked smile. 'Good to hear from ya. What you guys after?'

'Not sure just yet. We OK to have a look around?' Alex asked.

''Course,' Leon replied. 'Anything you want, I can deliver next Thursday. And you just add your usual discount to it all. OK?'

'Thanks, Leon,' Alex said with a nod. 'You're a good man.'

'Thanks to you,' Leon replied with a wink. 'I'll leave you to it.'

Cat watched the man walk off with a cheery whistle and then glanced at Alex. 'What's your usual discount?' she asked.

'Thirty per cent off the marked price,' Alex replied, leading her forward. 'Which is basically all his profit.'

'Wow,' Cat replied, slowing to look at an ornate mosaic-topped coffee table. 'That's very generous. How come he gives you that?'

A small smile lifted the corner of Alex's mouth. 'I did him a very big favour once.'

'Ah.' Understanding dawned. 'Like the kind of favour I asked you for?' Cat looked up at him again.

'Not quite the same but... sort of,' Alex answered, glancing back at her.

Cat nodded. That made sense. It was what the Capellos were best known for. Being solution men. Freelance fixers. It was something that should have shocked her. *Would* have shocked her, not so long ago. Back when the law was right and anything else was wrong. Back before she questioned such rigidity. But that had been before she'd found herself in need of services like theirs. Before she'd got to know Alex and Maria and Sophia. Before they'd taken her under their wing and had looked out for her and Orla in more ways than anyone in her previous life ever had. Save her father of course. Now she saw life, and the way the Capellos navigated theirs, from a very different viewpoint.

'Oh, look at this!'

Cat moved a chair aside to clear the way to a beautiful double dressing table. It was bleached wood with curly winding vines carved around the edges and, over the two matching mirrors, delicate leaves sprouted off, painted gold.

'Oh, Orla would *love* this,' she breathed. 'I could put it in my room for us both to use.'

'She would,' Alex agreed. He leaned over to pick up the price tag and angled it towards her. 'That's not a bad price either, after the discount.'

'It's brilliant,' Cat agreed. She bit her lip.

'What is it?' Alex asked, sensing her hesitation.

'I'm just wondering if it would fit in your car,' she admitted. 'I don't really want to wait until next Thursday.' She laughed.

Alex grinned and looked back at the piece of furniture

appraisingly. 'It would if we take it apart. I think it's in two pieces.' He knelt down and looked underneath.

Cat knelt next to him and peered under too.

'Yeah. See there?' Alex pointed to a join. 'That's hidden on top, but it comes apart. I could fit it in if we break it down and then put it back together for you at yours. Yeah.' He nodded. 'We'll get this home for you today.'

Cat suddenly felt overwhelmed with gratitude at his kind offer, and with a squeak she flung her arms around him. 'Thank you. Thank you, thank you, *thank you*,' she declared. 'Orla's going to love this so much.'

Slightly startled but with a smile, Alex turned his head to face her. 'You're welcome,' he said with a laugh. 'She deserves it.'

'She does,' Cat agreed.

Alex's warm eyes held her gaze, and Cat noticed, for the first time, just how many shades of brown and gold there were in them. This close observation, in turn, made her realise that she still had her arms around the man, and her cheeks immediately flushed pink.

'Oh God. I'm sorry,' she said awkwardly, pulling away. 'I didn't mean to fling myself on you like some complete weirdo.'

'That's OK,' Alex replied, straightening up and dusting off his hands. 'Happens all the time.'

Cat straightened up beside him, feeling embarrassed. 'Really?'

Alex chuckled. 'No. Not really. Probably a good thing though.'

'Yeah, of course,' Cat replied, trying to regain composure. 'I'm sure Bianca wouldn't love that.'

'No.'

At the mention of his wife's name, a cloud descended over Alex's face, and Cat immediately wished she could take the words back. Her brow briefly puckered, and she almost reached out to him but stopped herself.

He seemed so incredibly unhappy at times, in his marriage, and it pained her to see it. Alex was such a good man. He deserved to be happy. But that wasn't her business. She had to stop thinking about it, stop saying things like that. It wasn't her place to comment. She was, after all, just another employee. Family friend too, but certainly not one close enough to comment on his marriage.

Cat took a deep breath and tore her gaze from his. 'Shall we...?' She gestured towards the front of the building.

'Yeah. 'Course. Let's get going,' Alex replied.

He strode off, and Cat followed, feeling unsettled. She'd overstepped just then, and her mind had gone to a place it had no right to be. She needed to be careful around Alex. Very careful indeed. Because the Capellos had become her lifeline in recent months, in more ways than one. And she really couldn't afford to mess that up.

NINE

Bianca checked her rear-view mirror nervously as she circled the block one more time, then pulled into the underground car park beneath Antonio's building. As Alex's wife, she shouldn't even be talking to Antonio, let alone visiting him at home. And if she had her way, she'd have washed her hands of him, like the rest of them. But she'd always got on with her brother-in-law. More with him than the rest of them really. And perhaps, in part, this was because they were both so used to falling out of favour with the rest of the family. But this time was different.

This time Antonio had gone too far. He'd messed up big time, and in return, the family had completely cast him out. It had come as a huge shock to her. A wake-up call as to how vulnerable she really was. Because if they could do it to *him* – to their own blood – then they could certainly do it to her. She'd always felt fairly safe. Alex took his responsibilities in life very seriously – too seriously at times. And so, being his wife, the woman he'd vowed to love and protect until death, had given her a level of security reserved for very few. But even that wouldn't save her if he ever found out what she'd done. Which was the only reason she was here.

Bianca took the lift up to the top floor, nervously pushing her loosely curled light brown hair back behind one ear. The light behind the buttons moved up steadily, and as they neared Antonio's floor, she cast one more glance in the lift mirror. She ran a finger under the corner of one heavily kohled eye and smudged her red lips together, before pinching her cheeks. Of Italian heritage, her skin was a natural shade of warm gold, but today, the stress of everything had seemed to leech the warmth right out of her, leaving her complexion sallow and tired.

As the lift doors pinged open, Bianca heard the dull thuds of the dark angry rap music coming from Antonio's flat before she could even see the door. For a moment, she hesitated, wishing she could turn back and return when he was in a better mood, but she knew she couldn't. He had too much over her to be ignored. And he'd been growing increasingly impatient for her to find the time to slip away and come over. She sighed and marched down the hall, not bothering to knock before she walked in. He wouldn't hear her anyway.

The volume instantly increased to a level at which she could barely even think, and she closed the door quickly behind her. Turning to survey the large living area of his penthouse flat, Bianca squinted and wrinkled her nose. The place was dark, all curtains drawn, and the air was filled with a lazy haze of smoke. As her eyes adjusted and she finally located her brother-in-law, she let out a small sound of shock and disapproval, turning quickly away.

'Jesus *Christ*, Antonio.'

He sighed and pushed the woman – naked other than a lacy red thong and suspenders – away from him. 'What's the matter, Bianca?' he drawled, annoyed. 'You jealous?'

Out of the corner of her eye, Bianca watched the woman wipe her mouth with the back of her hand and shoot her a glare. Cringing, Bianca gritted her teeth.

'Plenty of me left to go around, if you ain't getting serviced well enough at home,' Antonio continued.

Bianca rolled her eyes and crossed her arms, turning a little to give the woman some privacy as she dressed. The music went off, and she heard a zip being pulled up before Antonio stood. He reached for a roll of cash on the side table and began peeling off some of the notes.

Hiding a sound of disgust, Bianca walked over to the windows and ripped open the curtains before throwing open the windows. The flat stank to high heaven of smoke, weed and stale aftershave, to the point that she was sure she was going to gag if she didn't get fresh air in soon. She waited at the window, breathing in the fresher air and steadily ignoring the exchange behind her, until Antonio's lady friend was gone. Then, as she heard him shut the front door, Bianca finally turned.

Now there was some light in here, Bianca could see that her brother-in-law was shirtless, his lean, well-defined muscles bared, along with the sharp V of his hip bones as they disappeared below his trouser line.

'Are you gonna put a top on or what?' she asked bluntly.

'Depends,' he answered. 'Want to finish what she started?'

'*Ugh*, would you *stop?*' Bianca exclaimed. 'I'm married to your brother, for God's sake.'

'Oh, fuck off, Bianca,' he replied breezily. 'We all know you would. You've already had half of London behind his back, why not carry on the trend with me?'

Bianca froze, and her eyes widened. 'What are you on about?' she asked, trying to feign ignorance.

But Antonio merely smirked. 'You might have him fooled into thinking you're as loyal as he is, but I've had your number for a *while*.' He sat back down and lit another cigarette. 'Had you followed on a few of your nights out. Quite a *busy* little bee, aren't ya?'

Bianca swallowed. 'You don't know what you're fucking talking about.'

'I do though.' Antonio took a deep drag and blew out a long plume of smoke. 'You, nipping off to the toilet stalls and back alleys with those young men you snap up. Seems you'll go anywhere, really, where you think you won't be seen. Except you *were* seen. And you also *were* photographed, my dear sister-in-law.' Antonio smirked again, clearly enjoying himself. 'You really should have been a bit more careful.'

'*What?*' Bianca uttered, naked fear on her face.

How had she been photographed? Who had seen her? If Alex found out, her life was over. She gripped the windowsill to keep herself steady as a strange light-headedness took over.

'Oh, don't worry. I've got the only copies. And luckily for you, I don't like my brother very much right now,' Antonio told her. 'So your secret's safe with me. Not that I need it anyway, eh? I've already got so much over you, you have to do what I say for the rest of your life.' He grinned, the action cold. 'Bit of a waste really. All this dirt on one person.'

'Fuck you, Antonio,' Bianca spat, her anger simmering as he tried to make her squirm.

'Like I said,' he retorted. 'Be my guest. Seriously, though' – he raised an eyebrow at her – 'that many men? You've got a fucking problem, mate.'

'Says the man who was just getting his dick sucked by a fucking prostitute,' Bianca shot back flatly.

'Er, it's sex worker actually. Have a bit of respect,' Antonio replied. 'And the difference between you and me is that I *know* I've got a problem. I'm just perfectly OK with it.' He shrugged.

Bianca took a deep breath in and released it before speaking again. There was no point trying to reason with Antonio. Not when he was like this.

'Still, I guess you need something to distract yourself from my brother's little fling with old Kitty-Cat, eh?' An amused glint lit up his eyes as he lifted a challenging brow.

The barb hit home, and Bianca snarled at him. 'He *isn't* sleeping with her.'

'Not all flings are physical, you know,' Antonio replied.

Bianca gritted her teeth as he twisted the knife further. 'What do you want, Antonio?' she asked, changing the subject. 'You asked me to slip away to come and talk to you, and here I am. So seriously, what do you want?'

Antonio took another deep drag of his cigarette then blew the smoke out sharply as he ground it out into the crystal ashtray next to him. 'I want you to do me a little favour,' he told her.

'What kind of favour?'

Bianca could feel her palms getting moist as her nerves began to jangle around her body. Antonio had warned her when he was cast out. He'd warned her that this day would come. The day she'd have to do whatever he asked or face the very real threat of him bringing her world crashing down around her ears. But for three months there had been nothing, and she'd stupidly relaxed, nestled in the bosom of a false sense of security. Now, though, it seemed her luck had finally run out.

'I want you to bring me something, that's all. Nothing major,' Antonio replied.

Something glinted in his eye, and Bianca felt a shiver run up her spine.

'If it was nothing major, you'd be able to get it yourself. Why do you need me?' she asked.

Antonio scratched at his cheek with his forefinger. 'Because it's something my brother and sister don't want me to have.'

Bianca clenched her jaw, her worry intensifying. 'Just get to the point.'

'Few weeks back, Alex moved the printing business over to a hotel in Paddington,' he told her. 'We own a share of the place.

Payment for a job. Alex had the smart idea of moving the whole production there. Our percentage of the place covers roughly one floor's worth of rooms, so we took over the top floor indefinitely, and now, from what I understand, he runs it all from there.' He stood up and tilted his head to one side with a grudging look of appreciation. 'Clever really. Hiding it in plain sight. With so many people coming and going, it don't look suss at all. And it's one of those hotels you need to put the key card in the lift, too, to get access to your floor. So only people Alex sorts out a key for can get up there.'

'When you say printing, you mean the funny money, right?' Bianca checked, her brow puckering slightly.

'Well, we ain't printing Christmas cards, are we?' Antonio responded, walking over to stand beside her at the window.

Bianca ignored the scathing tone. 'So, what do you want?'

'There are four sets of printing plates in the machines. Two sets for creating the fifties, two for the twenties,' he explained, leaning against the sill. 'I want you to bring them to me.'

'*What?*' Bianca asked, astonished. 'You're joking, right? You just said Alex has the floor locked down; he's hardly going to give *me* a key, is he? And even if he did, even if I somehow found some legitimate reason to have one – which I doubt I could – it would be a bit bloody obvious when two minutes later all the plates are gone!'

'Yeah, if you were that stupid that you announced it, I'm sure it *would* be bloody obvious,' Antonio agreed, rolling his eyes. 'You don't *ask* him for a key, Bianca, you *steal* one. And then you steal the plates.'

Bianca paled. 'How am I supposed to do that?'

'I don't know, and I don't care,' he replied seriously. 'But I need those plates. Those cunts have cut me out of everything except the drugs. And they only let me keep that arm of the business because they ain't got any idea how it runs. But by rights, a third of our family business belongs to me. So if they won't give me what I'm due, I'll simply take it. And fuck the lot of them over in the process.'

Bianca stared at him for a moment, wondering if he'd finally gone insane. She wasn't some master thief, for God's sake. The only thing *she* was good at breaking into was a decent bottle of fizz.

'No,' she said, shaking her head. 'No. I'm sorry, Antonio, I can't. I have no *idea* how I'd do that, and I know, if I tried, I'd definitely get caught. I'm *not* prepared to—'

But she didn't get to finish her sentence as Antonio suddenly lunged for her, pushing her back against the wall, one hand around her throat.

'I think you're forgetting one very important factor here,' he snarled into her ear. 'And that's that I *own* you. *You* were the one who told me where Cat's kid went to pre-school and what the password was to pick her up, remember? *You* were the one who suggested I take her. Remember *that*, Bianca? Eh?'

Cold fear gripped Bianca by the heart as he said the words out loud, and the fingers around her throat suddenly felt a little tighter. She nodded frantically as she struggled to draw in a breath.

'Yes,' she squeaked. '*Yes!* You've made your point.'

'And not that they know that *either* of us were involved in this one, but don't forget, *you* were also the one who asked me to go and set that fire at Cat's place. Remember that?' Antonio reminded her. He leaned in closer until she could feel his hot breath on her ear. 'I no longer have anything to lose with my family. But *you* certainly do. And I'd hate to see you cast out in the cold, Bianca. 'Cause we both know you wouldn't fare very well at all without my brother.' With that, he released her and stepped back, his chiselled face set hard as he stared at her.

Bianca's hand flew to her throat, where his grip had been just seconds before, and she swallowed. 'I'll, um, I'll figure it out,' she stammered.

'Good girl.' Antonio stepped forward and gently righted Bianca's leopard-print shirt. 'Let's all get a win out of this one, eh?' He touched his hand briefly to the underside of her chin and smiled. 'Keep me updated.'

Bianca nodded then began moving towards the door as Antonio turned away from her. She suddenly felt like a walking bag of jelly. As though the buzz of her nerves pinging around her body like a swarm of angry bees was the only thing still holding her up.

'Oh, and, Bianca?'

She turned at the sound of Antonio's voice, dreading whatever he was about to say next.

'Don't keep me waiting long,' he warned.

''Course,' she managed.

Not waiting to hear if there was any more, she moved as quickly as her jelly legs would allow, only releasing the deep breath she'd been holding, and bending over to lean on her knees, when she was inside the lift again.

What was she going to do? How on *earth* was she going to pull this off? Antonio wasn't bluffing. She knew him well enough to know he was more than capable of pulling her under the outcast bus with him if she didn't deliver. Except when *she* ended up under that bus, there wouldn't be a golden cushion to break her fall, like *he'd* had.

Cursing him under her breath, Bianca felt the first tears fall just as the lift doors reopened to reveal the underground car park. An old man stood waiting for the lift, and he blinked, startled, as he took in Bianca's devastated face. The startled look swiftly softened to one of concern, and he took a half-step towards her.

'Are you alright, love?' he asked gently.

Bianca stared at him for a millisecond before swiping away the tears with the backs of her hands and fixing him with a dark glare. 'Oh, go eat shit and die,' she snapped. Leaving him gaping at her in shock, she marched past him towards her car.

This *wasn't* going to beat her, she decided. She could do this. She'd survived marriage with one of the hardest and most powerful men in London for years. She'd *cheated* on that powerful man more times than she could count, right under his nose, and managed to keep it hidden, every single time. She played with fire every God damn day of her life, so was something like *this* going to be her undoing? No. Not if she had anything to say about it.

She was going to get those plates for Antonio, and then she was going to demand he cut her a piece of the pie for her troubles. Because if this little fright had taught her anything, it was that she needed some money on her side. Money of her own that Alex had no control over. Because if it ever really did go to shit, she needed a golden cushion of her own.

She unlocked the car and slipped in, feeling ten times better than she had just minutes ago. She could do this. She just had to figure out how.

TEN

Cat tapped her pen on the pile of papers she was looking at and loosed a long, contemplative breath. These accounts weren't in the worst state she'd seen so far, but they could definitely be better. All the various businesses under the Capello family empire seemed to have had different people running their double accounts, which certainly had its merits, considering the illegality of them. Tight circles like that meant that if one arm went down, the others were still protected. But this method had its drawbacks too.

'Whose system was this one?' she asked, looking up over the dining table at Alex.

They were at Sophia's house, who was currently busy cooking something that smelled delicious in her kitchen, at the other end of the large open-plan space. All the awkwardness she'd felt around Alex at the furniture warehouse the day before had thankfully disappeared, and they were back to normal, buried in their work.

'Mine,' Sophia called out, holding one arm up as if to claim her mark on it, whilst keeping her eyes trained on whatever she was mixing on the stove.

Cat nodded and caught Alex giving her a small knowing grin over the table. She quickly returned it, checking that Sophia hadn't seen, then cleared her throat.

'It's a great system,' she declared. The last person she ever wanted to offend with her true opinion was Sophia. She owed the woman so much.

'*Pah...*' Sophia swiped a hand in their direction as if to dismiss the compliment. 'It's a basic system, and it's outdated. I know this. You don't need to pussyfoot around me. Back in the day when I would help my husband – God rest his soul – hide the money, this was the *only* way to do it, if you wanted to be smart. But things have changed. This is too simple. You should change it.'

This was, of course, why Cat was here. She worked for the Capellos now, as the firm accountant. But she didn't want to seem too eager. Much as Sophia sounded like she was on board, Cat knew it was important to make it seem as though this was her idea. If Cat made it clear this was what she'd intended from the off, it might embarrass her.

'I don't know, it seems pretty good.' Cat chewed the end of her pen, as though considering it. 'But if you think it needs some work...' She trailed off with a shrug.

'Yeah, I mean, it wouldn't hurt to pull it into line with the others, just to keep things streamlined,' Alex added, as if in silent agreement with her to push this over the edge gently.

'It would make things quicker, I guess,' Cat said slowly.

'Exactly,' Sophia agreed. 'Listen, if you are happy to include those in your work with Alex and Maria, then please do. I always hated doing those accounts. They're a pain in the backside, so you'd be doing me a favour.'

'Yeah? OK, well, if it makes life easier for you, then of course I will,' Cat replied.

'You're an angel,' Sophia said, wiping flour off her hands. 'Right. I'll be back in a bit.'

Cat waved as Sophia walked out of the kitchen and then turned to Alex with a smile.

'Nicely done,' he said with a low chuckle. 'That would have gone a whole lot differently if you'd told her what you really thought.'

Cat laughed. 'I know.'

'So, where are we now?' Alex frowned down at a long line of codes in the notebook before him.

'I think we're pretty much there,' Cat replied.

Three months before, she had offered Alex her accounting services in return for assistance in getting back everything her soon-to-be-ex-husband had stolen from her. She'd already proven her loyalty by that point, having provided Alex with an alibi in a compromising situation with the police, and once she'd asked to enlist his services, she'd crossed the line of no return. He'd asked her, repeatedly, in those first few weeks if she was sure she knew what she was getting into. He'd reminded Cat that she came from a very different world. That she'd always lived within the safety net of the straight and narrow path of life. But what her ex had done to her and her daughter had changed Cat. It had hardened her and vastly altered her views on the world and on the people around her.

She'd made the decision then that she'd rather surround herself with people who were truly powerful, who would protect her and Orla at all costs, no matter the situation, than with people who acted righteous and obeyed the law but could stab her in the back the moment she didn't fit in with their plans. And so she had jumped in, head first and with her eyes wide open.

Alex had eventually stopped stalling and had slowly introduced her to the various parts of the business. They'd been working through all the different books together; Cat coming up with ways to better hide their money and suggesting more streamlined approaches in their general operations. And this, finally, was the last set of books she had to get familiar with and take over.

'I can have these straight within a few days. This side of things is simple enough,' Cat told him, closing the file. 'I do have a request though. Well, two actually.'

'Oh?' Alex arched one dark eyebrow at her.

Cat pushed a stray lock of her chocolate brown hair back behind her ear. 'I need an office. Somewhere to work from that isn't here and isn't my home. I don't mind running through things here sometimes, but it's too risky to have the books here all the time.'

'Of course,' Alex replied. 'I was going to talk to you about that actually. There's a nail salon in Paddington with a small apartment above it that we use for various things. We sorted out a bit of trouble for the owner, a while back. That was part of his payment to us. I've had one of the rooms made up into an office. You can work from there. There's no paper trail linking it to us, so it's a safe hideaway.'

'OK.' Cat smiled. 'Sounds great.'

'What's your second request?' Alex asked.

'I'd prefer the books to be kept off-site, away from that office and all your operations,' she replied. 'It reduces the risk of them being found significantly. Even if they did find the office and did decide to raid it. Or, you never know, the nail bar below might get raided. The last thing you want is for your cooked books to be caught in their crossfire.'

Alex watched her over the table, his warm brown eyes glazing for a moment as he nodded slowly. 'You'll have to meet me halfway on that one,' he told her. 'The reason I set your office up in Paddington is that I've had all the books moved to a location nearby.'

Cat mentally rifled through all the Capello locations she was familiar with and then frowned. 'The hotel?'

Alex nodded. 'We own a whole floor, and it's well secured.

Our interest in the place is hidden behind a string of offshore accounts, and even if someone did figure it out and raided the place, they'd never find the books.'

Cat bit her bottom lip as she calculated the risks of keeping them there. At the end of the day, it wasn't up to her. This wasn't her business; it was Alex and Maria's. They called the shots. She simply worked for them.

'If you're sure that's the safest option...' she said eventually.

'It is,' Alex confirmed. 'It's a very secure location. I mean, if that place ever got raided, the books would be the least of our worries. But even then, they'd be too busy with what was right in front of them to notice anything else. The books are very well hidden.'

'Where are they?' Cat asked.

'There's a housekeeping closet near the lift that's no longer in use,' Alex replied. 'There's a load of junk in there, but at the back, behind the shelves where all the cleaning products are stored, there's a loose wall panel. Behind that, there's a crawl space. Doesn't lead anywhere, which is perfect. So all the books are in there. You'll be the only one who has access, so you'll need to come back and forth with them, but it's only around the corner.'

Cat nodded. 'OK. That sounds like a good plan.'

There was a bang in the hallway as someone opened and shut the front door. Footsteps indicated that it was someone coming in, but neither bothered to look up. Cat knew it was likely Maria.

'I'll get you a key card for the hotel today,' Alex told her. 'Make sure you keep it on you at all times. Don't ever leave it unsupervised.'

'Of course,' Cat agreed.

'It will be plain, so it won't be obvious what it's for,' Alex continued.

Cat nodded and turned expectantly as someone entered the

kitchen. She almost smiled in greeting but then paused, her heart dropping as she saw who it was.

'Bianca,' Alex greeted her, sounding surprised. 'What are you doing here?'

'That any way to welcome your wife?' Bianca retorted, throwing Cat a narrowed glare before smiling sweetly at him. 'I was hoping I'd find you here. Take me to lunch? Thought we could have a redo of yesterday. Somewhere I don't have to cook.'

'Er...' Alex scratched the back of his head awkwardly, his handsome face scrunching into an apologetic grimace as he opened his mouth to let her down.

'You go,' Cat said, cutting him off before he could do it. 'It's fine. You can show me another time. I've got to get Orla from pre-school soon anyway.'

'You sure?' Alex's deep brown eyes searched her face, and Cat forced a smile.

''Course.'

'Alright then.' Alex stood up, straightening his fitted white shirt and then glancing at his watch. 'Where do you want to go?'

Bianca gave him a smug little smile and raised her chin in the air. 'There's that new Turkish down the road I wanna try. Take me there. Come on. Let's go.'

Turning on her heel, she gave Cat one last snooty glance down the length of her nose and then walked out. But just as Alex began to follow her, Bianca paused and walked back in. She pursed her lips and studied Cat for a moment.

'You and me,' she said unceremoniously. 'We should go for drinks sometime. You know. Seeing as you're now a permanent fixture around here.'

Cat's slim eyebrows shot upwards in surprise. Up till now, Bianca had been rude to her at best, and downright awful to her the rest of the time. She'd even been convinced, for some reason, that Alex and Cat were having an affair – which had been a laughable suspicion really. The only thing Cat had been able to think about, when she'd first arrived, was getting a roof over her and Orla's heads, after her cheating husband had scammed them out of everything. She certainly didn't want to be the cause of someone *else's* husband cheating. And even if she *had*, Alex just wasn't the type to cheat. He was too honourable, too good a person to do that. Bianca should have known that. But she'd accused them both anyway. Perhaps now, though, she'd finally come to her senses.

'Er, sure,' Cat said, trying and failing to come up with a reason she could use to get out of it. The last person she ever wanted to *go for drinks* with was Bianca, but she could hardly say no.

'Great,' Bianca replied with a quick tight smile. 'How about tomorrow?'

'Um...' Cat stalled. 'That might be tricky. I've got Orla, and there are some things I'm sorting out, but, er, maybe later in the week?'

'OK. What day works for you?' Bianca replied.

Clearly, she was not going to let Cat out of this, now she'd decided to befriend her.

'Um, I'll need to just check my diary. I left it at home, but I'll have a look tonight and let you know.' Cat smiled, hoping the other woman would accept this response.

Bianca rolled her eyes impatiently. 'Text me tonight then,' she demanded.

'Will do,' Cat replied cheerfully.

Bianca swept back out of the kitchen without another word, and Cat let out a long whooshing breath as Alex followed after her.

The front door slammed shut, and Cat stared down the hallway through the narrow side window, where she could just make out Alex opening the car door for his wife. Hopefully, Bianca wouldn't wind him up *too* much today. She always seemed to find reasons to fight with him. Reasons to piss him off and stress him out. The woman was pushing him further and further away, and she seemed not to even notice. Or perhaps she did. Perhaps she knew, as the rest of them did, that no matter how big a pain in his arse she became, he wouldn't leave her. That he'd stay in that miserable marriage because he was too honourable to go back on his vows.

Catching herself thinking too deeply on their marriage, again, Cat pursed her lips and looked away, walking back to the table. Picking up the paperwork, she neatly stacked it together and slipped it into her bag.

She really had to stop this. It didn't matter what her opinion was. At the end of the day, however much Sophia tried to act as though Cat and Orla were part of this family, they weren't. However good Alex and Maria were to her, however much trust they put into her, however deeply ingrained she now was in their firm, Cat knew she would still always be the outsider. An employee. So why, oh why, could she not just be sensible and get Alex's marriage troubles out of her head?

ELEVEN

Maria stepped off the busy London street and into the Sanderson hotel, turning right towards the long rectangular bar. The barman nodded to her in polite greeting as she took a seat with her back to the solid wall of windows. It had been a long and stressful day, and all she wanted right now was a non-stop stream of her favourite cocktails to take the edge off.

The barman made his way over with a small smile of recognition. 'Hello again. What can I get for you today?'

'I'll take a Lady in Red. Thanks,' she replied. 'And keep them coming.'

His eyebrows briefly rose and then fell as he set about collecting the ingredients. 'Bad day, huh?'

Maria rubbed her forehead tiredly. 'Bad would be an improvement.'

She trusted her men with her life, and she knew they'd do whatever it took to find out where Malcolm was keeping the negatives for those photos. But Malcolm wasn't just a normal mark. He was in parliament. There would be extra levels of security around his office and his home that, without help, she wasn't sure they could get into. As far as enemies went, he was the *last* person she wanted to be up against. He might look like a bumbling buffoon, but in reality, he was actually a very dangerous shark simply hiding behind a posh puffy mask.

She recalled the conversation she'd had with Alex. His face had been grim, not giving her the hope she'd needed.

'*We should just cut this off at the head,*' he'd suggested.

'*I really don't think you realise the media frenzy that would follow,*' she'd replied.

'*It doesn't have to be obvious. We do it quietly, make it look like an accident.*'

'*How?*' she'd asked, even knowing that it wasn't that simple.

'*We use the Viper,*' he'd said, holding her gaze.

Maria had stilled, running it through her head as their men exchanged glances. '*That doesn't solve our problem though. We still need those photos. If we don't, we have no idea who could get their hands on them, after he's gone.*'

Alex had shrugged. '*I think it's something to keep in mind. He's too much trouble to keep alive.*'

He was right, of course. Malcolm was a big risk, whatever way they looked at this. But, right now, there were too many risks all tangled up together to think about something like that. Right now, she had to focus on the main risk. The pictures. She *had* to get hold of them. She *had* to stop this build. Too many people depended on her. Their safety was in her hands, along with a business she'd spent years, and an extortionate amount of money, building. She couldn't let it go now. She just couldn't. There was too much at stake.

As she pondered her predicament, she caught the eye of the man in the suit sitting directly across the narrow bar from her. She swept her gaze past him, but he purposely moved back into her line of sight. She frowned and studied his face, checking to see if she recognised him.

She didn't.

He was handsome enough, in an average way. Smiling blue

eyes, dimpled cheeks, a five o'clock shadow and slicked-back brown hair. His suit was navy, an OK cut, and his Rolex glinted below his cuff, his arm resting beside his drink. It was an obviously purposeful show of wealth, and Maria restrained herself from rolling her eyes. She looked away, careful not to return his smile. She wasn't interested in playing this game tonight.

'Hey.' She heard a deep voice call to the barman. 'Put that on my tab, will you?'

Maria's gaze shot back to the man, who was still watching her with a smile.

'No. Don't,' she instructed the barman sharply. 'I pay for my own drinks.'

She glanced back over at the man, her expression hard, and he raised his hands in surrender. 'My apologies. No intention to offend.'

'No offence taken,' she replied flatly.

The barman handed over her drink, and Maria twisted in her seat, to face away from the stranger across the bar. She took a sip and closed her eyes as the crisp, icy-cold liquid slipped down her throat. This drink was one of her most favourite guilty pleasures, and she intended on enjoying it to the full. But as she opened her eyes, she saw that the man across from her had left his seat and was now rounding the end of the long bar, making a beeline for her. This time she didn't try to hide her annoyance, and she sighed – loudly.

'You know, I find independence very attractive in a woman,' he said as he reached her. 'I'm Jacob.'

'Right.' Maria sighed and put her drink down on the bar. 'Do you want to know what I find attractive in men, Jacob?'

'Do tell,' he replied.

'The ability to read the room.' Maria's stare turned icy. 'The ability to notice a person's body language, translate their actions and read between the lines when they speak. *That*'s sexy.'

'Oh, I completely agree,' he drawled, entirely missing her

point. Most likely on purpose, she decided. 'What is it you do, Miss, er...' He lifted an eyebrow in question.

Maria ignored the question and just stared at him, unmoved by his attempts to smooth past her clear rejection.

'OK.' He chuckled under his breath, and a twinkle shone in his eye, as though this was just a new challenge for him to overcome. 'I'm going to have to work a bit harder here, it seems. Well, that I can do. It's not often I come across someone as captivating as you, and I'd really like to find out more.' He paused, and his smile widened. 'Will you put me out of my misery and at least tell me your name?'

'Look, I get it,' Maria said, her tone matter-of-fact. She cast her critical gaze over him, noting the untanned dent on his ring finger and the strain of his buttons over his slightly protruding middle. He'd slipped his phone into his pocket as he'd approached, but not before she'd noted the photo on the screen of two young children smiling up at the camera. 'You're here, alone, at...' She checked the time. 'Nearly nine on a weekday. Which means you're probably staying here or nearby. For work, judging by the suit.'

His grin told her she was right. And that he had no idea how this conversation was about to turn.

'You're away from home for a day or two.' She smiled, the action not meeting her eyes, and turned her body to face him. 'Away from your most likely exhausted and overwhelmed wife, and the kids you left her to deal with alone.' He blinked, a little startled. 'And it probably feels good, right? To be here without them. To be all dressed up without worrying about cereal being poured down your suit. Without the constraints and chaos of the family *you* created. You probably feel like *you* again, right? *The man*. Suave and sophisticated and carefree.' Maria leaned forward with a conspiratorial whisper. 'And I bet she's not the woman you married, is she?' His expression changed, as if he was trying to work out whether this change of direction was in his favour or not. 'I bet she never has time for you, huh? Probably let herself go. Always focusing on those kids instead of giving her attention to you. It's probably all her fault that you cheat with whoever the fuck is dumb enough to let you pick them up in these bars. Right?'

Jacob barked out an embarrassed laugh, looking around self-consciously. 'Wow. OK. I was just trying to be nice, but clearly—'

'Why don't you try being nice to your *wife*, instead of strangers in bars?' Maria countered, cutting him off. 'Not that you'll take that advice of course.' She turned back to her drink. 'You'll continue trying to drown out the disappointment of your middle-management job that makes other men rich, by neglecting your family and picking up women while your waistline widens and your hair thins, until the point where your wife finds out and she leaves your sorry backside.'

His brow knotted and his expression darkened. 'What on earth do you think—'

Maria held a finger up to silence him without bothering to look round. 'I wasn't done. Because I'm going to tell you a secret. You want to know where that path leads? Right back here.' She tapped the bar. 'Where you'll then drown your sorrows, too old and broke to continue picking up young, attractive women. And that wife who left, she'll spend all that money she gets in the divorce picking herself back up and making herself feel pretty again, before getting out there to find a man actually *worth* her time. Someone who treats her like a queen and supports her, the way *you* should have. And those kids? They won't forgive you for what you did to her, so they'll drop you like a hot brick too. And you'll slink back off from the bar, every night, to an empty house, sad and alone. Just like you deserve.' Maria took a sip of her drink, watching his shocked face out of the corner of her eye. 'I'm no psychic, but I can assure you, that's a very accurate snapshot of your future, buddy.'

'Fuck you,' he spat under his breath before hurriedly turning away from her.

'Not even if yours was the last dick in the world, you sad, self-serving cunt,' Maria replied calmly, the corner of her mouth curling upwards in a small smile.

She drained the last of her cocktail, and the barman handed her a fresh one, just like she'd asked.

'Feeling better yet?' he asked with a grin.

'Actually, yeah.' Maria smiled back, amusement colouring her tone. 'That really hit the spot.'

Her phone began to ring, and she pulled it out of her bag, checking the caller ID before answering. 'Alex. Everything OK?'

'It is,' he replied. 'Bill Hanlon's on board. He's going to meet Danny tonight and give him everything we need to plant on Malcolm.'

Maria's smile widened, and she raised her glass to her lips. 'Well. This day is getting better and better.'

TWELVE

Cat slipped the key in the door and turned it with a smile. She still couldn't believe this place was really hers. It was the kind of house she'd always wanted. A Victorian property full of character. She loved the black and white flagstones leading up to the wide front door with its colourful mosaic windows and big brass knocker. The wide bay windows, either side, set into the pale, warm stone of the walls. It still needed a little love on the inside, but it was beautiful. And it was theirs.

She'd never chosen her own home before. She'd rented when she was younger, and then, whilst her father had paid for the house she and Greg had lived in, Greg had been the one to choose it. It had been a functional new build, not too far from the office. Not something *she* would have chosen, but it had made sense at the time, and she hadn't wanted him to feel like her family were calling all the shots in their marriage. So she'd gone along with it. Now, though, she never had to just *go along* with anything someone else wanted ever again. And that felt incredibly liberating.

'Nonna, you're going to fall,' Cat heard Orla say disapprovingly.

'No, I'm not,' came Sophia's voice, dismissing the idea. 'I'm fine, don't you worry, *piccolina*.'

'Maybe you should wait for Mummy,' Orla replied, sounding unconvinced.

Cat frowned and hurried her pace towards the large kitchen at the back of the house. As she entered the room, her eyebrows shot up in surprise.

'Oh my God! What are you *doing*?' She rushed over to steady the stepladder that Sophia was precariously balanced on.

'I'm cleaning the top of your cupboards, Catriona,' Sophia told her, as if the answer was obvious. 'Honestly, they are *disgusting*. Whoever owned this house before, they lived like pigs.'

Cat exhaled heavily, knowing there was no point arguing. Sophia was like a little Italian household Hitler when it came to cleanliness.

'You really don't need to do that,' Cat told her. 'I can sort it at the weekend.'

'You're too busy for things like this,' Sophia replied with a tut. 'I have the time. Let me help you.'

'You've helped me too much already,' Cat chided gently as Sophia reluctantly descended the steps. 'Seriously, you've already picked up Orla from pre-school again today for me – for the third time this week. You won't even let me *pay* you.'

Sophia turned and grasped Cat's face between her hands. 'What have I told you? You're *family* now. And family helps each other.' She gave Cat a quick smile and then turned back to Orla. 'Why don't you show Mummy the picture you made at school?'

'Oh yeah!' Orla scurried off excitedly.

'Your ex-husband turned up, by the way,' Sophia said quietly. 'Asking if he could see you. I told him to sling his hook.'

Cat laughed. 'Did you really?'

'I certainly did,' Sophia confirmed, her expression one of

disapproval. 'He didn't even ask to see her. Only you. What kind of a father doesn't ask after his only daughter?'

'The kind that only cares about himself,' Cat replied with a sigh. She walked over to the kettle and flicked it on. 'Coffee or tea?' she asked.

'Tea,' Sophia replied. 'I'm not drinking that instant piss-water you try to pass off as coffee.'

Cat chuckled and shrugged off her raincoat, hanging it on the back of a chair. Then she quickly tied her long brown hair up in a ponytail and set about making the teas. As the kettle came to a boil, Orla ran back in, clutching a colourful and slightly screwed-up piece of paper.

'Mummy, look what I made!' She thrust it at Cat eagerly.

Cat took it and smoothed it out, casting her eye over the jumbled swirls and slashes of colour. 'Wow, that's amazing! You did this?'

'Yeah!' Orla bounced up and down in glee. 'Do you love it, Mummy?'

'I do,' Cat confirmed, walking across the kitchen. 'In fact, I love it so much, I think we should keep it right here, in the middle of the fridge. What do you think?'

'Good idea,' Orla agreed. 'Can you tell what it is?'

She peered up at her mother with suspicion in her eyes, and Cat froze. This was a test, and if she didn't pass, Orla would be bitterly disappointed.

'Of course! Um...' Cat winced at the mess of colours, trying to pick out shapes, to make sense of it. 'It's a, er, it's...' She glanced up at Sophia, who was making frantic hand motions behind Orla.

Hot, Sophia mouthed, waving her hand at her face.

'It's very hot,' Cat said slowly.

Sophia immediately shook her head and held her arms up in the air, arcing them out to the side and meeting her hands in the middle. *Hot*, she mouthed again, followed by *balloon*.

'It's a hot air balloon!' Cat declared with a wide smile.

'You got it, Mummy!' Orla squealed in delight. 'Well done. You're very clever.'

Happy with her mother for guessing correctly, Orla toddled off out of the room, humming under her breath.

Cat let out a quiet laugh. 'Thanks for that.'

Sophia chuckled. 'I've been there, my friend. We mamas know.' She tapped the side of her nose with a knowing look. 'I remember once, when Antonio...' She trailed off, her smile disappearing.

Cat bit her lip. Antonio was a sore subject for them all. Sophia had lost a son. The fact it had been due to his own actions and that she had been the one to cast him out didn't make that fact any easier. And as for Cat, Antonio was the man who now haunted her nightmares. Who haunted her daughter's nightmares. Orla still woke up screaming sometimes, and Cat still had to hold her in her arms until morning came and the darkest shadows of their past melted away.

'Well, anyway,' Sophia mumbled, subdued. 'These days are precious.' She smiled sadly. 'Make the most of every moment. They grow up far too quickly.'

'I know.' Cat squeezed Sophia's arm.

Sophia patted Cat's hand and walked over to the kitchen table, taking a seat there. She watched Cat for a few moments as Cat poured the tea. 'Your ex. Greg. He seemed very interested in where you were earlier.'

'Makes a change,' Cat replied. 'He was never that interested when we were together.'

'What will you do if he asks you back?' Sophia asked, her words careful.

Cat blew out a breath through her cheeks. 'I've never really thought about it,' she replied honestly. 'But I guess I don't really need to. I was the one to leave, before all of that drama with the house and my dad's business. I already knew about his mistress.

Well. One of them at least.' She crooked a half-smile and shook her head. 'Going back to him is the last thing I'd do.'

'Are you sure that's the right decision?' Sophia asked quietly.

Cat blinked and turned, surprised. 'What do you mean?'

Sophia shrugged. 'I'm just asking the question. Is it what's best for your family? Maybe all of this could have made him realise what a big mistake he made.'

Cat frowned and turned back to stir the sugar into her tea. 'He cheated on me, Sophia. With not one but two women. And not once but ongoing relationships, behind my back.'

'I know, I know,' Sophia agreed. 'I just...' She sighed. 'Men are idiots. Most of them at least. Sometimes they're hopeless cases, but sometimes they are good men who have just made stupid mistakes. My husband, Ivano. He was a good man. He made many mistakes. Some that I nearly left him for.' Sophia suddenly looked tired, her olive skin losing some of its lustre. 'Some maybe I *should* have left him for. But we always worked it out. For the family.' She looked up at Cat. 'For the children.'

Cat swallowed, finding it hard to hear Sophia suggest she forgive Greg all that he'd done to them. 'Greg isn't a good man, Sophia. He wasn't a good father or a loving husband. He isn't someone who just messed up. He's always been a very selfish person who loves himself above all others.' Cat turned and walked over to the table, a tea in each hand, and placed one in front of Sophia before sitting down. 'There is absolutely no chance of me ever allowing him back into our lives, beyond the occasional times he bothers with Orla.'

Sophia nodded. 'OK. I just wanted to remind you that things aren't always black and white. I'm not saying you're wrong about Greg,' she assured her. 'But just remember that men are very different creatures to us. Men don't think like we do, so we can't follow their reasonings with female logic. It's always worth just considering men's actions from another angle, if we want to understand them. In relationships, in business. Anywhere really. It's something I always told my girls when they were growing up.'

'Girls?' Cat frowned. Sophia only had one daughter. Maria.

'Oh.' Sophia started, and her cheeks flushed red. 'I meant my children. It's something I always told my *children*.' She shrugged and picked up her tea, casting her gaze away.

Cat picked up her own tea and took a sip, watching her friend across the table with a small frown. Because that didn't seem like something Sophia would have need to tell her sons. It didn't make sense. And there was a strangely guilty expression on Sophia's face. In fact, Sophia was now looking distinctly uncomfortable, as though she'd said something she really didn't mean to. But what did *that* mean? And if her accidental slip was the truth, then where on earth was her other girl?

THIRTEEN

Alex's car swept up the drive outside the front of his house, and he clocked the fact that the space next to his was empty. Again. He sighed and stared up at the neat brick house with the two white pillars either side of the front door. The engine idled as he considered whether or not to go in.

It was supposed to be a home. A big, warm family home. That's what he'd envisioned when he'd bought it for himself and Bianca, years before. But things hadn't quite gone the way he'd hoped. He didn't mind that Bianca didn't want kids yet. He understood the commitment that would be for her. He didn't mind that she wanted to live her life wild and free, for the most part. But coming home every night to a cold, dark, empty house was chipping away at his soul much harder than he'd thought it could. More than that, it was full-on depressing. He stared at the darkened windows, no movement behind them.

Unable to bear the thought of another evening eating alone, in silence, Alex put the car in reverse and pulled back off the drive. He'd cook for his mother tonight. Grab some food on the way over and make something nice for them both. Perhaps Maria would drop in too. She often did in the evenings. The thought perked him up, and he smiled, turning towards the nearest supermarket.

Half an hour later, Alex stood at the front door of Sophia's house with a frown. She wasn't home and wasn't answering her mobile either. He grimaced up at his old family home and pondered what to do. He'd stupidly left his keys at home and couldn't be bothered to drive back to get them. In all likelihood, his mother was probably over at Cat's new house, pottering around and taking over, the same way she'd done when they'd all moved out and got their own places. It had annoyed Maria so much that one day she'd simply stolen the key back from her mother when she wasn't looking and had never replaced it. To this day, Sophia still didn't know Maria had done that and had simply given up reminding her to cut her another one.

Making a decision, Alex got back in the car and drove the five minutes around the corner to Cat's. Night had well and truly fallen now, the late January darkness making it feel much later than it really was. Knowing Cat usually put Orla down at this sort of time, he was careful not to make too much noise as he approached the door and knocked softly, instead of using the large knocker or the bell.

A full minute passed before he saw the shadow of a figure walking down the hallway towards him, and then the door opened, and Cat smiled out at him.

'Hi.' Her smile swiftly dropped to a look of concern. 'Everything OK?'

'Yeah, sorry to disturb you.' Alex rubbed the back of his neck with his hand. 'I'm looking for my mum. Is she here?'

'No, it's Wednesday,' Cat replied, as if that explained where Sophia was. The look on his face must have shown that it didn't. 'Wednesday night. Art club.'

'Ahh, yes.' Alex slapped his forehead. 'I'd forgotten she

signed up for that. I'm surprised she stuck at it actually. She's never enjoyed painting.'

Cat's mouth quirked up into a grin. 'I take it you haven't heard what they're painting then.'

Alex winced. 'Do I want to know?'

'Nope.' Cat tried to bite back another smile, but her amusement shone through anyway.

'OK.' Alex glanced back out at the empty road. That put paid to his plans then.

'What did you need her for?' Cat asked, pulling the long cream cardigan around her a little tighter against the cold air. 'Is everything alright?'

'Yeah. Yeah, it's fine. I was, er...' He glanced back at the bags on the passenger seat of his car. 'I was going to surprise her with dinner. In hindsight, she'd probably have already eaten anyway.'

Cat followed his gaze towards the bags. 'You were going to cook?' Her eyebrows shot upwards in surprise.

Alex laughed. 'You don't have to look so shocked.'

'No, I'm not,' Cat replied, matching his laughter. 'Sorry. I think that's a really nice thing to do.'

'Yeah, well. You know.' Alex shrugged, feeling embarrassed. 'It's nothing really.' There was a short silence, and Alex scratched his neck, turning on his heel. 'I'll catch you tomorrow.'

'Wait,' Cat called as he began moving towards his car.

Alex turned and lifted one dark eyebrow in question.

Cat held her hands out to the sides and then dropped them. 'I was about to cook, myself, if you want to join me? Orla's in bed, and I haven't had time to eat yet, so...' She trailed off and shrugged.

'Er, I mean, I don't want to put you out,' Alex said, not wanting to take her up on a pity invite. He had *some* pride.

'You really wouldn't be,' Cat replied. 'Honestly, it would be nice to have some adult company for once. That's the curse of being a single parent unfortunately. Most nights you eat on your own.'

Alex studied her. He hadn't thought about that before. Now that he *was* thinking about it, he realised Cat must have to deal with a *lot* on her own. And that had to be hard. Yet she still turned up with a smile, every single day, making life look easy. His admiration for her suddenly went up a notch.

'What were you going to cook?' he asked, taking a step back towards her.

'I was just going to pan-fry some chicken and make a salad,' she told him. 'But there's more than enough for both of us.'

Alex scoffed and shook his head. 'No. OK. Here's what we'll do.' He turned back to the car and grabbed the bags from his passenger seat. '*You* pour the wine, *I'll* cook the food. You have wine, yes?'

'Yes,' Cat answered with a laugh, moving out of the way so he could pass her. '*And* it's Italian. Your mother made me get rid of the French stuff I had in the cupboard.'

'Rightly so!' Alex joked, making his way through the hall. 'She's going to regret missing out on this dinner when she realises what I cooked.'

'Oh, I don't know,' Cat countered. 'You haven't seen Pablo.'

'Pablo?' Alex placed the bags on the kitchen counter and gave her a confused frown.

'Pablo,' Cat repeated, a humorous glint in her eye. 'The poser.' She waggled her eyebrows up and down, and what she meant suddenly clicked in Alex's mind.

'Oh! *No!* Ahh, I did *not* need to know that,' he said, shaking his head as if trying to erase it from his memory.

Cat laughed and darted out of the way as Alex half-heartedly flicked a tea towel towards her. 'Now, that's enough scarring me for life. Tell me where you keep your apron.'

. . .

An hour later, Cat collapsed on one end of her new burgundy sofa and placed both hands on her overly full stomach with a groan.

'That was the best...' Cat frowned. 'Actually, I don't know what that was. What was it?'

'Pasta alla puttanesca,' Alex told her, sitting down on the other end of the sofa with his wine.

'That was the best pasta alla puttanesca I've ever tasted,' Cat confirmed.

Alex smiled. 'I'm glad you liked it. Better than a chicken salad at least.'

'Miles better,' Cat agreed.

She looked across at him and wondered, as she had all night, why he was avoiding going home. And that was very clearly the case. Sweet as it was to want to cook his mother dinner, it wasn't something people usually went all out for on a whim.

'So, where's Bianca tonight?' she asked, careful to sound casual.

The content expression on his face instantly faded into subtle tension. Someone who didn't know him well might not have noticed the shift, but Cat certainly did. She pursed her lips and looked away to hide her expression.

'Out with friends somewhere, I think,' he replied, his tone equally casual. 'We don't live in each other's pockets, as you've probably noticed.'

Cat simply nodded, feeling bad for him that he felt the need to explain their situation like that. Not wanting to embarrass him any further, she changed the subject.

'I went over to check out the office today, by the way. Thanks. It's a great space.'

Alex waved a hand. 'It's not much, but the location is practical.'

'No, seriously, it's great. I really like it,' Cat told him

honestly. She pushed a stray lock of hair back behind her ear. 'It's nice to have my own office again. It's been years.'

Alex watched her for a few moments. 'I still don't know why you want to do this. Don't get me wrong,' he swiftly continued as she opened her mouth to speak, 'I'm glad to have you. It's great to have a proper accountant running the books. I'm just surprised that with all the options you have right now, *this* is what you want to spend your time on.'

Cat exhaled slowly and sat forward, reaching over to the coffee table for her wine. She knew what he meant. And she could see why it looked odd. After selling her father's business, she was now rich. *Very* rich in fact. So rich that neither she nor Orla would ever have to worry about money again. They could live a life of pure luxury and barely make a dent in what she now had in her various accounts. A lot of people would have jetted off to some paradise somewhere and never looked back. But the thing was, those people likely had a family to come back to at Christmas, and on holiday or birthdays. They probably had parents and siblings and groups of friends to tell all their amazing stories to. Those people had anchors, and anchors gave people a sense of security. Gave their new lives a deeper meaning.

Cat didn't have any of that. Her ex had slowly separated her from all her old friends, over the years they were together, and her only family had been her dad. When he'd died and her marriage had ended, she and Orla had been left entirely alone in the world. That was, until a chance encounter with Maria had led them both to the Capellos. After all Cat had been through, they'd stood by her. Helped her fight. Been there for her when no one else had. And although she knew she would never be blood, they had become like family.

Cat could jet off tomorrow if she wanted. She could let the world swallow them up as they drifted through adventures, or pick up and start afresh somewhere new. But because they *weren't* blood, she and Orla would soon fade from Sophia's and Alex's and Maria's thoughts. They wouldn't be family anymore. They would just be some old friends the Capellos helped out of a tight spot once. And that thought – the thought that this treasured bond with the only people who truly cared about them in this world could disappear – was too painful to test. She and Orla didn't need a life of private beaches and plane rides, with no one around to care. They needed family. They needed love and security and a village. And this was now their village.

But this was too much to voice out loud. And so instead, she simply said, 'This is just where I want to be.' She smiled. 'Plus, I hate not being busy. It's good to actually use my mind and, well, distract myself from...' She paused, the shadow that was always there in the background hovering a little closer, once more. 'Well, you know. Just, stuff.' She looked away.

There still wasn't a day that went by when Cat didn't look over her shoulder each time she left the house. When she didn't triple-check all the windows and doors were securely locked and her alarms were on. It would be a very long time indeed before she stopped fearing Antonio's return. Because while Alex assured her that she was safe now, that she was officially under their protection and couldn't be touched, Cat didn't trust that this, alone, would stop Antonio from coming for her again. His family had disowned him and then taken her under their wing. In his warped mind, she was sure he must blame her.

The doorbell rang, and Cat tensed, her forehead furrowing in a confused frown. Alex caught her eye and mirrored her expression.

'Maybe Mum?' he offered.

Cat shook her head, glancing at the gilt clock on the mantelpiece. 'Her class doesn't end for another twenty minutes.'

She stood up and walked through to the hallway, flicking on the light as she approached the door. She heard Alex stand up and follow her, a few steps behind, and as she neared the door, she was suddenly very glad of his presence. Because although she couldn't make out any detail through the stained-glass window, the yellow streetlight clearly illuminated the silhouette of the man outside her door.

Like a flash of lightning through her brain, Cat was transported back to that dark, soulless room, the one Antonio had forced her into, the night he'd taken Orla. Ice-cold dread flooded her veins, and her breath caught in her throat. It was him, she was sure of it. But it couldn't be, could it? He didn't know where she lived. Unless he'd had her followed? But she'd been careful. Bought a house that was tucked away at the end of a quiet cul-de-sac, watched in her rear-view mirror for any cars that could be tailing her, anytime she came home.

So how on earth had he found her?

FOURTEEN

Alex caught her up but remained a step behind as she steeled herself and twisted the key in the lock. It was going to be OK. Alex was here. He wouldn't let Antonio do anything. But what if he had backup? Alex was here with her, alone. Her hand trembled, but she forced herself to open the door, and as she did, as her unwelcome late-night visitor came into view, her breath whooshed out of her lungs.

'Greg,' she said with deep relief and a tinge of annoyance. 'What are you doing here?'

'I...' He paused and stared at something behind her. At Alex, she realised. 'Who's *this* guy?' His pale blue eyes narrowed as he frowned.

Cat's eyebrows rose, and she crossed her arms over her middle. Greg actually had met Alex, once before, but as Alex had been wearing a ski mask at the time, Greg was still blissfully unaware that this was the same person who'd forced him to hand Cat back everything he'd taken.

'None of your business,' she replied tartly. 'What do you want?'

Greg hadn't bothered to pick Orla up again, the weekend

before, despite it being his weekend to have her. That was the second of his weekends in a row that he'd missed, meaning he now hadn't spent any proper time with her in over a month. He'd picked her up from pre-school a couple of times and taken her for dinner before dropping her home swiftly after, but that had been the extent of his attempts to be a dad lately.

'I just wanted to see you,' Greg replied. 'I miss you, Cat. You and Orla both. I thought...' He sighed and ran a hand back through his sandy blond flop of hair. 'Listen, if you're seeing someone new, then I think I have a right to know.' He sounded so put out that Cat almost laughed. 'Especially if that someone is in my daughter's home.'

Now Cat did snort. 'Are you serious?' She narrowed her eyes. 'It was only a few months ago, Greg, that you threw us out on the streets without a care *where* we went or *who* we were around. *Then* you moved your side piece into our home and had *her* playing happy families with *my* daughter. On the *one* occasion you grudgingly took her for the night of course. Remember that?'

Greg had the grace to momentarily look away, his cheeks flushing. 'That was different, Catriona. Orla *knew* Jeanie.'

Cat let out a sharp bark of amusement and looked up to the heavens. 'Oh, Greg.' She shook her head. 'You lost *any* say in our lives a long time ago. And not that it's any of your business, but Orla knows Alex too.' Greg didn't need his assumption that she was dating Alex corrected just yet, she decided. 'In fact, at the rate you've been dropping your visits with her, since we split, she's starting to know Alex a lot better than she knows you.' This wasn't a lie either. 'So if you want to change that, start actually turning up when it's your weekend. But as for me? I couldn't give a shit if you miss me. I miss *you* about as much as a hole in the head. In fact, I think I'd probably prefer that to *any* of amount of time in your company.'

There was a low sound of amusement from behind her, and

Greg's gaze flicked back to Alex, growing darker with brooding annoyance.

'Catriona, listen,' he said, stepping forward as he tried, once more, to gain control of the conversation. 'I just want to talk. I know it's been a tough few months for us. But I believe our marriage is stronger than—'

'Our *marriage* is non-existent!' Cat exclaimed. 'What don't you get? It's done with! Over!' She shook her head incredulously. How could he believe there was any chance of coming back from all he'd done? 'You need to stop this now.'

He made a sound of disbelief and placed his hands on his hips, looking away and then back to her. 'So you've really moved on?' he asked accusingly. 'After all these years, despite the fact we have a *family*, you've just thrown it away after five minutes and moved on with *this* guy.' He gestured towards Alex.

Cat opened her mouth to correct him, but Alex stepped forward and rested his arm across her shoulders, squeezing her arm.

'She has, Greg,' he replied firmly with a smile. 'That's what happens when your wife finds out you've been fucking everything that moves and then you publicly try to screw her out of everything she has.'

'Mate, piss off, will you?' Greg snapped. 'This is a conversation between me and my *wife*.'

'I'm not your wife, Greg,' Cat interjected. 'The paperwork is there, waiting for you to sign it so we can be done with this. And then as far as I'm concerned, other than being civil when we have to, for Orla's sake, I never want to speak to you again.'

Greg glowered at them, his eyes darting from one to the other and back again. 'Well, we'll just see about that. Maybe I'll have my lawyer take another look at the situation.' He jutted out his chin and looked down his nose at her coldly. 'You've done *very* well out of your old man's death. And well protected as he may have left things, I'm *sure* there must be some marital loophole in there somewhere.'

Cat felt her insides freeze as he left the threat hanging in the air between them. As Greg's true colours shone. *This* was the real reason he was here, trying to patch things up. He wanted her money. Not her. She'd known that already of course, but seeing his mask slip this way made it feel all the more ugly.

'How's things with Rachel?' Alex asked, his voice quiet and deadly.

Cat looked up to see him watching Greg intently, his gaze boring into the lesser man. She flicked her gaze over to Greg and saw him frown, confused. He still hadn't clicked that Alex was one of the men who'd threatened him that night. And who'd dropped him and his girlfriend at his *other* mistress's house as a little bit of revenge icing on the cake. Cat hid a smile and waited. Greg opened his mouth to reply, but Alex continued, cutting him off.

'I always wondered, did she forgive you, after we dropped you there with Jeanie that night? Or did she kick you to the kerb, like any self-respecting bit on the side would, after finding out they weren't the only one?'

Alex's words were laced with venom, but it was Greg who Cat watched, waiting for the penny to drop. Suddenly, his eyes widened, and his face paled.

'You,' he breathed. He took a half step back.

Cat smiled as fear flooded his features. 'That's right, Greg. You've met before.' She lifted her chin up defiantly. 'And we both know how that worked out for you.' She paused to let her words register. 'Sign the fucking papers and be done with it. Because one way or another, you aren't getting a penny out of me.'

Alex moved forward, pulling Cat closer to his side and

shooting Greg a wide smile. He lifted the hand that had been holding Cat's arm and gave a little wave.

'Bye, Greg,' he said merrily. And then swiftly shut the door in his face.

They stood there for a few moments, watching the shadow on the other side of the door dither, and then turn and leave. And once she was sure he was safely out of hearing, Cat turned to Alex and burst out laughing.

'Oh my God, his *face*!' She covered her mouth as more giggles came out, not wanting to wake Orla.

Alex grinned, stepping back and resting his hand on the banister. 'Well, I doubt he'll go through with trying to steal your inheritance again at least.'

'Yes, he's *definitely* not got the balls to go up against you after that reminder,' Cat agreed.

Alex looked past her to the door and shook his head, his grin fading. 'You and Orla deserve so much better than that.'

Cat watched him, her expression softening slightly. *So do you*, she thought.

She pushed her hair back behind her ear and smiled as he looked back to her. 'Well. Thank you for being my fake boyfriend for the evening.' She laughed but it felt awkward suddenly. Because it *had* felt like that, she realised. Even before Greg had turned up.

Alex stared at her, his hard, handsome face unreadable, and she held his gaze until her attention was caught by something glinting in the hallway light. His wedding ring, she realised. His eyes followed hers, and he quickly stepped back with a tight smile.

'Glad I could help. Hopefully you won't have any more bother, but if you do' – he picked up his jacket from the coat hook behind the door – 'just give me a shout.' He glanced over his shoulder towards the lounge and scratched the back of his neck. 'I'd best make a move. Bianca will probably be home soon.'

Cat nodded quickly, plastering a bright smile over her face. "Course. Thanks again for dinner.' She wrapped her arms tightly around her middle. 'I'm sorry you didn't get to cook for Sophia, but I was happy to be the stand-in.'

'Right. No probs,' Alex replied, clearing his throat. He opened the front door and briefly raised a hand. 'Catch you tomorrow.'

'Yeah, catch you tomorrow,' Cat echoed as he jogged away through the light rain that had just begun to fall.

She watched him until he reached his car, and then closed the door and turned around. Closing her eyes, she leaned back against the wood.

'What the fuck are you doing, Cat?' she muttered to herself. She sighed and then opened her eyes again as she heard the car purr away. 'You need to pull yourself together. Because he is *not* yours to think about like that.' She pushed off the door and pulled in a deep, bracing breath. 'You are *not* going to be one of those women.' She shook her head, her resolve strengthening. '*Not* now, not *ever* and not for *anyone*.'

FIFTEEN

Maria fought the urge to tap her heel on the floor as she waited outside Malcolm Ardley's office. His secretary kept shooting her glances and looking her up and down with a sour twist to her mouth and the occasional full sneer. Subtly appraising her, Maria decided she must be another of his many affair partners. She definitely fitted the bill. Self-important, prissily dressed and with a clear air of someone who was past their prime and desperate to feel attractive again. Exactly Malcolm's type. The low-hanging fruit he seemed to gorge himself on everywhere.

As the door finally opened and Malcolm gave her a sickly smile with a little wink, Maria's suspicions were confirmed. The woman brightened and preened under his gaze, then soured again when she turned back to Maria.

'Miss Capello,' Malcolm said, gesturing into his office. 'Shall we?'

Maria stood up, forcing a pleasant smile, and walked into the room. She took a seat at the desk, opposite Malcolm's chair, and crossed her slim legs, waiting while he closed the door and joined her.

'So,' he said, heaving his considerable bulk into a comfortable position. 'What is this offer you want to put to me?'

Maria smiled. 'I can't reveal all the details just yet, but if I can pull this off, it would land you with a contract for several million. A contract you don't have to do anything at all to fulfil, but that is completely kosher and through the government books.'

'That sounds too good to be true,' Malcolm replied sceptically.

That's because it is, Maria answered silently.

'It does, but yet here I am, offering it to you on a plate. And all for just a little bit of land that really means nothing to you.' She smiled again winningly.

Malcolm chuckled, his eyes glinting dangerously. 'You aren't, though, are you? You haven't actually offered me *anything* yet. Explain your plan to me.' He sat back and laced his fingers together over his protruding belly.

'I can't do that yet,' Maria replied, lifting her chin.

'Then why are you here?' he asked with a frown.

'To make sure you're holding up your end of the deal. That you've kept that spanner in the works, with regards to that land. Because I'm not going to waste my time and resources pulling this all together for you if my interests aren't safe.' Maria mirrored his body language, relaxing back and lacing her own fingers.

A knock at the door interrupted them, and the sour-faced secretary poked her head in. 'Apologies, Mr Ardley, I'm just going to take my lunch and wondered if you needed anything before I disappear?' She eyed Maria as though staring at a particularly offensive bug.

'No, no, all good here. Thank you, Ellen,' Malcolm replied.

Ellen smiled at him and retreated, closing the door again.

Maria hid an amused smile. 'Ellen seems like a real ray of sunshine,' she quipped.

'Ah, well...' Malcolm cleared his throat. 'She gets a little protective when there are, er, attractive women around. On my wife's behalf of course.'

'Oh, of course,' Maria replied with a hint of sarcasm.

Malcolm eyed her, and she put on a show of innocence. He clearly didn't buy it, but they both pretended he did, continuing their little dance.

'Your interests are safe,' Malcolm said, answering her earlier question. *'For now.'* He eyed her with a steely expression. 'You asked for a week, and you have *exactly* a week, from the moment you asked. And not one minute longer. So if you're here to ask for more time...'

'Not at all,' Maria said smoothly. 'Everything is on schedule.' She swallowed and touched her throat. 'Sorry, could I get a glass of water? I've just realised I'm absolutely parched.'

'Well, I'm about to take lunch myself. If you'd like, we could grab a drink in the—'

But Maria cut him off. 'Unfortunately, I have to rush off to another meeting. If it's not too much trouble, I just need a glass of water. Then I'll be on my way.' She cleared her throat, to push home her point.

'Right.' Malcolm glanced reluctantly towards the door. 'Er, OK. I'll, er, *I'll* have to go. Just wait here a moment.' He eyed her suspiciously, then his gaze flickered briefly towards his computer.

Maria hid a victorious smile. *Oh, Malcolm. You'd make a terrible poker player.*

'I won't be two ticks,' he said pointedly. 'The kitchen is just across the hall.'

'Great. Thanks,' Maria replied.

She waited while he crossed the office and then another full five seconds after he disappeared. Then, with deft hands, she pulled out the tiny device Danny had given her earlier that day. It was no bigger than a five-pence piece and as slim as one too.

'All you need to do is make sure it's within a foot of the hard drive. OK?' he'd told her.

'So it doesn't need to actually connect to it?' she'd checked.

'No. Bill said it just has to be in reach. Then you send over an email with an attachment that he must open. The attachment carries a bug that connects to the device. Malcolm won't see what it really is, but once he's opened it, and the device is active, we'll be able to get in.'

Reaching under the desk, Maria found the lip of the wood and quickly pulled the sticker backing off the little round device. She slipped the backing into her bag then bent over to double-check that where she was sticking it wasn't visible. It wasn't.

'Here we are.' Malcolm's voice drifted through as he began to push open the door.

Out of time, Maria pressed the device hard against the wood and darted back upright, just as Malcolm's face came into view.

'Thank you!' she exclaimed gratefully.

'You're most welcome,' he replied, handing the glass to her and glancing back at his computer again. Finding it locked, just as he'd left it moments before, the anxiety on his face turned to a pleasant smile. 'So, if that's all there is, then...' He trailed off, leaving the prompt hanging in the air.

'Actually, there was one more thing,' Maria replied. 'I've been eyeing up another piece of land nearby that I thought might make a suitable alternative to your buyers. You never know, it could be a win-win situation for you, if you can make it work.'

'Oh?' A glimmer of interest lit up in Malcolm's eye. 'Where is it?'

'I've just emailed you the details, a few minutes ago. I know the current owners and could potentially have a conversation with them, if it appealed to you,' she offered.

Malcolm clicked his mouse, and the screen in front of him came to life. He glanced up at her and covered the keys with one hand.

'Oh, of course,' she said politely, turning her head away.

'One can't be too careful when you're in a position like mine,' he told her by way of explanation.

'I can imagine,' she replied.

'Let's see. Ah, here we go.'

Maria turned back to him expectantly as he clicked open the attachment. There was a long silence as he read through the details she'd planted there earlier, and then he let out a grunt of disappointment.

'Ah. No. OK. I'm afraid it's too low,' he said with a sigh.

'Low?' Maria queried innocently.

'Yes, too low to build on unfortunately. It's all to do with the water table. It's rather boring really. Don't worry your pretty little head with it,' Malcolm responded with a dismissive wave.

Maria nodded along seriously. 'I see. OK. Well.' She lifted her arms and then dropped them again. 'It was worth a try.'

'I do very much appreciate the thought,' Malcolm said, looking at her in a much less guarded way than before. 'I can see you're really trying to make this all work. It's admirable.'

Maria smiled and stood up, pulling her handbag up over her shoulder.

'Who knows what lies ahead of us?' Malcolm added as he walked her towards the door. 'Maybe we'll end up with a very long and lucrative working partnership after all.'

'Who knows?' Maria echoed, her smile dropping and her eyes shooting daggers into the back of his head as he walked ahead.

Except I do know what lies ahead, Malcolm, she added silently. *And it's most definitely not the future you were hoping for at all.*

SIXTEEN

Glasses clinked over chilled bottles of champagne, and quiet chatter filled the air of the upmarket cocktail bar where Bianca had invited Cat to join her. Cool grey-and-white marble-topped tables matched the central bar, brightened by the afternoon sun shining through the window wall at the front. The barmen were smartly dressed with silver waistcoats and claret ties over crisp white shirts, and the menu was appealing and expensive. It was a nice place. Not really Bianca's usual scene. It was too quiet, too full of old-money toffs for her liking. But, of course, that was why she'd chosen it.

'I really am *so* glad we're doing this,' Bianca gushed as she sat down at the small round table opposite Cat.

Cat gave her a tight smile. 'Me too. Thanks for inviting me.'

Liar, Bianca thought caustically. 'So, how's your week been?' she asked with a sweet smile.

Not that she cared in the slightest. She didn't like Cat any more than Cat liked her. Personally, Bianca couldn't understand what they all saw in her. She was a boring, basic cow with no life.

'It's been OK so far thanks,' Cat replied. 'And yours?'

It was painful already. If she hadn't had good reason for this pretence, she'd have told Cat as much and ended the torture. But she *did* have good reason. And she couldn't afford to show her hand.

'Oh, you know.' Bianca crossed one leg over the other and leaned back in her chair, running her hand through her long chestnut curls. 'I've kept busy.'

Even the clothes Cat wore were boring, she decided. At least Bianca had made an effort. In her cherry-red pleather skinny jeans that perfectly accented her curvy behind, her favourite off-the-shoulder leopard-print top and matching stilettos, she *knew* she looked a million dollars. Partnered with some gold hoops and smoky-rimmed eyes, she'd turned heads the moment she'd stepped out of the cab. But Cat, with her high-waisted navy suit trousers and plain high-necked navy jumper, was a stark contrast indeed. She hadn't even bothered to jazz up her poker-straight hair or apply any more make-up than the usual basic nude palette she used so sparingly on her pale face.

The silence was becoming awkward, and Cat gave her another tight smile before picking up the cocktail menu. 'Nice place. I haven't been here before.'

'Yeah, it's alright, ain't it?' Bianca looked round, feigning appreciation.

She'd picked somewhere so different from her usual haunts because she couldn't risk bumping into one of her boy-toys with Cat in tow. If she got even a *hint* that Bianca was doing something she shouldn't, that snake would grass on her for sure. And she had *no* intention of letting her late-night amusements ruin her marriage.

Bianca didn't see what she did while she was out as cheating. She wasn't emotionally attached to any of them or engaging in an ongoing affair. They were simply tools to scratch an itch when her husband was too busy to. It was something to make her feel special for a few minutes. Because she needed that. No, she *deserved* that. So as far as she was concerned, what Alex didn't know wouldn't harm him.

'I think I'll go for a Violet Kiss,' Cat said. She passed the menu across to Bianca.

'Ooh, that sounds good,' Bianca enthused. 'I might just join you.'

Cat pushed her hair back behind one ear and glanced away for a moment before looking back at her. 'I must admit,' she said, 'I was a bit surprised that you wanted to do this. I know we, well... that things between us started off on the wrong foot.'

A corner of Bianca's mouth tugged up in wry amusement. 'I'm sure you can imagine how it felt to be told the alibi my husband used to evade arrest involved being in a bathtub with *you.*'

'We were never actually in the bathtub together,' Cat replied, her expression open and sincere. 'We just made it look like that. We had no time to figure anything else out. I wouldn't do that. *He* wouldn't do that. You know that.'

'Hmm.' Bianca pursed her lips.

She knew they hadn't done anything. Cat was right – Alex *wouldn't* do that. He wasn't the type. But still, she couldn't stand the woman. Because although she believed Alex wasn't screwing her, he still seemed to act like the sun shone out of her arse. He still laughed at her stupid jokes and listened when she talked. He barely even looked Bianca's way when *she* talked anymore. And it wasn't just him. Sophia thought a lot of Cat too. Much more than she thought of Bianca, her own daughter-in-law. Antonio had become so obsessed with the woman he'd almost lost his damned mind! And where had that landed him? Ostracised by his own family. Cast out by his own blood, all because of *her*. And it *was* her fault. Not his.

Sure, he'd gone a bit far. He'd taken her kid and used her as bait to lure Cat into a trap. But it wasn't like he would have actually *hurt* her, for God's sake. And what had Cat's problem really been anyway? That she'd caught the attention of a rich, powerful, handsome man? If Cat had been smart, like *Bianca* had been, she'd have stopped being such a prissy little nun and leaned into it. And if she'd played her cards right with Antonio, she could have landed herself a very comfortable position in life. She could have landed herself a Capello man and all the perks that came with it. But *no*, the stuck-up cow had thrown a hissy fit instead and had run crying to Alex about it. It was pathetic.

Her annoyance at Cat's audacity in thinking she was better than Bianca rose inside her, but Bianca pushed her poisonous thoughts away. She couldn't let her true feelings show tonight. She had to keep up the act. Because she had a job to do. And while Antonio might not be her *favourite* person right now, he was still someone she liked a lot more than Cat. And even if that wasn't the case, it wasn't like she had a choice. Antonio had been cornered in more ways than one in the fallout from all of this. Which made him even more dangerous and unpredictable than ever. And right now, with all the information he had on her that could blow her own life apart, she couldn't risk pissing him off.

She smiled. 'I know. I know Alex would never do that to me. And I also know what you went through with your ex must have been really hard.' Bianca forced a look of sympathy. 'That sort of thing leaves its mark. It really can't have been easy. Especially with Orla. I know I've not been the most welcoming person, but since I heard the full story – and then all that with Antonio...' She sighed and shook her head as if unable to comprehend it. 'I just, I've really felt for you actually.'

'Thank you,' Cat said softly. She looked down for a moment, her expression unreadable but definitely less guarded than before. 'I appreciate that.'

Bianca reached across the table and squeezed her hand, pouring as much sympathy as she could into her smile. 'I invited you here because I'd really like to start over. It would be good to have an actual friend in this family.'

She forced a laugh, fighting the urge to curl her lip. Cat wasn't *family*. But Sophia kept telling her she was, so for the sake of tipping Cat over the edge in this conversation, Bianca would jump on the bandwagon. Just this once. It seemed to work because Cat laughed a little in return.

'I'm sure you've got more friends in the family than you think,' Cat offered.

Not since you ousted my only ally I don't, Bianca mentally growled.

'No, not really. But that's OK. I get it.' Bianca shrugged. 'Mamas and their *boyyyys*, right?' She rolled her eyes and forced another laugh. 'Anyway. We should order these drinks.'

'Yes, let's do that.' Cat craned her neck and caught the eye of one of the waiters, lifting a hand to signal them over.

Bianca glanced at Cat's handbag on the floor beside them. She needed to get Cat away from it somehow. Because what she needed was inside.

The waiter appeared with a tall bottle of water, two glasses and a smile. 'Good afternoon, ladies. Some water while you wait?'

And as though God himself had answered her prayers, her way of getting what she needed was suddenly right in front of her.

'Sounds good,' she enthused. 'I'm parched.'

'Of course, madam,' he replied. 'Let me pour you a glass.'

'Nah, that's OK.' Bianca almost snatched it out of his hand. 'I can do that.'

The waiter hesitated for a moment then placed the glasses down in front of her. 'OK. What else can I get you?'

Bianca stayed quiet, focusing on pouring the water into one of the glasses, so that Cat would order first.

Cat picked up the cocktail menu and glanced at it, taking her attention away from the table. 'Er, I think I'll have the...'

Seizing her opportunity, Bianca finished pouring and then, with the bottom of the bottle, quickly knocked the entire glass of water flying in Cat's direction.

'Argh! Oh my God!' Cat spluttered as it drenched her with full force.

Bianca set the bottle down and put her hands to her mouth, as though she was in shock. 'I'm so sorry! Ah, man, you're drenched. Oh *Gawd*. I'm so clumsy.' She grimaced apologetically across the table as Cat grabbed the two small napkins. They did nothing against the half pint that had soaked her to the skin.

'It's OK,' Cat managed, looking down at herself in dismay. 'Accidents happen.'

'You should get under the dryers. Go on, go dry yourself off, before that leaves tide marks on your top.' She stood up as Cat did and ushered her towards the bathroom before the other woman could remember her bag. 'So sorry, Cat. I feel terrible.'

'No, honestly, it's fine,' Cat assured her. 'Don't worry about it. I'll be back in a minute.'

She disappeared, and Bianca turned back to the table with a small smile of triumph. She paused as she noticed the waiter still standing there, looking on with worry.

'Is she OK? I can—'

'She's *fine*,' Bianca snapped, cutting him off. 'It's water, not fucking battery acid.' There was a short silence, and Bianca widened her eyes with an aggressive look. She didn't have time for this. 'Well? Can I *help* you? The water all went on her, so there's nothing to clear up and nothing to see here. As for the drinks, we'll have two Violet Kisses.' There was a brief pause as he looked towards the bathroom and then back to her. She sighed loudly. 'You can *go*.'

The waiter's eyebrows shot up in surprise, and then he

backed away, shaking his head as he turned to walk back to the bar.

Bianca rolled her eyes and sat back in her seat, one eye on the bathroom door as she grabbed Cat's handbag. She quickly rifled through it, checking the worn brown leather wallet before discarding it and going through the various side zips of the main bag. Her fingers knocked against something smooth, and as she felt for the edges, she realised it was a card.

'*Bingo,*' she muttered, pulling it out.

It was a plain white card, no markings, no serial number, just as Alex had described to Cat when she'd overheard him talking about it. It was definitely the right one. Not wasting any time, she slipped it into her bra and zipped the bag back up, placing it back on the floor exactly as Cat had left it.

A few minutes later, as the waiter returned with two martini glasses filled with a purple-tinged concoction, the bathroom door reopened and Cat walked out, looking a little damp still.

Bianca smiled at her and tilted her head. 'All OK?' she asked.

'Yeah, it's fine,' Cat replied. 'It's just a bit of water. It'll dry. You OK?'

'Oh, I'm fine,' Bianca said, the first genuine smile she'd given since arriving here creeping across her face. 'I'm absolutely fine.'

SEVENTEEN

The end of the tightly rolled fifty-pound note touched down on the white, clouded mirror and was tilted at a perfect thirty-degree angle before Antonio bent down and swiftly sniffed the thick fluffy line of cocaine up into his left nostril. Straightening up, he breathed in deeply a couple more times, to ensure he hadn't missed any, before collapsing back into the battered old coffee-coloured armchair.

'Me nan used to have this suite,' he observed, fingering the silky fringe that edged the arms. 'Fucking horrible set. It was fucking horrible even when it was fashionable in the seventies, let alone now. Why haven't you changed it, for God's sake?'

His question was aimed at the beaten and bloodied man now cowering on his knees in the middle of the small room. The man glanced up at him with real fear in his eyes. He licked his split lip when he realised Antonio wanted an actual answer.

'I – I don't know,' he stammered. 'Money, I guess.'

'Money. Mm,' Antonio grunted. He nodded slowly. 'Funny thing, money, ain't it? More controlling than any human being could ever be. Makes us do all sorts of things.'

Antonio stared at the man for a few seconds, watching him

begin to shake under his gaze. This fucker needed to worry a little bit longer before he got to the point. With a glint in his eye, Antonio suddenly smiled.

'And this carpet.' He chuckled with deep amusement. 'Honestly, I don't know how you can actually *do* drugs here, without it making things proper trippy. Look at it.' He sat forward, the wide grin still in place. 'All those green and orange swirls, they're proper fucking trippy. Go on.' He stood up and walked over, watching the man wince back in fear as he approached. '*Look* at it.'

He slammed his hand down on the back of the man's neck and shoved his bloodied face hard into the carpet, ignoring his cries.

'Bit dirty down here, ain't it?' Antonio wrinkled his nose. 'Don't you own a hoover? Bloody stinks. Then again' – he released the man with one last vicious shove – 'this whole place is a shithole.' He stood up and sniffed, looking around at the chipped, dented door and the peeling textured wallpaper. 'Your poor nan. I bet she'd be right ashamed of you, letting it get into this state, eh?'

The man had been pulled back into a kneeling position by Ben and Harvey, the two men whose loyalty Antonio had managed to keep after the family firm had split.

When he didn't answer, Antonio shot him a look of question.

'Yeah, she would, to be fair, Antonio,' he conceded in a level tone, wiping the fresh blood coming out of his nose with the back of his hand.

Antonio nodded then paused as if a thought had suddenly occurred to him. 'She die here?'

'Yeah,' the man answered. 'In that chair actually.' He nodded to the chair Antonio had been sitting on, and they both stared at it for a moment.

'Huh.' Antonio took a deep breath in and then turned his

gaze dismissively, sitting down in it anyway. 'So. Liam.' His gaze hardened again, the change so swift the other man blinked and then swallowed hard.

There was a long silence, and in the few moments he took to gather his thoughts, Antonio suddenly felt the cocaine kicking in. It felt like a rush of fresh, clean air sweeping through his body, leaving an electric tingle in its wake. He pulled in a deep breath, the action energising him more than it ever could have without chemical help. And then suddenly his brain cleared of the day-to-day fog, his focus now razor sharp on the man in front of him.

Antonio nodded with a grudging appreciation. 'It's good shit.'

Liam blinked, clearly unsure how to react to this statement.

'But that don't excuse you taking it from another dealer.' Antonio's voice lowered to a dangerous growl. 'Whose fucking product is it?'

Liam's mouth gaped open once then twice, and his eyes darted around as he began to shake more violently.

'I asked you a fucking question.' Antonio waited, his gaze blazing with cold, quiet fury.

When Liam still didn't answer, he sniffed and looked around at the picture frames scattered around the room. Most of them were old, but a few were more recent. He picked out one that displayed two young children at a beach, a smiling young mother sitting behind them.

'That your daughter, is it?' Antonio pointed at the picture. 'With the two little ones.'

Liam paled, and his body turned still, his fear surpassing his body's need to react, it seemed.

'Maybe *she'd* know.' The corner of Antonio's mouth curled upwards into a cruel half-smile. 'Maybe I should ask her.'

'M-Mickey Flynn,' Liam stuttered. 'It – it's Mickey Flynn's gear.' He cowered back with a pained cringe. 'I— He *made* me take it. He made me sell it instead of yours. I had no *choice*. He collared me and put me in a fucking *van*.'

'He put you in a *van*?' Antonio asked, feigning indignance. 'Well, why didn't you *say* so? That's all alright then, ain't it?' He cocked his head, his sarcasm now shining through. 'That's OK. Couldn't be helped, mate. I'll just pack me bags, shall I? Just *fuck off* to some other city and let that Irish cunt take over my gaff here, yeah?' He pushed up off the chair and grabbed Liam by the face, digging his fingers into the other man's cheeks as he bellowed. 'Who the *fuck* do you think I *am*? Who the fuck do you think you've been *working* for all this time?'

'*I'm sorry*,' Liam yelped, squeezing his eyes shut. 'I'm *sorry*, Antonio, I'm *sorry*! Please just don't kill me – I have a family.'

He was sobbing now, and Antonio dropped his face, disgusted. He wiped the blood and tears that now dirtied his hand on the other man's shirt. Turning around, he walked a slow, tight circle and sighed.

'I'm not gonna kill you, Liam,' he eventually said, his voice quiet.

A mixture of hope and surprise lit up Liam's face. 'You ain't?'

'Nah. No point, is there?' Antonio held his stare and saw the confusion flicker as Liam tried to work out what was going on. 'Why go to all the bother of cleaning up the mess when I can just leave Mickey Flynn to do it?'

'What?' Alarm now registered on Liam's face as he realised he wasn't getting off so lightly after all.

Antonio tilted his head towards the hallway and caught Ben's eye. 'Help our friend here through to the kitchen,' he ordered.

Walking through ahead of them, Antonio picked up the blue plastic bag from the table and took it over to the kitchen sink. Dumping it on the side, he turned on the tap and let it run for a few seconds, turning around to wait for Liam to be seated.

Ben and Harvey dumped him unceremoniously on a wooden chair at the kitchen table, each keeping a heavy hand on one of his shoulders. Liam looked nervously up to each of them in turn, then slid his wary gaze to Antonio for a second before the flowing water caught his attention. Instantly, his eyes flared wide.

'*No,*' he whispered, shaking his head. 'No, no, no, *please*. Antonio, *please*, I beg you. Don't do this. I'll give it back. I'll – I'll do anything you want, just *please* not that. Please, he'll...' His eyes met Antonio's again, naked fear written there. 'He'll kill me.'

'Exactly,' Antonio replied. 'And for this amount of marching powder' – he glanced at the coconut-sized ball of pure cocaine – 'he'll probably take that little family of yours too.'

'No, *please!*' Liam begged.

Antonio turned and, with a theatrical flourish, dumped the ball into the sink, right under the running water.

'*No!*' Liam cried in an almost feral scream.

There was a scrabbling noise as he tried to break free from the chair the others held him in, and then a pained grunt that segued into a low keening as Harvey punched him hard in the stomach.

Antonio stabbed at the sticky crumbling ball with a dirty knife from the draining board, watching as it all slowly melted into the water and slipped away down the drain. When he was done, when the last of the powder was no more than a whitish residue at the edge of the flowing water, Antonio finally turned it off and moved to face the broken wreck of a man, now crumpled in a sobbing heap on the floor.

'When Flynn comes looking for his money, do make sure you tell him hello from us, yeah?' Antonio picked at an invisible speck on his black shirt.

'What have you done?' Liam sobbed, his thin voice cracking with despair.

'I think you know exactly what we've done.' Antonio looked down on him with quiet contempt. 'You won't be seeing us again. And just to be clear, you ain't affiliated with or protected by me anymore.' Antonio looked up at his men and cocked his head towards the door. They silently filed out. 'Goodbye, Liam,' he called out brightly as he walked. 'I'll catch you later, in hell.'

As he strode out of the run-down 1930s house and down the street, his phone beeped in his pocket, indicating he had a text. He pulled it out and quickly scanned the message, a small smile growing with every step he took.

I've got the key card. Will keep you updated. B

Pulling in a deep, bracing breath of air, he let it out with a loud, content sigh.

'All good, boss?' Ben queried from his left.

Antonio glanced at him, his smile wide. 'You know what, boys? Yeah. Things are definitely looking up.'

EIGHTEEN

'OK, come on. Let's go, kiddo.' Maria pushed her hands down into the pockets of her long burgundy coat and waited as Orla fumbled with her zip.

Eventually, Orla looked up at her with a small pout. 'I can't do it.'

'Yes, you can,' Maria replied frankly. 'I've seen you do it before, so don't try and pull that with me. Come on. Try again. You are a strong, independent woman, remember?'

Orla sighed and went back to fumbling with the zip. Eventually, after a few painstakingly long attempts, the zip caught, and she pulled it up with a squeak of achievement.

'See? I told you you could do it.' Maria waited for Orla to start walking and then the pair of them made their way down the pre-school path and up the road towards her car.

'How come you're picking me up today?' Orla asked, trotting alongside her.

'Your mama's busy working,' Maria replied. 'I'm just dropping you off to her, so she has a bit more time to finish up.'

'Why aren't *you* busy working?' Orla asked, curiosity filling her young voice as she glanced up at her.

'I *am*,' Maria told her. 'I'm just taking a break. I don't work normal hours.'

'Yeah. Me neither,' Orla replied sagely.

They turned the corner, and Maria rested her hand protectively over Orla's slim shoulders as they passed an old lady walking her dog.

'I'm going to be four soon, you know,' Orla continued.

'I heard.' Maria glanced both ways up and down the street and then guided her young ward across. 'What do you want for your birthday?'

'Are you getting me a present?' Orla asked.

''Course!' Maria declared. 'What kind of honorary aunt would I be if I didn't get you a present?'

'Not a very good one,' Orla agreed.

'Exactly. So, what are we thinking?'

Orla thought about it for a moment. 'I've always wanted a dog.'

Maria crinkled her nose. 'You know you have to walk them every day, even in the rain and the dark, right? *And* you have to clean up their poo.'

'*Eww!*' Orla cried, mimicking Maria's expression. 'OK, maybe I don't want a dog.'

'Goldfish are pretty low maintenance, if we're looking at pets,' Maria offered. As they drew near, she pulled the keys to the car out of her pocket and unlocked it.

'I like fish,' Orla mused.

'I'll speak to your mum about it. See what we can do,' Maria promised. 'Right. In you get.'

After helping Orla into her car seat, which she'd earlier installed in the front, Maria reached across and secured the strap, making sure to give it a quick safety tug before she shut the door. As she rounded the car and got into her own seat, Orla turned and studied her, a small frown puckering her otherwise baby-smooth brow.

'Mia?' Orla used the version of Maria's name she'd adopted when they'd first met and she'd been unable to pronounce her actual name.

'Mm?' Maria started the car and pulled out onto the road.

'Why don't *you* have kids?' she asked.

'Because I don't want them,' Maria replied in a matter-of-fact tone.

Orla's frown deepened. 'Why?'

'Because I don't have time to teach zippers or to deal with broccoli meltdowns. And I have a lot of breakable things in my house, which I don't want to have to get rid of,' Maria replied.

Orla considered this for a moment and then shrugged. 'Yeah, that's fair. I break lots of things in my house.'

Maria grinned and glanced across at the little girl sitting next to her. 'Besides, it's much more fun being a cool auntie. I get to do things like buy you goldfish and take you for ice cream and give you advice about boyfriends.'

Orla frowned again, this time looking a little outraged. 'I don't have a *boyfriend!*'

Maria waved a hand dismissively. 'You will, later. And then, when you need advice – and you *will*, trust me – there I'll be. *That*, my little friend, will be my time to shine.'

Orla cocked an eyebrow and cast her an odd glance. 'If you say so. So, the ice cream bit, we can do that now?' she added hopefully.

Maria tilted her head and rounded the next corner. 'Mmm. Go on then. But only if you promise you'll eat all your broccoli later.'

'Promise!' Orla exclaimed, bobbing up and down with glee in her seat.

Maria glanced sideways at her with an indulgent chuckle. 'Fibber.'

. . .

An hour later, Maria pulled up outside Cat's new house and walked behind Orla as she ran up the front path to the door. It opened as she reached it, a smiling Cat looking out at them both.

'Mummy!' Orla cried, jumping into her arms.

'Ahh, there you are.' Cat hugged her tiny daughter close, closing her eyes briefly with a warm smile. 'You've been ages. Where have you...' She paused and sniffed the crook of Orla's neck, then her eyes narrowed. 'You smell very sweet.'

'Thank you,' Orla replied happily.

'Have you had ice cream?' Cat asked.

Orla sat up and looked her mother in the eye, guilt written all over her face. 'Well... we didn't *not*,' she said slowly.

Maria laughed. 'It's my fault,' she admitted. 'I led her astray.'

'Yep,' Orla confirmed. 'Mia let me be a tray. She actually let me have *two* ice creams, 'cause she didn't finish hers.'

'Hey!' Maria wrinkled her nose at Orla in an expression of mock annoyance. 'Snitch.'

Cat laughed and shook her head. 'OK, well you'd better eat all your dinner, young lady.'

Maria shot Orla a glance as if to say, *Told you so*.

Orla simply sighed defeatedly.

They all walked through to the kitchen, and Maria put Orla's backpack on the table before walking over to sit at the polished oak breakfast bar. 'Get everything done?'

'Yeah. Thanks for that,' Cat replied. 'Fancy a coffee before you go?'

Maria glanced at her watch, mentally sifting through what else she still had to do that day. 'Yeah, why not? I've got a bit of time. What you got in?'

Cat pulled two mugs out of the cupboard. 'I've got that stuff your mum brought round last week, or I've got iced vanilla latte sachets – but for God's sake, don't tell her. The last lot got culled in the *that's not real coffee* raid.'

Maria laughed. 'Has she asked for a key yet?'

'Well, I gave her one for emergencies. You know, in case...' Cat trailed off as Maria gave a loud comical groan. She pressed her lips together in a thin line. 'Was that *not* a good idea?'

'You will never get rid of her,' Maria replied. 'I gave her a key to my place when I first bought it, years back. She drove me up the *wall*. So one day I just stole it back and let her think she'd lost it. She still doesn't know, to this day.' She laughed again, her face softening at the memory. 'Had to pretend I kept forgetting to get her another one cut for months of course. She gave up in the end.'

Cat pulled in a deep breath and blew it out through her cheeks, one hand on her hip. She glanced at the mugs on the side then up at Maria. 'Wine?'

'Yeah, go on then,' Maria agreed.

Cat put the mugs away and pulled out two glasses instead, followed by an already open bottle of white from the fridge. She poured both glasses and handed one to Maria, and for a few moments, the pair drank in companionable silence.

'So, how's things?' Cat asked. 'Any juicy cases you can talk about? Or juicy *dates*...?' She drew out the last word, a twinkle in her eye as she grinned at Maria.

Maria rolled her eyes. 'No. You know I don't have time for dates. I make the odd gentleman friend but no one worth keeping around. I can't be bothered with the hassle.'

'Don't you ever get lonely?' Cat asked.

'Not really,' Maria replied without pause. 'I have my work and my family. That keeps me busy enough. I don't need someone else to look after too. But I could ask the same of you. Do *you* get lonely?'

She'd expected the answer to be much the same as her own,

knowing how happy Cat was these days, how full her life was, with purpose. But to her surprise, it was not.

Cat shrugged. 'A little. Don't get me wrong, I love my life now, and I'm so glad I don't have Greg dragging me down anymore. But it can get lonely in the evenings. It would be nice to have someone to share it all with at some point. Someone actually worth my time.'

Maria's eyebrows rose in surprise, but she simply nodded.

'You know, your mum said something funny the other day,' Cat said, tilting her head with a small frown, as if something had just occurred to her.

'Humorous funny or nuthouse application funny?' Maria asked.

Cat grinned. 'Neither actually. It was just' – her brow knitted further – 'she was talking about you guys when you were little, and she said *my girls*.'

Maria froze, feeling a frisson of cold shock run through her. She swallowed and quickly schooled her expression. 'Oh.' Looking down at her glass, she rested her fingers on the stem. 'Probably a slip of the tongue. She most likely meant to say kids.'

'No, she didn't.' Cat shook her head. 'Because it was, like, specifically girl related.' Her face scrunched, and she looked upwards as she said the words, as though she was trying, and failing, to find a better way to describe what she was saying.

But she didn't need to find a better way because Maria already understood exactly what had happened. Casting her eyes downwards, she took a carefully slow sip of her wine before replying. 'Weird. So, back to you being rid of Greg... have you heard any more from him since he turned up to proclaim his undying love for your new fortune?'

Cat laughed as Maria's attempt to distract her and move the conversation on worked.

'No, thank *God*.' She sighed and ran a hand back through

her shiny brown hair. 'I honestly don't know what I ever saw in that arsehole.'

'Arrogance? A wet blanket?' Maria offered with a teasing grin.

Cat rolled her eyes with a sheepish expression. 'I can't even defend myself here. There's literally nothing good that I can recall.'

Maria laughed and was grateful that Cat didn't seem to notice that the sound was brittle and thin. Because her heart wasn't behind it. Not after hearing what her mother had accidentally said out loud. Because that slip of the tongue meant only one thing. It meant that her mother was thinking about it all again. It meant that she was thinking about *her*.

NINETEEN

Bill Hanlon lived for two things in life – his wife, Amy, and whatever cutting-edge technology could undermine anything and everything in the legal world. He'd made a very lucrative career out of the latter these past few decades. And with the speed that technology was now advancing, he knew he had a very long and very bright future ahead of him for the next few too.

Bill's services were available, for a hefty sum, to anyone in the murky depths of the London underworld who was on the right side of the Tyler firm. The Tylers were reigning underworld royalty. Whilst other players still lorded over their own territories across London, the Tylers were the biggest and most influential of them all. Not many dared to go against them. While not technically a part of the Tyler firm himself, as he preferred to stay a free agent, this was where Bill's loyalties lay. And so, when he went through the photos he'd found on Malcolm Ardley's computer, he took a while to consider what they could mean to his close friend and current head of that firm, Freddie Tyler.

Placing his elbow on the desk, Bill rested his face in his

hand and sighed heavily through his nose. Then, making a decision, he picked up his phone and found Freddie's number. It rang twice, and then a low voice spoke.

'Bill. Talk to me.'

'Alright, Fred,' Bill greeted him. 'I've come across something on a job. Something you might find interesting.'

'Gimme a sec.' There was a short silence from Freddie as the background noise faded and a door was closed. 'Whose job is it?'

'Maria Capello's,' Bill replied, lowering his deep craggy voice slightly as he glanced out of the window.

'Go on,' Freddie instructed.

'Some politician's been blackmailing her. I helped extract the damning photos from his computer. And they *really are* damning,' Bill revealed.

'What we talking? Locations? Product?' Freddie asked.

Bill shook his head. 'Nah. He's got her blowing up a pub, somewhere east. It's no man's land so they've not stepped on any toes, but these photos... They're practically a signed confession.'

There was a long silence before Freddie replied. 'Make copies. Keep them in the vault for me.'

'Got it,' Bill replied.

A car pulled up on the road outside his house, and he turned back to his desk, hitting a key to bring the screen back to life.

'Good stuff. You're coming to Anna's birthday bash tonight, yeah?' Freddie checked.

''Course. Wouldn't miss it for the world. I'll catch you later,' Bill replied, quickly reopening the file he'd made for Maria.

'Catch you later.'

The line went dead, and Bill dropped the phone, quickly copying the files over onto one of his external hard drives. The doorbell went, and he disconnected the hard drive, putting it away in a cupboard before locking his screen and standing up. That would go into the special vault of leverage files *hopefully* never to be used again. But as Bill and Freddie both knew, you could never say never in their game. Even when it came to allies. And it was always better to be prepared.

He could hear Amy talking now, welcoming Maria into their home and asking all the usual questions. How was the family? Had life been treating her well? How had they not seen each other in years and yet Maria hadn't aged a day?

Bill glanced in the mirror and smoothed his thin hair down before straightening his shirt collar. Broad and stocky with a heavily lined, naturally serious face, Bill had long ago accepted he'd never be classed as handsome, but he still took great pride in the neatness of his appearance.

Bill walked out of his office and down the hallway to the kitchen, where Amy, his adoring wife and love of his life, was already bustling about pulling out mugs.

'Here he is!' Amy exclaimed with a wide smile. 'Maria's here to see you. I was just about to make some tea. Do you want one, love?'

'Nah, I'm OK thanks.' He smiled warmly at her and then turned the same smile to Maria. 'Good to see you. How's things? You keeping well?'

'Yeah, all good thanks, Bill,' she replied. 'And thank you so much, Amy, but I'd better not. It's only a flying visit. I've got a meeting in an hour I need to prep for.'

'Oh, OK.' Amy looked disappointed, but she hid it quickly with a smile.

Maria looked like she'd come straight from the office, Bill noted. She cut a smart figure, dressed in a deep green trouser suit, with a cream satin blouse and an assortment of long gold necklaces draped over it.

'How are you two doing?' Maria asked, smiling at them both in turn. 'It's been an age since we last caught up.'

Bill wasn't fooled by the smile. It was warm and easy but a little too polished. Politeness rather than true interest. He didn't blame her though. Maria was clearly desperate to find out how much Bill had managed to do with the photos, and he didn't want to keep her hanging in suspense for too long. He knew, all too well, how stressful that could be.

'We're good thanks, love,' Amy replied. 'Same old, same old over here. Nothing very interesting to report. We're quite boring really.' She laughed.

'Well, there's a lot to be said for that,' Maria replied. 'Boring is highly underrated! I could do with a bit more of it, to be honest.'

'Wouldn't want it any other way,' Bill confirmed, shooting Amy another warm smile. 'And on that note...' He met Maria's gaze and tilted his head towards the hallway. 'I've got something to show ya.'

'Yes.' Maria turned to follow him as he walked out of the room. 'Catch you later, Amy,' she called over her shoulder.

They walked through to Bill's office, and both their smiles dropped away to more serious expressions as he shut the door behind them.

'So.' Maria took the seat to the side of Bill's desk and cast her gaze across the wall of screens and various technical devices. 'How did you get on?'

Bill lowered himself into his chair and pulled it in, touching his hand to the keyboard. The main screen in front of him came to life and, on it, a picture of an East London street.

Maria blew out a long breath through her cheeks as she stared at it. 'So he wasn't bluffing.'

'No. He definitely wasn't.' Bill clicked through the photos, and they watched together as Maria exited the pub, Danny following right behind. They crossed the road to stand with Joe, moving closer to the photographer.

She shook her head. 'I was so sure there was no one there.'

'There probably wasn't,' Bill told her with a sympathetic grimace. 'At least not close. Nowadays, some of these cameras have a seriously long range and the quality is crystal. You likely wouldn't have spotted him even if you were looking right at him.'

As if on cue, Bill clicked on a photo of Maria looking directly into the camera.

'Fuck's sake...' she muttered, wiping a hand down her face.

They continued to look through the photos, a stilted slideshow of that day at the pub. Maria and the two men by her side turning to look back at the pub. Half of the building erupting in a huge explosion, followed by debris falling from the sky all across the street. Maria and her men in the aftermath, no sign of a reaction from any of them. A handful of other men stumbling out of the pub. Maria turning and addressing someone just out of shot, handing over two brown packages that were very obviously filled with money – then very calmly walking away from the scene, her two men following her.

Bill swivelled in his chair to face her. 'That's everything he has.'

Maria nodded. 'Can you tell where it came from?'

'They were downloaded directly from an SD card. Likely the one it was saved on in the first place. Wouldn't be much call to copy them to another – it would be easier to email or copy to a cheap USB if the owner wanted to keep the originals,' Bill told her. 'And they don't appear to have been sent on either. There's no trace of any of them being emailed or uploaded to the cloud.'

'Good,' Maria said with a tinge of relief. 'That's good.'

'That don't mean he hasn't downloaded them onto another device of course,' Bill warned. 'He could have stored them on another computer somewhere. And even if he hasn't, he'll still have the SD card somewhere. So that's something else you'll have to get around. If you can,' he added.

'I know,' Maria replied. 'Danny and Joe have been watching

the house. I'm pretty certain it's in there.' She sat back and folded her arms, chewing the inside of her cheek for a moment. 'Knowing Malcolm, he won't have told anyone else about this. It's a dirty move, and he can't afford for his political status to be threatened by that knowledge. But he'll have been smart enough to keep the copies and the SD card in different places. There is a chance it could be at one of his mistresses' houses, but I don't think so. He wouldn't want to lose that level of control.'

'Well, I hope you manage to figure it out,' Bill told her. 'Don't forget, you'll need to get back into his office to remove that bug. They sweep the place and it'll be found. And while it's not directly linked to any of us now it's burned out, it's still a loose end.'

Maria nodded. ''Course.'

'I've wiped these copies and any trace of them ever being there, so that part's done with at least,' Bill continued.

Maria squeezed his arm with a grateful smile. 'Thanks, Bill.' She reached into her handbag, pulled out a thick stack of notes wrapped in brown paper and placed it on the table between them. 'As agreed. Feel free to count it.'

'Nah, I trust you, Maria.' Bill smiled.

They both knew Bill didn't work with anyone he didn't explicitly trust. And they both *also* knew that Maria would be a fool to short-change him, considering he was the best in the business and they were all swimming in a very small pool.

'And for your piece of mind, here's the deletion of *these* copies.' Bill moved the mouse and tapped a couple of buttons, deleting the files in front of her.

Maria looked instantly relieved. 'That's great. Thanks, Bill.' She slapped her hands down on her thighs and released a loud breath before pushing up off the chair. 'Right. I'd best be off. I need to be in Central in half an hour.' She glanced at her watch and pulled a face. 'Sorry I can't stop.'

'No worries at all,' Bill assured her. He stood to open the door and found Amy hovering in the hallway. 'Amy will see you out. You take care now.'

'You too.' Maria gave him one more smile and walked out of the room, then down the hall with Amy.

Bill watched her go and then sat down, his eyes resting on the blank screen. After a second, his gaze moved up to the cupboard where he stored his external hard drives. He hadn't *lied* when he said he was deleting those copies. He'd done exactly that. But, of course, he hadn't said a word about the ones he'd stored away for a rainy day.

TWENTY

Cat bit her lip as she stared at her handbag. She was sure she'd left the card in the inside pocket, but she'd searched the damn thing three times now and she *still* couldn't find it. But where could it be? She hadn't taken it out – of that she was completely sure. Alex had been explicit in his instructions, and she'd followed them to the letter. To keep the card on her at all times and never let it out of her sight. And she hadn't. She truly hadn't. She hadn't even left her bag alone with Orla, though she'd questioned her anyway. But Orla hadn't rifled through her bag, she was sure of it. Aside from the way she'd not shown an ounce of guilt whilst protesting her innocence, the bag had been tidy, all the zips still fastened. If Orla had been through her bag, there would be telltale signs of disarray.

At first, she'd thought maybe she'd put it somewhere else. She'd had to have done, *right?* But even before she'd finished searching all the pockets in her jeans and jackets, and the drawer of her bedside table, she'd known. She *hadn't* put it somewhere else. She wouldn't have. She was too organised a person to do that when she'd already made the decision to keep it where it was. Which meant someone else must have taken it. There was literally no other explanation for it. But who? And why? And *when?*

'You OK?'

The voice stirred Cat from her thoughts, and she turned to see Sophia staring at her with a frown. 'Fine,' she insisted, forcing a smile. 'Can I help you with that?' She gestured to the pots and pans bubbling away on the hob.

'No, no. You go and relax with the others. I'm pretty much done,' Sophia insisted.

They'd been invited round for Sunday dinner, and today it was a full house. Maria and Alex were in the lounge, along with their two cousins on their father's side, Marco and Lucia, and Bianca. Lucia's husband, Gio, was also there, along with their five-year-old daughter, Alice. Orla had been instantly taken with Alice, who was nearly two years older and therefore cooler and clearly in possession of much more superior knowledge of the world. Orla was now trailing around after her in the garden, playing whatever game Alice had decided they should play. Cat glanced out the window at them.

Sophia followed her gaze. 'Go on,' she urged. 'I'm watching the girls. They can't get up to much out there, and the side gate is locked. They're alright.'

Cat nodded with a grateful smile at the reassuring words. Sophia knew how anxious Cat could get about Orla's safety, and despite the fact Cat knew her worry was overkill a lot of the time, Sophia had never once berated her or told her she was being silly. She understood. And that meant a lot.

'OK. Call me, though, if you need me,' Cat said, reluctantly walking out of the kitchen towards the lounge.

'But yeah, business is pretty good right now,' Marco said as she entered the room and perched on the end of one of the sofas.

He smiled at her, and she mirrored his expression, casting her gaze over him subtly as he turned his attention back to Alex. Marco looked a lot like his cousins. The same thick, raven-black hair, striking bone structure, full lips and almond-shaped eyes. He could easily pass as Alex and Maria's brother. Even more so, she thought suddenly, than Antonio. The reminder of him sent a shiver through her, and she determinedly pushed him from her mind.

'Are you cold?' came a soft voice.

Cat looked up into Lucia's concerned eyes and quickly plastered a smile on her face. 'Oh no, I'm OK. I don't know what that was. I'm fine.'

'My mum always says spontaneous shivers, like that, are someone walking over your grave from a past life,' Marco chimed in, his dark brown eyes focused back on her.

'She also says if you don't throw salt over your left shoulder every time you use some, someone you care about will die in some horrible, violent accident,' Lucia threw in. 'And that's never happened, so I'd take what Mum says with, well' – she paused for effect – 'a pinch of salt.'

Marco turned to look at her, a half-smile playing on his lips, and Alex chuckled.

'I said what I said,' Lucia claimed with mock defiance. 'You guys aren't the only ones who can run with a good dad joke.'

Cat grinned. She'd warmed to Lucia instantly when they'd arrived. She came across as kind and easy-going, and her husband seemed the same. Lucia looked completely different to her brother and cousins, with long auburn hair, blue eyes and a slender face that perfectly fitted with her slight frame. The only similarity Cat could see between them was when she smiled.

'Anyway, how's the consultancy going, Alex?' Marco asked, changing the subject.

Alex cleared his throat and shifted in his seat. 'Yeah, all good thanks,' he answered.

'Maria was telling me Antonio has decided to take a bit of a back seat for a while,' Marco continued, his expression inquisitive.

Cat watched Alex and Maria exchange a quick look, and Bianca stopped typing on her phone long enough to glance up at the pair of them before Alex answered.

'Yes, he has. He's still looking after a few clients, but he's exploring some other things right now.' Alex's smile was tight.

He'd warned Cat before they arrived that this side of the family lived very different lives than they were used to. Marco ran a second-hand car dealership, and Lucia had worked in marketing before she'd given that up to be a full-time mum. They probably suspected that there was more to their cousins' businesses than was spoken about, Alex had told her, but they didn't outright know. They had no idea who Alex and Maria really were or the kind of things they really did. And this was how they wanted to keep it. To keep things simple, they'd come up with the story that they were business consultants. It was easy enough to keep vague, and the closer to the truth they stayed, the better. If anyone probed too hard, Maria simply hijacked the conversation and began talking about her law firm. *That*, at least, was real.

'I see,' Marco mused. 'Is that why you've brought Cat on?' He turned back to her. 'Are you taking over the rest of Antonio's clients?'

'Er, no,' Cat replied. 'Actually, I'm an accountant.'

'Yeah, Cat's come on board to streamline the way we run our accounts,' Alex added. 'The way we were doing things before was a little outdated.'

Alex smiled at her, and Cat shot him a grateful smile in return. Bianca briefly looked up from her phone again, and Cat automatically tensed, but then she relaxed as Bianca shot her a friendly wink.

'Wow. Good-looking *and* intelligent,' Marco said, pulling Cat's attention back. 'That's a rare combination these days.'

Cat blinked, realising he was flirting with her as a slow smile spread across his face. His dark eyes held hers, and she felt heat rise in her cheeks at the unexpected attention.

'Oh.' She laughed nervously and pushed her hair back behind one ear, feeling awkward. 'I don't know about that.'

'No, don't do that,' Marco insisted. 'Don't put yourself down. You're a very attractive woman, and you certainly have some brains if you're an accountant. This world could do with more of that.'

Alex shifted in his seat and shot Marco another tight smile. Cat glanced at Bianca again and noted that she was now carefully watching Alex.

'I fully agree,' Maria chimed in. 'This world has *far* too many self-important men in positions of power, running around messing things up. It's about time you all moved over and let us women run things for a change.'

'*Ooh*, now, I never said that,' Marco teased.

Maria rolled her eyes.

'War would be a thing of the past,' Lucia chimed in.

'Everyone would stop comparing the size of their nukes,' Bianca added, without bothering to look up.

'Equal pay would be standard,' Maria said, nodding. 'Women's healthcare would get sorted out.'

'Oh *God*,' Gio said in mock despair. '*Look* what you started, Marco! It's a bloody revolution!'

'A well *overdue* one,' Lucia stated, turning on him with a frown.

He immediately threw his hands up in surrender. 'And one I fully support! I totally agree. You guys would do a much better job than us. We're idiots.' He turned a pleading expression on her. 'I was just hoping we could have dinner before you take over the world, babe. I'm *starving*.'

Lucia tilted her head in acceptance and then patted his leg. 'That's fair.'

Sophia popped her head around the door. 'Come on, Gio. I'll feed you all now, and then this lot can carry on with their plans for world domination.'

'Sounds good to me,' Maria said, grinning at Cat as she stood up and walked past.

Cat waited for the others to file out and bit the inside of her cheek as her mind moved back to the missing key card. Bianca slipped her phone away and followed the others, and Cat took the opportunity to catch Alex's eye.

'Hey, can I grab a quick word?' she asked quietly.

'Sure.' He hung back and waited until everyone else was out of earshot. 'What's up?' He glanced at the doorway with a small frown. 'Is it what Marco said? He can be a bit—'

'No. No, it's not that.' Cat cut him off. 'It's, *ugh*. It's the card you gave me,' she whispered, cringing internally. 'For the hotel.'

Alex's frown deepened. 'Right?'

'It's, well, it's gone missing,' she admitted.

If she'd felt terrible about it before, she felt ten times worse now. Alex's eyes widened in alarm, and then his face dropped as he stifled a groan.

'I'm so sorry,' she said hurriedly. 'I don't know what happened. I put it in my bag, and my bag hasn't been out of my sight, but it just' – she pulled her shoulders in tight and held her hands out in a helpless gesture with a grimace – 'disappeared. I don't know what to say. I was careful. I just—'

'It's fine,' Alex said, cutting her off. But it was clear from his expression and the loud, stressed sigh he released that it was anything but fine. 'Look, hopefully it just fell out of your bag somewhere random. If that's the case, then it's plain, so it won't be obvious what it's for.' He ran a hand back through his hair. 'I'll get you another one, but just, *please*, make sure this doesn't happen again. You *know* how much is at stake if that were to fall into the wrong hands, Cat.'

'Of course,' Cat replied with a hurried nod. 'I'm so sorry, Alex. It won't happen again.'

Alex just sighed and walked off into the hall, and Cat watched him go, cringing at how painful that had been. She was still so new here. She was still trying to show him, show *all* of them, that she was an asset. Someone worth having around. Someone they could trust. And now, here she was, letting them down at the very first hurdle. Failing the simplest of tasks.

Keep this safe at all times. That's what he'd asked of her. And she couldn't even do that.

Placing her hands over her eyes, Cat suppressed a groan. What must he think of her? Now she was going to have to work even harder to prove herself capable. To prove herself worthy of this job. Worthy of his friendship too. And she realised, suddenly, that this mattered more than the job. Because she'd grown so used to having him around. To talking to him and laughing with him. Having him in her and Orla's day-to-day lives.

It hit her, then, how much she'd come to need him around. And this sobered her. She had no right to him. No more than anyone else in her position. She put her hands to her cheeks as it dawned on her that this need for him to be around stemmed from feelings she shouldn't be having. Feelings that had crept up on her so slowly she'd not noticed them until now. Feelings that went against everything she believed in and that could only lead to pain and disappointment. Because there was no alternative.

What was she doing? How had she allowed this to happen?

Lowering her hands, she pulled in a deep breath. This had to stop, and it had to stop *now*. She was stronger than this. She wasn't some silly little schoolgirl – she could quell a crush. And she would. Starting immediately.

With a fresh feeling of determination, Cat gritted her teeth and followed the rest of them to the kitchen. She would work out what to do with this later. Right now, they had a family dinner to attend.

The aroma of roasted meats and rich gravy made her mouth water, and for the briefest of moments, she felt comforted as she caught sight of Orla eagerly jumping onto a chair at the dining table and Maria pushing it in. To see her daughter so at ease here, surrounded by people who cared about her, was worth more than anything after all they'd both been through.

But as her eyes swept across to the woman pouring herself a glass of water at the other end of the table, something jogged in Cat's memory, and she froze. She'd been so sure she hadn't left her bag unattended since Alex gave her the key, but that wasn't strictly true. She *had* left it for just a few moments, while she'd been out with Bianca.

Bianca caught her eye and smiled, gesturing to an empty seat beside her. Cat forced herself to smile back, but the action left a sour taste in her mouth as she replayed those moments in the bar. As she replayed Bianca spilling that water, how dramatic it had all been. And suddenly she realised that it *had* to have been Bianca who took it. It was the only feasible explanation. All this talk of being friends, of starting afresh and moving on, it had seemed odd, but it hadn't been unwelcome. Had it all been a lie? Had this all been part of a bigger plan?

But if it was, what kind of plan? And, more importantly, why? Anger began to bubble up inside as she realised what a fool she'd been, if she was right. And suddenly, she had the awful all-consuming feeling that she was. Oh, how easily she'd been played. How had she been so blind?

Bianca glanced over with a swift smile, and though the action only served to fuel her indignant rage, Cat swallowed it down and forced a smile back. Because, right now, she couldn't prove it. Right now, she might still be wrong about it all. But if this *was* all one big game, Bianca's streak of running rings around her was about to come to an end. Because now she knew, Cat was more than prepared to enter the ring. And when it came to her future within this family – within this firm – she was absolutely not prepared to lose. No matter what.

TWENTY-ONE

Maria picked up the ringing phone with anticipation and listened as her men confirmed that they were all in place.

'Good. I'm going in now. And then...' She stared up at the tall building with a cold smile. 'Then we wait.'

Slipping the phone back into her bag, she took a deep, bracing breath and walked inside. Her heels tapped out a sharp rhythm on the marble floor as she crossed to the lifts, then she travelled up to Malcolm Ardley's floor.

The lift pinged as the doors opened, and she marched straight over to Ellen's desk, her chin jutting out determinedly as she reached the startled woman.

'I'm here to see Malcolm,' she declared.

'Er, well, you don't have an appointment,' Ellen replied, sounding flustered.

'I know,' Maria agreed. 'But I also know he's in and that he'll see me if you tell him I'm here. Please do so.'

Ellen's puffy cheeks began to colour, and her face contorted a little bit at the brazen directness. 'Well, I don't know who you think you—'

The doors opened, and they both turned to see Malcolm's frowning face peep round.

'Everything alr— Oh. Maria.' His frown deepened as he looked at her. 'Er, did we have an appointment?' He glanced at Ellen.

'No, you did *not*,' Ellen replied vehemently before shooting Maria a purse-lipped glare.

'I am sorry to bother you unexpectedly like this,' Maria said more gently, offering Ellen an apologetic smile. 'I was just in the area, and it's rather time sensitive. I won't take too much of your time, Malcolm. I only need five minutes.'

'Ah, OK.' His frown disappeared, and his expression now displayed much more interest. 'I'm assuming it's about this deal we were discussing. It's OK, Ellen.' He turned his most gut-wrenchingly wet smile on her, and Maria had to stare at a fixed point behind him to avoid grimacing. 'I can take it from here. I was about to break for lunch anyway. Do come in, Miss Capello.'

Maria smiled. 'Thanks.'

Marching past him into the room, she made a beeline for Malcolm's desk, quickly reaching underneath and ripping off the tiny device she'd planted there as she lowered herself into the chair. Malcolm closed the door and ambled over, none the wiser, and Maria slipped the device into her handbag with a smile.

'So,' Malcolm said as he sat down. 'Am I to assume you have an update on the situation?'

'Of sorts,' Maria replied.

'I'm all ears,' Malcolm told her, lacing his hands together and resting them on his rounded middle.

Maria's smile widened momentarily before dropping completely. 'There is no deal, Malcolm. There never was. I just needed to buy myself some time.'

The look of interest on Malcolm's face faded into one of

annoyance. 'Well, that's not very good news at all,' he told her. 'Especially for you.'

'Don't you want to know *why* I needed time?' Maria asked.

Malcolm's eyes narrowed. 'It doesn't really matter, does it? I hold all the cards.'

'Do you?' Maria's eyes glinted with amusement.

'Stop playing games, Maria. You know I do,' Malcolm replied. But the conviction in his tone had been replaced with a note of doubt.

'Why don't you check your computer?' Maria suggested.

For a few moments, Malcolm simply stared at her, but when she didn't break her gaze away, his own flickered towards his screen.

'This is ridiculous,' he muttered. But he logged on, just the same.

Maria rested back in her chair and waited, watching his eyes narrow and then widen when he found the file was gone.

'*What?* How did...' He mashed his lips together and kept searching, his typing growing more frantic as he failed to find it, time and again. His cheeks reddened, and his breathing grew faster as his anger built up. 'How *dare* you hack a *politician's* computer?' he seethed. 'How *dare* you? I'll have you arrested for this.'

'You could *try*,' Maria offered. 'But how on earth would you prove it? And even if you could, what would you say exactly? That I stole back photos of illegal activity that you were holding on to so you could blackmail me?' Maria tutted and shook her head. 'Not sure that will be looked upon very kindly by the police, Malcolm. Plus, of course, I'd then have to release the footage I have of *you* with all those women.' She wrinkled her nose. 'That would get very messy very quickly for you, wouldn't it?'

Malcolm's face had reddened further and further as she spoke, to the point he now reminded her of an overcooked beetroot. 'You stupid bitch,' he spat. 'Did you really think this was the only copy I have? *Nothing* has changed. This was just the backup; I still have the original.'

Maria allowed a slow smile to spread across her face, holding his gaze in hers as she spoke her next two skilfully loaded words. '*Do* you?'

Malcolm stared at her over the desk, cold fury in his eyes and his jaw working overtime. Then, without another word, he stood up and strode out of the room, grabbing his jacket on the way. Maria stood and followed, pausing at the door to watch him slam out of the hallway towards the lifts.

Ellen was on the phone and barely seemed to look up as her boss left, Maria noted. This was good. Careful not to draw any further attention to herself, Maria closed the office door behind her and made her way to the door that led to the stairwell. Once she was safely down the first flight of stairs, she pulled her phone out and placed a call.

'He's on the move.' She glanced over the handrail, both up and down, to make sure she was alone, and lowered her voice. 'Stay on him and keep me updated. I'll be right behind you.'

* * *

Ten minutes later, Malcolm swung his car over into the next lane, ignoring the angry horn that blared at him from the driver he'd just cut up. He didn't have time for road manners today. Not when his entire future was at stake. He was furious. Furious at the world and at Maria. But mostly he was furious with himself. He'd *known* he shouldn't have trusted her. This promise of a better deal than the one he'd already been offered had seemed too good to be true – and he was smart enough at this point in his life to know that if something seemed too good to be true, that it most likely *was*. But Maria was beautiful and charming and smart, and he'd always been a sucker for attractive women. They were his Achilles' heel, and his judgement had been clouded.

'Get out the fucking *way!*' he roared as a slow driver dared to overtake someone in front of him.

He had to get to that SD card. It was his only hope now. She had to be bluffing. She just *had* to. How could she *possibly* know about his little village bolthole? Even his *accountant* didn't know about it. And that had been no mean feat to pull off, but he'd done it, just in case his wife ever did make good on her threats to leave him one day, and he was wrung out through the divorce courts. This place was hidden through a trail of paperwork so long that even *God* would be hard pressed to find it. So there was no way on earth that Maria Capello could have, as good a lawyer as she was. But she'd seemed so confident in his office that suddenly he was questioning everything. *Could* she had found this place? Had he missed something? His accountant, his wife, they had no particular reason to dig around, to suspect he had a hidden property, but Maria had very good reason indeed. And she was far from stupid. Suddenly, it seemed all too feasible.

What seemed like an age later, Malcolm pulled onto the gravel driveway of his hidden cottage and barely waited for the engine to shudder to a stop before he jumped out of the car and raced to the front door. He pulled his keys from his pocket and then dropped them in his haste, swearing as he bent to pick them up.

So intently focused on finding the right one, he barely registered the sound of another car stopping on the road just beside the drive. It was a sleepy village, but there was still traffic, so it was nothing out of the ordinary.

The footsteps on the gravel gave him cause to pause though, and as he turned to see who it was, his brow furrowed. Two men he hadn't seen before were headed his way, up the drive.

His irritation grew. He didn't have time to hear about whatever they were selling. Not today.

'Hello, Malcolm,' one of them said in a gruff voice.

Malcolm opened his mouth to tell them he was too busy to hear them out but then paused as they used his name. 'Who—'

But he never got the chance to finish his question as, with a dull clang, something hard hit him on the back of the head, and the world went black.

TWENTY-TWO

Cat stared down at her sleeping daughter, stroking her soft, silky hair and marvelling, as she often did, at how lucky she was to have her. Sure, Cat had been through the mill with Greg, and part of her would love nothing more than to erase him from her history forever. But the bigger part of her wouldn't swap all the hell he'd put her through for the world. Because if she hadn't met him, she wouldn't have this perfect little slice of heaven currently snuggled up in the crook of her arm.

She continued humming Orla's favourite nursery rhyme under her breath, even though she was now firmly asleep, content to stay in this perfect bubble just a little while longer, until a sound downstairs caused her to pause. She frowned. *Had that been the door?* A few seconds passed and then another tentative knock sounded, confirming her suspicions.

Cat gently eased Orla off her arm and manoeuvred her onto the pillow, then tiptoed out of the room and down the stairs. As she approached the door, she saw the outline of a man through the stained glass and frowned. If Greg was here to pester her again, she wasn't in the mood. Sighing, she swung open the door, ready to give him a piece of her mind, but then she stopped short. It wasn't him. It was Alex.

Alex grinned. 'Hey. Hope I wasn't interrupting anything.'

'Oh. No, I've just put Orla down,' Cat replied. Her heart lifted at the sight of him, and she scolded herself, pushing it back down. Pulling her cardigan further around herself, she crossed her arms over her chest. 'So, what's up? Everything OK?'

'Yeah, everything's fine.' Alex's gaze flickered to her arms, clearly noting her defensive stance. 'I was just at a loose end tonight, and I remember you saying you don't get out much, with Orla. Thought you might be up for some company?' He held up a bottle of wine that she hadn't noticed he was carrying. 'It's not Italian though.' He leaned in conspiratorially. 'Just don't tell Mum.'

Cat couldn't help but laugh at that, but then she caught her bottom lip with her teeth. She so badly wanted to say yes. She enjoyed his company immensely, but that was the problem. She liked it too much. She cast her gaze away with a rueful expression.

'You know, I, um...' She searched for the words. 'That sounds lovely, but I think I'm actually going to just get an early night tonight. It's getting on a bit.'

Alex glanced at the clock behind her, and she followed his gaze with an internal cringe. It was barely seven o'clock.

'I'm just really tired today,' she continued. 'I don't know if maybe I'm coming down with something.' She touched her throat, feeling guilty for the lie. 'I didn't sleep well last night.'

The last part wasn't a lie. She'd been up late, again, raking over all her past interactions with Bianca, checking that there was nothing else she'd missed. She still couldn't work out if what she'd realised really *was* a realisation or whether she was just looking for connections out of sheer desperation. Her intuition was telling her she was right. That Bianca *had* stolen that card. But logic kept wading in, asking her why Bianca would need to steal it in the first place? It didn't make sense. Bianca would have no reason to act so deviously against her own husband's firm – against her own family. And if she did, there were surely simpler ways to do so.

And if Bianca was gunning for Cat, this seemed a lot of effort for very little return. Besides, it wasn't even her style. Bianca, they all knew, liked things blunt and dramatic. Still, her behaviour had been off recently. Unpredictable, for a change. And the more Cat looked back at it, the more staged that water spill now seemed.

'Sure,' Alex said, taking a step back and forcing Cat's thoughts back to the present. 'Of course. No worries.' He looked down at the bottle of wine and twisted it around in his hands. 'It was just on the off chance. Another time.'

'Yeah, maybe,' Cat answered.

She watched him catch the word and turn it over in his head. *Maybe*. It sounded reluctant even to her own ears, and she wanted nothing more than to recover this conversation and say what she *really* felt.

Yes! Any day! Every day! I love it when we hang out. I wish we could do it all the time.

But she couldn't. It would be wrong. She'd be as bad a person as the women who'd participated in the affairs her own husband had had behind her back. And she would *never* be one of them. Not that Alex would do that to Bianca of course. He was a good man. He wouldn't cheat. He had no idea at all that these thoughts were swimming around in her head. This was *all her*. And this spiralling thought process was exactly the reason she had to start distancing herself from him, outside of work.

'OK. Well, I'll see you tomorrow,' Alex said, his voice a lot less sure than it had been a moment ago.

'Yeah. Um, Alex? I actually need to just crack on tomorrow, really. I think I'm good to go. I probably won't come to the house. I'll just head to the office, if that's OK?' she added, remembering in time that he *was* still her boss.

'Oh. Of course. If you have everything you need, then that's great. I'll see you...' He trailed off as if trying to work it out.

'I'll just give you a shout when I'm done with those and you can direct me on where you want me next,' Cat told him. 'I don't want to take up too much of your time. I know how busy you are.'

Alex stared at her for a moment, his brows puckering slightly as he tried to understand this three-sixty attitude change. Until now, Cat had always been happy to get involved and join him or Maria as they went about their various tasks, keen to understand how their businesses worked so that she could continuously come up with better ways to hide their money. It was unusual for her to be so detached. But he didn't question it. Instead, he simply nodded slowly.

'Right. Well. You know where I am,' he told her.

Cat forced a bright smile and nodded back at him. 'Yep. Catch you soon.'

Alex walked away, and Cat shut the front door, instantly turning and leaning back against it, closing her eyes. She felt rotten. Her insides roiled in protest against her decision to push Alex away, and her heart felt heavy. But though she felt miserable, this only served to enforce that her decision was the right one. Alex would never be hers to pursue or even to think about like that. It was better this way. Better to disappoint herself now than break her heart completely later.

Besides, Cat couldn't spend the evening looking him in the eye and acting normal, pretending that she wasn't about to shatter the fragile peace that had formed between herself and his wife. Because she was. She couldn't continue to sit idly by, not knowing if Bianca really was causing chaos for her from the shadows. Not when she was taking such dangerous risks every day. Working for the Capellos, Cat had to know that she was surrounded by people she could trust. She didn't have to like Bianca, but that trust was non-negotiable. There was far too much at risk, for her and for Orla.

So she would get to the bottom of whatever was going on there. And Cat knew that whatever step she took now, the outcome wasn't going to be pretty. Because either she was wrong and she'd, once again, make an enemy of Bianca – and possibly even Alex, which was something she couldn't bear to think about – or she was right. And the Devil himself wouldn't want to be around for that fallout.

TWENTY-THREE

Maria relaxed into the terracotta wing-backed armchair, one leg loosely crossed over the other as she patiently waited for the man on the single bed across the room to wake up. It wasn't a particularly large room, but it was cosy enough. A colourful home-made peg rug covered a large portion of the floor, and printed pictures of beautiful places all around the world brightened up one of the walls in a large collage. Danny stood beside the door, behind her, hands clasped and a hard look on his face. He was the only one she ever allowed in here, other than Alex, now. The only one outside of her bloodline who she trusted with these particular secrets.

Eventually, Malcolm stirred, and after a moment of shifting and groaning, he finally opened his eyes. He blinked blearily and then sat up in a sharp, jerky motion that instantly made him groan and close his eyes again.

'You might want to move a bit more carefully,' Maria offered. 'You had quite a fall.'

Malcolm forced his eyes open again, gingerly touching the back of his head as he glared at her. *'You,'* he snarled. 'What the *hell* do you think you're doing?'

'Right now, making sure you don't have a concussion,' Maria replied. 'How are you feeling?'

Malcolm snorted, easing himself up to lean against the wall. 'You vindictive bitch. I take it you never actually had the SD card?'

Maria shook her head. 'Thank you though. For leading us straight there. It didn't take us long to find it once we got inside.' She lifted the tiny card into the air and studied it, before slipping it away in her inner jacket pocket. 'Honestly, behind the bathroom mirror?' She smiled. 'You need better hiding places.'

'I demand that you let me out of here, *right now*,' Malcolm declared, ignoring her comment.

'Of course,' Maria replied calmly. 'You can walk out that door anytime, Malcolm.'

His eyes flicked warily to Danny.

'He won't stop you,' Maria assured him. 'He's just here in case you got a bit cranky with me when you woke up.'

Malcolm let out a short, humourless laugh. 'I don't need to hurt you physically, Maria. I'll get you back in other ways.'

'Yeah?' she asked, arching an eyebrow.

But Malcolm didn't answer straightaway. Instead, he shuffled forward off the bed and stood up, taking a second to find his balance before stumbling towards the door.

Maria watched him go, not moving from her seat until he'd opened the door and walked into the hallway beyond. She heard him curse, and a smile curled up her face. Joining him, she followed his gaze to the two doors at the end of the dimly lit hallway.

'Oh, don't worry. I'll show you the way.' She walked slowly on, waiting for him to fall in beside her. 'Then you can go home, get cleaned up and forget any of this ever happened. You no longer have anything over me, but I still have everything over you, Malcolm. So it really is in everybody's best interest that we simply go back to where we were before. Wouldn't you agree?'

She paused and turned to face him. To her disappointment, there was no look of defeat on his face. Only a simmering anger and hot defiance.

'Oh, I'll get cleaned up and back on form, Maria. But this is far from over. I will *get* you for this. You are so fucked. And I won't rest until you get what's coming to you. You've made a *big* mistake here today. *Big*. And you want to release those videos of me with my mistresses? *Go ahead*,' he spat. 'I'll get someone to confirm it's all just a fabrication put together by AI because you wanted to blackmail me for the land. And if that doesn't work and my wife leaves me, then so be it. I'll be a bloody rich man by then. I'm sure I'll get over it.'

Maria lifted her eyebrows. 'Nice. What a lucky lady Mrs Ardley is.'

Malcolm narrowed his eyes and curled his lip in hatred but didn't bother replying. He took another step towards the two doors, one hand touching his head again, where they'd hit it. '*Well?*' he growled.

A faint smile coloured Maria's lips as she stared at the two doors. Then she pointed to the one on the right. 'This way, Malcolm.'

Striding forward, she unlocked the door and held it open for him to walk through, Danny hot on his heels.

Malcolm stopped a few feet in and looked around with a curious frown. 'What is all this?'

Maria joined him and cast her gaze over the rows and rows of plant life, hydroponic systems and special lighting, under the corrugated iron roof. 'You asked me, a while back, why I needed that housing project stopped. Well, this is why.' She took a couple of steps forward to a side table where some small clippings were drying out under a lamp and touched her fingers to the leaves. 'We're about fifteen feet underground right now. From above, all that people can see is a field and an old barn. A dirt track leading up to it. But in that old barn, there's a hidden entrance that tunnels down here, into a series of connected containers, that form a ring of rooms around a steel-supported dugout.' She gestured at the supports. 'Which is where *we're* standing. The people who work here live in the container rooms, and they all work together, looking after these very special plants.'

Malcolm snorted. 'You went to all that trouble to protect your fucking weed operation?'

'Oh no,' Maria replied, a cold smile pulling up the corners of her mouth. 'These aren't cannabis plants, Malcolm.' She felt a small thrill shoot through her at the confusion on his face. 'They're so much more than that.'

'What are they?' Malcolm peered at them as if trying to make sense of it all. He stumbled forward a bit and cursed, placing his hand back up on his head once more.

'Each marked area holds something different,' Maria told him. 'A lot of these plants are illegal in this country. Some are very rare. Most of them are deadly, when used in the correct manner.' She picked up a leaf and smiled.

'Most are *deadly*?' he repeated with a wide-eyed frown.

'Yes,' Maria replied. 'The ones that aren't are here to create antidotes against the effects of some of them. Not all of them of course. For some there *is* no antidote.'

Malcolm blew out a long, stressed breath and winced as he clutched his head a little tighter. 'Why are you telling me all this?' he asked.

Maria let out a small sigh as she turned to him. 'You could have gone through the left door, Malcolm.'

'What are you *talking* about?' he demanded, pulling at the neck of his shirt to loosen it as he stumbled forward again. He caught himself on the edge of the table and rested his weight against it as sweat began to form on his brow.

Maria walked on to the next row of plants, gently touching the purple petals at the tip of the long stem. 'I gave you the option to leave and for us to move forward in *peace*. If you'd just been agreeable, you could have gone out through the left door and never discovered what's in here. I'd have slipped you the antidote to the poison I gave you earlier that's now slowly working its way through your body, and you'd have been none the wiser. But you made it very clear you wouldn't stop coming for me and that you wouldn't stop that build. And I just can't have that. As well as my business, I have people to protect here.'

'*Poison?* Your... *business?*' Malcolm asked, sounding completely confused.

'Yes. *This* business,' Maria said, gesturing around her. 'I'm guessing your airways are beginning to feel a little tight right about now.' She watched him desperately try to create more room between his shirt and his neck. 'And I imagine the room is spinning pretty heavily.' She walked towards him slowly, each step precise and deliberate. 'Your head will be thumping like there's someone with a hammer inside your skull, and your muscles should be weakening.'

As if on cue, Malcolm fell gracelessly to his knees, his breaths coming out in short, sharp rasps.

'It won't be long now. And it won't be painful,' she promised him. 'You'll pass out before anything really happens.'

'*Please*,' he begged. 'I'm... *sorry*. I won't...' He clutched at his neck.

'I know,' Maria said quietly. 'But it's too late, I'm afraid. You know too much. Goodbye, Malcolm.'

She watched as he tried to crawl towards her, one arm outstretched, but then he slumped forward, collapsing in a red, sweaty heap, and became still. She looked down at him and shook her head with a sigh.

'Where d'you want him?' Danny asked, stepping forward.

'Put him in the chiller for now. Just until I figure out what to do with him,' she instructed.

'Yes, boss.' Danny clicked his fingers, and one of the men

who lived and worked there jogged forward to help as Maria turned away.

'You alright?' another man asked, materialising from a doorway to her right.

She'd asked them all to stay out of her way until Malcolm was dealt with, but now they were all slowly reappearing to get back to their day-to-day tasks.

'I'm fine,' Maria answered calmly.

She stared back at Malcolm's motionless body, her heart hardening as she thought about everything and everyone she'd just protected by killing him. She raised her chin defiantly. This was who she was. Who she *really* was. The face behind the veil of smoke. The person they only whispered about in the dark circles of the underworld. The nameless ghost who ran London's deadliest poison game.

'He made his choice,' she said. 'And as everyone knows, no one outside these walls ever meets the Viper and lives to tell the tale.'

TWENTY-FOUR

Alex dropped his unconscious wife down on top of the bed a little less gently than he probably should have and then straightened up for a moment to look down at her. Her mascara had smudged down over one cheek, and her red lipstick was all over her chin. Her low-cut top had twisted to one side, revealing half of her bra, and she'd lost one of her gold hoop earrings at some point along the way. None of this, though, was as bad as the smell. She reeked of stale alcohol and smoke and the musky scent of what he imaged was cheap club bathroom perfume. It certainly wasn't one he recognised from her own collection.

He shook his head unhappily and sat down beside her, leaning forward to rest his weight on his thighs. This was the third time in the last week he'd had to pick her up like this, each time rearing for a fight and making no sense in her rantings as he dragged her to the car. And, as always, she passed out so hard he could never wake her when they got home. How many more times could he do this?

It wasn't the embarrassment that got to him, though that was bad enough. It wasn't the inconvenience of it all either. Alex would happily have picked her up from Timbuktu on a weekly basis, if it meant her coming home safe from somewhere she'd enjoyed being. But this constant state of aggressive drunkenness was wearing him down. As were the arguments that always inevitably followed. They weren't even started by *him*, though he had every right to kick off, if he'd wanted to. It was Bianca. She'd wake up in a few hours, miserable and feeling sorry for herself. And when he wasn't there to pamper her and pander to her every need, she'd round on him as though he were the devil incarnate.

Up till now, Alex had just made sure to avoid her during those times, as much as possible, unable to feign sympathy for her constant self-sabotage. But the problem was, he couldn't keep this up forever, and he was getting to the very end of his tether with it all. This wasn't the marriage he'd signed up for. If it could even be *called* a marriage. He'd spoken to her time and again, asking her to rein it in a little. To make at least *some* effort. To meet him in the middle, so they could try and get back to a better place together. But it never happened.

He sighed heavily and looked down to his ring, turning it around on his finger. Once upon a time, it had felt like the symbol of their very own happy ending. Now it simply felt like the shackles of a curse. One that had him trapped by the weight of honour and responsibility.

He stared for a moment at the bedside table, contemplating leaving his wedding ring on it. Contemplating calling it a day, the way he so desperately wanted to. But then he reached into his pocket and pulled out a thick wad of cash, dropping that down instead. It should ease her pain when she woke. And, in turn, hopefully his too.

His phone beeped, and he looked down at the screen. It was his cousin Marco again. He slipped the phone back into his pocket without bothering to read the message. Marco had messaged a couple of times now, asking if Alex was free for a drink, but it was the last thing Alex wanted to do right now.

Because he knew what was behind it. Curiosity. The nosy need to delve into what was *really* going on in the Capello household. He'd been way too curious about Antonio's absence and Cat's appearance. And whatever the underlying motivation for that was, Alex just didn't have time for it.

Standing up, he made to walk out of the bedroom but, as he did, Bianca stirred and muttered something unintelligible. He paused and then continued moving a little more quietly, not wanting her to wake until he was gone. But as he pulled the door to, she muttered one more word. And this one was as clear as day.

'*Antonio.*'

Alex paused, shock zapping through him. *Was that...?* Yes. Yes, he'd heard correctly. But why on earth was Bianca dreaming about Antonio?

A knock on the door cut through Alex's spiralling thoughts, and he glanced at the stairwell, then back at his wife's sleeping form. He contemplated waking her, demanding to know what was going on in her life that caused her to dream about his brother, but the second knock tore his attention away again.

Perhaps it was for the best, he decided. No good ever came of waking a drunken Bianca. Besides, even if there was some reason for it, she'd be unlikely to actually tell him. With a deep sigh, Alex closed the door and padded down the thickly carpeted stairs towards the front door.

Opening it, he frowned. 'What are *you* doing here?'

'Nice to see you too, cousin,' Marco replied sarcastically with an awkward grin. 'Look, I did text, but, um...' He turned and glanced back at the street nervously, rubbing at the side of his neck. 'Well, I really need to talk to you.'

'Er, now's not a good time,' Alex told him reluctantly.

'*Please,*' Marco begged, a tinge of desperation creeping into his tone. 'I don't know where else to go. I don't know anyone else, like, you know. Like *you.*'

Alex frowned. 'What do you mean, *like me?*'

'Ah, come on, man,' Marco said, releasing a stressed breath. 'You know what I mean. I *know*. Alright? I know. You really think you guys can get as big as you are in your game and that no one else in this family would hear your name? I know you're fixers. I know you're probably a few more things too, but that much I know for sure. And I need your help.'

Alex's gaze sharpened as Marco said the words, and he quickly looked around to make sure no one else was in hearing distance. 'Come— *Ugh*, right. OK. Get inside.'

Alex moved aside and gestured for Marco to go in then quickly closed the door before he rounded on him. 'Don't *ever* say those words out loud again, do you hear me?' he said menacingly. 'You don't know who's listening.'

Marco threw his hands up. 'OK, no problem.'

'No, I'm serious.' Alex stepped towards him, pulling himself up to full height and shooting daggers at his cousin. 'I don't want to hear that you've said those words ever again. Not to me, not to other people, not even whispered to yourself in the fucking mirror, *do you understand?*'

'I *hear* you,' Marco stressed, holding Alex's eye contact.

Alex nodded. 'OK.' He mussed up his hair with his hand and let out a quiet groan, then walked through to the kitchen. 'Come on. We'll talk in here.' He sat at the kitchen table and offered Marco the seat opposite, waiting for him to sit before he continued. 'Where did you even *hear* that?'

A muscle in Marco's jaw worked back and forth. 'I've known for a while. I once caught Antonio in the middle of a run-in with someone in a back alley. He didn't see me. I hid behind a bin and heard him lay down the law. Saw how the men around him respected him, even though what he asked them to do was, well, crazy, to say the least. It wasn't until recently, though, that I heard that term. The, er, what I called you on the doorstep.'

'That we're fixers,' Alex confirmed.

Marco nodded. 'I was working late at the lot, and I was on my own. Two kids with masks stormed in, demanded I open the safe. And I was going to do it. I mean, I have insurance for that kind of thing. I wasn't going to be a smart-ass and get myself stabbed. But then the bigger one saw my name plaque and freaked. Started ranting to the other that I was a Capello, and that the Capellos were big fixers. They scarpered without another word.'

Alex's eyebrows rose. It was annoying that these little idiots had outed him, but at least the outcome had been positive. 'Well, that sounds like a good thing.'

'Yeah, it was,' Marco agreed. 'Except they were wrong of course. Because I'm not one of *the* Capellos, am I? But that was fine. I was more than happy to be mistaken that night. And I didn't say anything to Lucia, or my parents, by the way. I kept that little nugget to myself.' He bit his bottom lip and then released it. 'A week ago, we had a visit from some men who say our business is in their protection territory. They demanded we start paying them thirty per cent of our profits in return for their security, otherwise they'll let it be known we're unprotected. Started putting the pressure on.'

Alex frowned. They ran protection rackets in their own territory, but it was a choice that businesses made for themselves – they didn't force people. And they never charged above ten per cent.

'Thirty per cent is extortionate,' he mused. 'And they shouldn't be pressuring you.'

'I agree. On both counts,' Marco replied. 'But that's what's happening. When we said no, they beat Dad up. Gave him a black eye and a fractured rib.'

'*What?*' Alex sat up and leaned forward. 'Are you serious?'

'Unfortunately, yeah,' Marco replied. 'We told Mum he'd fallen down the stairs. Didn't want her to worry. But that was just the start of it. Two days later, we came in to all the car alarms going off. Someone had caved in half the windscreens on the forecourt with a bat.'

Alex felt anger rise in his chest. Their car lot was in North London in an area that was under the jurisdiction of a long-established Greek firm. But they'd never had any beef with each other, and the Greeks had always left the car lot well alone, out of professional respect. Why would they suddenly start messing with them now?

'Who was it?' he demanded. 'Who came to see you?'

Going to war with another firm was the last thing he wanted to do right now, with Antonio only recently gone. Their position was much weaker than it once was. But perhaps that was why they'd hit out now. Perhaps they wanted to start something while they had a fighting chance of actually winning.

'Irish guy. Maloney, his name was,' Marco replied.

Alex blinked. 'Irish?' he repeated.

'Yeah. From that new Traveller community over in Wood Green,' Marco confirmed. 'They said it's their turf now. So, can you help me? Can you, you know... fix this?'

Alex let out a long, slow breath as the implications all began crashing down in his brain. He couldn't say no. This was his family. But of all the people in the world they could challenge and feel confident about coming out on top, the Irish Travellers were definitely not high on that list. They were the most unpredictable and dangerous group of people Alex had ever come across.

'Fuck, Marco,' he breathed. 'This is some deep shit you've found yourself in here.'

'I know,' Marco replied. 'And, er, I should tell you, my dad doesn't know I'm here. He told me he didn't want to burden you. But, of course, he doesn't know what I know.'

'Oh, he knows,' Alex told him. He saw the look of shock pass over his cousin's face. 'They were brothers, remember.

Both so young when my dad started this firm. Your dad didn't agree with it, and they parted ways professionally, so he could pursue a more honest living. But he knew. He just kept it from the rest of you.' Alex stood up and walked over to the cupboard where they kept the alcohol, pulling out a bottle of whisky. Grabbing two tumblers, he sat back down and poured them each a generous glass. 'But whether he likes it or not, you both need me now. Because you certainly won't find a way out of this without me.'

'But we can *with* you, yeah?' Marco checked, sounding tentatively hopeful.

Alex released another long breath, unsure how to answer that honestly. 'I hope so, Marco. I really fucking hope so.'

TWENTY-FIVE

Cat shuffled out from under the shelving unit and pushed the wall panel back into position, making sure there were no visible cracks around the edges before placing all the cleaning supplies back in place again. It was the second time she'd taken the books out, done the work and placed them back in their little hidden spot. And it really was a clever place to hide them. Having explored this floor of the hotel and seen what was in these rooms, she now knew exactly why. If police ever raided this place – God forbid – they'd be so busy with the jackpot find of the printing presses that they'd likely see no reason to dig much deeper.

The floor was a hive of activity, and Cat marvelled at it each time she came here. The hallway looked like any other in this hotel, but the insides of each of the rooms all held pieces of one very big secret. There were two printing machines in the largest room – huge, hulking monsters that looked old and sturdy and complicated. That room had been soundproofed to avoid the real guests of the hotel detecting the production noise. Then there were three drying rooms with rows and rows of racks surrounded by industrial dehumidifiers to dissipate the strong smell of the chemicals. The next room along was a storage room with long tables and boxes of different dyes and chemicals, and trays carrying an assortment of tools of the trade. Finally, the two rooms at the end were where they cut, concealed and packed the finished notes.

Alex had explained to her that once they'd printed and dried out the sheets of notes, these notes were cut precisely into sheets of three, then concealed between the pages of fresh bibles. Cat had laughed when he told her that, but he'd explained it was the easiest way to keep them hidden in transit. He purchased the bibles from a charity, in bulk. The charity took the extra income gratefully and asked no questions. Then they added the money, repackaged them and sent them off to their various clients across the UK, who bought them at less than half the monetary value printed on the notes. From there, those clients had their own operations in place to launder and use it.

It was a terribly clever operation, and despite the criminality of what the Capellos were doing here, Cat couldn't help but admire the genius of it all. It had occurred to her, more than once lately, that her boundaries of what was right and wrong had slipped so very far from where they used to be. But although some small part of her worried about that, the bigger part just didn't seem to care. Because she'd learned, recently, that the law and what was right were often two very different things.

Brushing off her hands as she stood, Cat turned around to leave. She didn't want to be here any longer than necessary tonight. It felt too eerie. At this time, the small group of people who worked here had gone home and all the activity had ceased for the day. Or, rather, had ceased for the next few days, as it was Friday and no one worked here over the weekends. Besides, she'd already worked much later than she'd intended to tonight. She'd just been so absorbed in it all that she'd forgotten the time.

Or perhaps, subconsciously, she'd done that on purpose. Buried her head in work so that she didn't have to think about Orla.

Greg had finally bothered to pick her up from pre-school today and was having her overnight. And even though Cat knew this was a good thing, even though she *wanted* him to bother with Orla, for Orla's sake, it still left a knot of worry in her stomach. Was Orla alright? Did she feel safe and loved, or would Greg ignore her in favour of his phone all night, like he used to? Would Greg feed her something she liked or shout at her if she didn't eat whatever he'd made? Would he read her a bedtime story and leave a night light on, or leave her to settle herself alone, in unfamiliar surroundings? He'd only had this place a few weeks. Orla had only been there once before. Worry squeezed her insides and wrung them out as all these questions flooded her mind.

Her spirits a little low, Cat walked back through the hotel and out through the front door. Luckily, her car wasn't far away. As she'd come over so late, she'd risked driving and had lucked out, grabbing a spot just across the street, a little way down. Reaching into her handbag, she scrabbled about for the keys and then pressed the button to unlock the little silver BMW. It was new. Something she'd decided to treat herself to, after the money had come in from the sale of her father's business. Cat hadn't been sad to see her old car go. Like her old home, there had been too many bad memories attached to it.

Cat chucked her bag across to the passenger seat, then closed the door and rubbed her hands together for a moment, glad to be out of the cold. It was a bitter night. She moved her hand to the start button and was about to press it when a movement at the corner of the street caught her eye. She paused and squinted. There was something familiar about the quick, tightly spaced steps the person was taking. Whoever it was wore an oversized hoodie with the hood up and their face lowered, arms wrapped defensively across the middle. And it wasn't until they walked under the next streetlight that Cat realised exactly who it was. There was only one person she knew who wore leopard-print jeans with bright red shoes. Bianca.

Cat's hand slowly lowered away from the start button, and she caught her lower lip between her teeth as she watched Bianca look furtively around and then dart into the hotel. This was it. This was the moment she'd been waiting for. Proof that she *hadn't* just been imagining it. Bianca *had* taken her card. She had to tell someone. Explain it all. She should call Alex. Yes, that's what she'd do.

She reached for her phone but then stopped. What if he already knew Bianca was here? What if she was simply running an errand for him? This was her husband's place of business, after all. It wasn't an unreasonable place for her to be. For all she knew, Alex had left a favoured jumper there, and Bianca had offered to pick it up. Or maybe she'd come to just check up on things. There was no CCTV inside, even on a closed circuit, to ensure at least some people's identities were protected, should the worst ever happen. Cat could be entirely wrong about it all and then she'd have made herself sound like a crazy, paranoid fool.

Or even if she was right about Bianca taking the card, what if the other woman still had a good reason to be here and Cat revealed her hand too early? Bianca would then know Cat was on to her and close ranks. Make sure there was no opportunity for Cat to uncover her little secret. Then again, what if this *was* her chance to out Bianca? What if she *was* here doing something sinister and Cat missed her chance because she was out here panicking about whether or not to do something? Her insides twisted with anxiety as she pondered the dilemma.

A couple of minutes passed as Cat tried to work out what the best course of action was, and then suddenly, Bianca reappeared. Cat's hands flew to the steering wheel, and her gaze sharpened on the other woman as Bianca gave another suspiciously furtive glance down the street. This time, the large bag that had looked flat as she'd walked in now strained on her shoulder and had filled out at the sides. She was carrying something out, but what? It certainly wasn't a jumper, Cat decided, from the awkward bulkiness of it. Her heart thumped. Everything was telling her this wasn't right, but she knew she only had one shot at proving it. She couldn't mess it up.

Torn for a moment between Alex's warnings never to take any photos or videos of this place, and the inner voice telling her she needed proof, just in case, Cat eventually decided it was worth it.

'Fuck it,' she muttered, reaching for her phone.

But she was too late. Bianca rounded the corner and disappeared out of view.

'Shit,' she hissed, mentally kicking herself.

Cat stared at the corner for a few seconds, trying to work out what to do, then made a snap decision. She would follow Bianca. See where she went from here. If all she did was drive home, then clearly all was fine. She would have misjudged the situation, but she wouldn't have blown it.

Decision made, Cat started the engine and slowly pulled away from the kerb. She crawled to the corner and peered around, relieved when she saw the back lights of Bianca's car just pulling out of another space, a little way down. She waited for Bianca to pick up speed then pulled out behind her, careful to keep a good distance between them. Silver BMWs weren't uncommon, but Cat needed to make sure she didn't get close enough that Bianca would be able to see her face.

Bianca turned off the main road, and Cat followed her safely far behind for the first ten minutes. They were definitely *not* going in the direction of Bianca and Alex's home, which bolstered Cat's resolve. She was right. She *knew* it.

Bianca came to a set of traffic lights, and Cat cringed as she slowed to creep up behind her at a glacial pace. She slid down in her seat as she neared the back of Bianca's car and dipped her chin, trying her hardest to disappear from view. But thankfully, Bianca seemed too preoccupied to even glance in her rear-view.

They moved off again, and Cat let out a whoosh of relief as she was able to increase the distance between them once more. They drove for another fifteen minutes, until Bianca pulled into the underground car park of a tall apartment building. Cat slowed to a stop on the side of the road outside and looked up at it. It looked fairly new and expensive. She wondered who lived there. Suddenly, it hit her that this might not even be to do with Bianca sneaking around the hotel at all. Who would the woman be visiting at home at this time of night? Was she having an *affair*? Her eyebrows rose as she looked up at the building again, suddenly wishing she hadn't come across Bianca tonight at all.

This wasn't her business. Bianca's life, Alex's marriage, none of it. She didn't want any part of that. Then again, if her old neighbour had thought that way when they'd discovered her ex, Greg, was having an affair, they might never have told her either. And had that been the case, Cat could still be trapped in that marriage. The thought made her feel physically sick, and she glanced up at the building again with a groan. Lifting her phone, she reluctantly took a photo of the building and then turned the car around and left.

But she left feeling a hell of a lot heavier than she had felt driving in. If she spoke up and this turned out to be a huge misunderstanding, she'd be left looking like a lunatic. If she didn't and it turned out to be something big, she'd be letting Alex down. So what the hell was she supposed to do now?

TWENTY-SIX

Alex walked into the Black Bear pub, a place known as a neutral meeting ground for most of the London underworld. Of course, there were always exceptions. But unless a firm was being particularly difficult or had made many untimely enemies, everyone in their world was welcome through its doors.

As the door swung shut behind him, Alex breathed in the familiar scent of wood polish, leather and beer, and quickly took stock of who was there. A couple of his own men sat in the corner having a quiet beer, and they started when they saw him. One made to rise, but Alex motioned with his hand for him to stay seated. He wasn't here for them. At the table next to them, watching him with interest, were two men he'd never met, but he knew them to be Finn and Sean Logan. Old-school faces who'd once been run out of London by a firm run by Alex's two-faced uncle, Mani Romano, and who'd later returned to claim back what was theirs. Alex nodded to them, both in respect and as a reminder that he held no ill wishes towards them. The Capellos had never aligned themselves with the Romanos. The

Logan brothers nodded back, and Alex continued sweeping his gaze across the room.

There were a few faces he didn't recognise. Younger men, he noted. Most likely fresh blood in the ever-growing larger firms throughout the city. Lastly, in one of the booths that edged the length of the pub, he spotted who he was looking for. Pausing only to ask the bartender to bring a pint and another of whatever his guest was having over, Alex made his way to the booth and took a seat opposite a man who was clearly tall and lean but with such well-defined muscles they may as well have been sculpted from stone.

'Seamus,' Alex greeted him with a nod. 'How's things? Still boxing?'

'They're very good, Mr Capello, t'anks for asking. And, of course. Though mainly I teach the younger lads these days. Get the good ones ready for the big fights.' Seamus glanced at one of his hands as he said this, and Alex noticed a scar there.

Alex nodded. 'Well, thanks for meeting me.'

"Tis no problem at all, Mr Capello,' he replied in a thick, melodic Irish accent. 'What is it that I can do for ye?'

Seamus worked for the Tylers, but he had family in the Traveller community. Something Alex had remembered hearing whispers about a few years back, when Seamus had recruited their services to help the Tylers out on a job. It had been a one-off, as that community preferred to keep to themselves, but it showed that there was willingness to connect, should there be a need.

'My cousin has a car lot, just off the North Circ, near Wood Green,' Alex told him. 'Recently, a new community of Travellers moved into the area and are now squeezing him for protection money. When he said no, they jumped his dad and smashed a lot of windscreens. And they've made it clear they'll be back. Now, Wood Green ain't your territory—'

'It falls under Cos, the Greek,' Seamus interrupted. 'I'm

well aware. You want to know if I can help ye because I'm a Traveller.' His serious clear green eyes stared at Alex unblinkingly, and his expression was unreadable.

Alex nodded. 'Yeah. That's exactly what I'm wondering.'

Seamus's clear gaze pinned him for a few more seconds before the other man spoke. 'We're aware of them moving in, and we know who they are. But unfortunately, Mr Capello, none of mine will have nuttin' to do with 'em no more. Not after one of theirs ran off with me sister's mother-in-law's favourite dog a few years back. T'was a bad falling-out, that one.'

Alex's heart fell. He'd really been hoping to find a way in. To sort this amicably. 'I see.' He nodded. 'No worries. I thought it might be worth an ask.'

'That's not to say I can't help ye though,' Seamus added.

Alex blinked. 'It's not?'

They fell silent as the barman walked over with their pints. Lager for Alex and Guinness for Seamus.

'Thank you very much,' Seamus said with a nod. He took a sip and then made a noise of appreciation before he sat back and appraised Alex. 'D'ye know who your cousin's been having these problems with specifically?'

'Man called Maloney,' Alex replied. 'I don't have his first name.'

But Seamus was already nodding in recognition, a grim look on his face. 'Yea, I know the dryshite. Ain't nuttin' but cotton between his ear holes and a pair o' hams for arms. No skill to his game, there's not. Tried to compete in a bare-knuckle match at a big meet-up once. Me cousin took him out with one punch.' Seamus shifted in his seat and leaned forward. 'OK. This is actually good news.'

Alex frowned. 'It is?'

''Tis. And here's why.' Seamus pointed his finger down on the table. 'He's pissed off a lot of people. Even his own ma's sick of the sight of him. If he was one of the serious ones, someone higher up the food chain, you'd have yourself a problem. But this guy, no one would be unhappy to see him take a knock. He's also a classic bully wit' no balls. If ye strike back, put on a show of strength and give him something to cry about, he'll not bother your cousin again.'

Alex squinted. 'Are you sure? The last thing I need is to bring the wrath of his whole community down on my cousin's head.'

But Seamus shook his head confidently. 'This is why I said it's good news that it's Maloney. It's up to you, friend, but that's the advice I have to give ye. You do that and your problem will be solved. Now...' Seamus lifted his pint and took another deep sip. 'I'm sorry I can't help you more, but hopefully that advice was worth this pint of the good stuff.'

Alex smiled. 'I'd say it was, Seamus. Thanks.'

'No worries,' Seamus replied. 'Now, if you do go ahead, you must let me know. I'll buy you one back, so's I can hear all about it.'

'Absolutely.' Alex lifted his pint to his lips and stared off into the distance.

So he had to teach this guy a lesson the old-fashioned way. Well, if that's what he had to do, that's what he had to do. He was, after all, one of the best fixers in the game.

TWENTY-SEVEN

'Wake up.'

Something shockingly cold and wet hit Bianca's face as she was forced awake. Alarmed, she sat bolt upright, coughing and spluttering as the water that had been thrown over her filled her mouth and nose.

'*What the fuck?*' she screeched in a voice now hoarse and broken from all the celebrating she'd been doing the night before. What or who that celebration had been for she couldn't now remember.

The room was still dark, and her vision was blurred, her caked-on mascara half sticking one closed eye, and she rubbed at it with her hands. A second later, a blindingly bright light filled the room as someone drew the curtains, followed by a cool gust as they opened the window.

'Smells like a fucking whorehouse in here,' someone muttered.

Sophia, Bianca realised.

She blinked away the blurriness and winced to focus on her mother-in-law. Sophia was now taking a seat in the chair on the opposite side of the room, a hard look on her face. Irritation flooded through Bianca, alongside a pounding headache and a feeling of rolling nausea. *How much had she had to drink last night?*

'What are you doing here?' Bianca asked groggily, pushing sodden strands of hair back off her face. 'Did you – did you pour *water* on me?' She stared down at herself with an incredulous look.

'You looked like you needed it,' Sophia replied drily. 'And I'm here because I wanted to see why I woke up to find my son asleep on my sofa again this morning.' She looked Bianca pointedly up and down.

Bianca followed her gaze and saw she was still dressed – if the haphazard way the clothes still clung to her could be described as such – in the same skimpy outfit she'd worn out the night before. Next to her on the bed were her heels and clutch bag, and to her embarrassment there was a half-eaten box of kebabs spilled all over one of the pillows. Bianca sighed, wishing she could just roll over and sleep off the raging hangover that was now making its appearance, but it didn't seem that was a likely option right now.

'What are you doing, Bianca?'

The words were surprisingly gentle from the woman Bianca knew hated her guts. So gentle that, for a moment, she felt a prickle of emotion at the corner of one eye. But she quickly blinked it away.

'Well, I *was* sleeping, until *you* arrived,' Bianca replied sullenly.

'That's not what I meant,' Sophia replied. 'What are you doing with your *life?*' There was a short silence before she continued. '*Look* at you. Is this really what makes you happy?'

'Oh please,' Bianca snapped. 'Like you care what makes me happy.'

Sophia nodded, her sharp brown eyes not moving from Bianca's face for a second. 'OK, maybe I don't. But I do care what makes my *son* happy. I care that more often than not, I come down to find him on my sofa. He shouldn't be sleeping on my sofa, Bianca.'

'Don't pretend you don't love having him there to cluck over,' Bianca shot back, screwing her face up hatefully. 'You love it.'

'I love my son,' Sophia countered. 'And I want him to be happy. But he isn't. Because he keeps coming home to *this*.'

She gestured to the kebab-covered bed, and Bianca felt her cheeks flush with embarrassment.

'This is a one-off, Sophia,' she replied, rolling her eyes. 'I don't usually fall asleep with food up here.'

'I'm not talking about the food.' Sophia stood up and walked over, taking Bianca's chin between her thumb and forefinger. 'Get out of bed. Wash your face, put on some clean clothes, clear up this mess and then take a good long look in the mirror.' She released her and stepped back. 'You know, you have everything most women dream of. You have no worries in life, enough money to do whatever you want, a husband who loves and is loyal to you. But even Alex has his limits, Bianca. And I don't want to see him reach them any more than you do.'

'You'd love to see me fail,' Bianca replied, narrowing her gaze.

Sophia sighed. 'Actually, believe it or not, I'd love to see you succeed. I'd love to see you step up and be the wife my boy deserves. The one I used to think you *could* be.' Sophia's eyes searched Bianca's face. 'That girl still has to be in there somewhere. Find her. And bring her home to us. Because, Bianca, we would *all* be much happier if you did. You more than anyone.' Sophia walked towards the door and then paused to look back. 'For the record, while I don't like *you* very much, I'm rooting for that girl.'

With that, Sophia left, and Bianca clamped her jaw shut as those simple, meaningful words hit her heart like a poisoned barb. Tears filled her eyes, blurring her vision, and an ache deep down in her chest threatened to rip it apart. But it wasn't until she heard Sophia close the front door behind her that Bianca let out the first sob. The second and third swiftly followed, and she buried her head in the kebab-free pillow to muffle them as they gave way to a tsunami of cries.

Because those words, those well-meant, priceless words of encouragement were far, far too late. That girl was well and truly gone. She'd let her go too long ago to remember, sometime between the first time she'd cheated on Alex and Friday, when she'd stolen from him. And the monster that she had become was all that was left.

TWENTY-EIGHT

Maria woke slowly that Sunday morning, languishing in bed for a few minutes longer than usual as she stretched and thought about the day ahead. She felt lighter now that the Malcolm problem had been dealt with. He was gone, and therefore so was his threat. His computer was clean, and she had destroyed the SD card. She'd seen the missing persons alert go out for him the day before, when people finally noticed his absence, but this didn't worry her. This wasn't her first rodeo. His body was still safely underground in one of their chillers, until they decided what to do with him and ensured there were no links between them, other than professional ones. He'd been careful, always worried about his own position, never to mention the underhand dealings going on between them, over text or email.

For once, Maria had no plans, which was a welcome change. A whole day ahead of her and all the choices in the world. She might see if her mother wanted to go for a mani-pedi and a facial, she decided. They hadn't done that for a while. And she'd pop in on Cat and Orla later too. Maybe take Orla for a babyccino and a walk around that pet shop with all the bunnies in it that she loved so much, if Cat needed a break.

This thought cheered her greatly. It still surprised her how much that funny little girl had grown on her these past months. Yes, she would do all of that. Just as soon as she'd got rid of last night's entertainment.

She turned to look at the handsome man still sleeping soundly in the bed beside her and watched him for a moment. Chiselled jaw, designer stubble, great hair – even greater body – he'd been a lot of fun. But fun like that was for Saturday nights and it was now Sunday morning. Now, all she wanted to do was get him out of here before he started trying to engage her in inane conversation, or worse, try to woo her with his basic breakfast-making skills. She couldn't bear to sit through another one of those and pretend to be impressed. It always felt like listening to a child looking for praise from its mother.

You made me eggs? Oh, well done, you! You're such a clever cook, managing to get them in the frying pan like that! And you didn't even burn yourself on the stove...

Even the thought made her shudder a little, and she sat up promptly. 'Hey.' She prodded him gently with one hand and attempted to tame her wild mane of dark, caramel-streaked hair with the other. 'Hey, um... *Dan?*' She winced, suddenly unsure if that had been his name.

Maybe-Dan stirred and opened one sleepy eye with a slow smile. 'Good morning, gorgeous,' he murmured, his deep voice rumbling warmly as he reached for her.

Maria skirted away and swivelled to get out of bed. 'Hi,' she replied bluntly. 'So, listen, um, I have a really busy day planned, and it's already' – she checked the clock and winced – '*wow*, nearly seven. I'm actually running really late. So...'

'It's only seven?' Maybe-Dan queried.

'Yeah, it's really getting on,' Maria pushed, nodding wholeheartedly. 'I need to get moving.'

'Mmm.' Maybe-Dan groaned and pulled a sad face which made Maria internally cringe. 'Come back to bed. It's Sunday.'

'I'm going to head downstairs,' she replied, ignoring his comments. 'Get your clothes on and then come join me?' she asked. 'I'll make you a coffee.' She could afford to be a little nice.

'OK. You drive a hard bargain, Maria, but if that's what you want, I'm in,' he replied with a small chuckle.

She smiled as he sat up and swung his legs off the edge. 'Great. See you down there.'

Marching briskly across the room, Maria flicked the light switch with a flourish, ignoring the sound of protest from the bed behind her. In truth, she was probably just going to turn the light back off and grab another hour's sleep, after Maybe-Dan left. But for now, she needed all the help she could get to boot out the man she'd brought home last night as politely as possible.

Humming quietly to herself, Maria made her way downstairs to her slate-grey and white open-plan kitchen and flicked on the coffee machine. Her place was neat and tidy, modern and minimalist. Exactly as she liked it. Expensive art was dotted around the place, pieces that matched the aesthetic perfectly. Not overpowering but decently thought provoking, whenever someone stopped to properly look at them. Not that many people did. Maria didn't have people over often, and when she did, such as last night, she wanted to get rid of them quickly. Because this was her inner sanctum. Her safe space away from the stress and chaos of life. Somewhere she could close herself away and truly unwind. Where she could fully be herself, without anyone else knowing what that looked like.

Maria padded through the hallway to the front door and picked up the post. She was halfway back to the kitchen before she halted and looked down to the package in her hand with a frown. It was too early for the postman. And it was Sunday, which meant she shouldn't even be getting post today anyway. Her bright hazel eyes flickered around the packaging, and she realised that whilst it had her name and address written on it, there was no stamp. Someone had hand delivered it.

Quickening her step, she closed the distance between her and the kitchen island, then set about ripping it open. Steps sounded behind her as she pulled out the contents, and then she froze, her mouth dropping open, as she realised what she was looking at.

'OK then,' Maybe-Dan said, clapping his hands together as he glanced around her kitchen appreciatively. 'I'll tell you what, why don't I make us breakfast?'

'Get out,' she breathed, barely able to tear her eyes away from the items clutched in her hand.

'What?' he asked, tilting his head to the side with an unsure smile.

'I said, get out, Dan,' Maria said, more clearly this time. Her voice rose sharply. 'Get out of my house. Right now.' She no longer had time to play these games. She just needed him gone.

'Er, wow, um. It's actually *Will*,' he replied, affronted.

'I don't care,' she replied impatiently, not even bothering to look up this time. 'And I don't have time for this. Just get out of my fucking house.'

'Wow.' Will took a step back and shook his head, then turned and walked out, muttering something under his breath that Maria didn't care enough to catch.

She waited until the front door slammed and released a long, slow breath, trying to calm her racing heart. She wetted her lips and then took the items over to the kitchen table, staring down at them in fear and confusion. The first item was a high-resolution print of her outside The Raven's pub, just as the explosion lit up the scene in the background. The second item was a cheap generic phone. She picked this up and turned it over in her hand for a minute as she tried to think it all through.

What was going on? Malcolm was dead. He hadn't shared the images with anyone. She'd destroyed the SD card. So who the *hell* still had copies of this? And why were they playing games with her?

Maria swallowed hard and pressed the home button on the phone, watching as the screen came to life. She checked the call log. Nothing. Then the texts. Nothing there either. This was a brand-new burner, clearly bought especially for this. Pressing the contacts icon she saw the single number saved there, a full stop where the name should have been. Maria wiped a hand down her face then took a deep breath before placing the call. As it rang, she put it on speaker and laid it down on the table in front of her. It was picked up on the fourth ring, and for a few moments there was total silence, as whoever was on the other end waited.

'We both know you didn't go to all this trouble not to speak to me,' Maria said in a low tone. 'So speak.' Her heart rose to her throat as she waited in the silence a few seconds more. *Who the hell was this?*

'I don't know what you've done with Malcolm,' came a thin male voice. 'If your track record is anything to go by, I'm sure it can't be good.'

Maria frowned as she didn't recognise the voice. And what did he mean?

'But honestly,' he continued, 'I don't really care. If he's not around, then our deal's void, and you're fair game. And he was an odious man anyway. I'll tell you who *wasn't* though. Paul Walker. Remember him?'

Maria's frown deepened. The name did ring a bell, but she couldn't quite place it. She bit her lip and remained silent, hoping he'd continue.

'Unbelievable,' he spat. 'You really kill *that* many people, huh?'

Maria's expression opened up in surprise. That certainly narrowed it down a bit. Suddenly, it hit her, where she'd heard the name. 'The photographer,' she said slowly.

'Yes,' the man confirmed bitterly. 'The *photographer*. The one your brother kidnapped, and then you killed and disposed of.'

'No, that's...' Maria trailed off with a sigh and shook her head.

It hadn't been her who'd killed Paul Walker; it had been Antonio. A bloody disaster that could have so easily been avoided, had he not been off his head on coke and looking to vent some of his pent-up psychopathic rage. She *had* disposed of the body though. She had cleaned up the mess Antonio had made, just like she'd always done, until three months ago. Paul now lay eight feet underground. A couple of feet below the true grave of an old friend of hers, in a cemetery just a few miles away. Much as she'd hated to desecrate her friend's final resting place like that, it had been too clean an opportunity to miss. No one would ever think to look in a graveyard for a dead body that wasn't supposed to be there.

'That's not quite what happened, Mr...?' She waited, but he laughed.

'Do you really think I'm stupid enough to give you my *name*, after what you did to Paul?' he asked. 'I don't want to be the next on your long list of hits, *Capello*.'

She nodded slowly, expecting as much. 'Then what *are* you going to tell me?' she asked. 'If you were going to hand this picture in to the authorities, you'd have done it by now. But you haven't. Instead, you sent the photo to me. Which means you want something. What is it?'

She heard a sniff on the end of the line and a muffled curse.

'Do you know what kind of person he was, Maria?' the man asked with a shaky sob. 'Do you how *good* he was? How *kind* and *loving*? How *hopeful* he felt about this awful world, despite all the ways it constantly let him down? Of course you don't. He was just another nobody to you. A slab of meat you could do away with as you fancied.'

Maria's gaze dropped, and her forehead crinkled as a heavy sense of sadness washed over her. Taking a life – any life – wasn't something she enjoyed. It was something she, and all of them, only did when it was absolutely necessary. And, unfortunately, there were times in their world when it did become necessary. Or when it was part of their job. They were not perfect people, and they did not live perfect lives. Their souls were tinged with something dark and cold and heavy, and that was just the way it was. They had chosen to follow their father down this path, and that came with hard decisions and difficult sacrifices. But the fact that her brother was behind yet another killing that was so unnecessary was a difficult truth to carry. In fact, Antonio's unnecessary body count was really starting to weigh her down.

'What do you want?' she repeated, though a little quieter this time.

'I want him *back*,' the man replied, anguish in his tone. 'I want *justice*.' He sighed, and when he spoke again, the despair had vanished and a hard anger now came through in its place. 'But there are many other ways to make someone like you suffer. To make you pay. So, yeah. I could just hand this all in and watch you go down. But I think I've come up with a much better idea. Something a bit more drawn out.'

A cold trickle of dread crept up Maria's spine.

'From this point on, you will begin paying me a hundred grand a month,' he continued. 'For each month you hit that payment, you get to keep your freedom. Miss just *one*, or have that money for me even a day late, and all those photos go straight to the police, along with the identities of the two young homeless men you paid off that night.'

Maria sucked in a sharp, silent breath, and her eyes widened. She'd paid those men to scarper, to never say a word or return. And that's exactly what they had done. They'd seen what she could do – there was no way they'd risk their own safety by gossiping. But that had been easy for them, while no one knew they'd been there. When no one had seen them leave. How would they fare in an interrogation room full of police officers? They weren't hardened criminals bound by a code. They were just a couple of unfortunate souls who'd been in the wrong place at the wrong time.

'I imagine you're currently weighing up how well they'll hold up in front of the police,' the man on the phone correctly guessed. 'Not great, is the answer to that question. They didn't ask for this. They just got caught up in the crossfire of *your* mess, so they'll most likely sing like fucking canaries. Best thing I did that day was follow those two.'

Maria closed her eyes and began rubbing her temples. 'How exactly do you expect me to access a hundred grand a month?' she asked. 'You're setting this up to fail, straight off the bat. Ask for something more reasonable.'

'This isn't a negotiation,' he snapped. 'It's a demand. I hold the power here, not you. Remember?'

Maria rolled her eyes. 'You can demand all you want, but I don't have a hundred grand a month.'

'Then sell everything you've got,' he replied. 'That nice house of yours will buy you, what? Eight, nine months? Sell it. Your car will get a couple of weeks. And I'm sure you have more assets hidden away.'

'You want me to sell my entire life to pay your extortionate blackmail rates?' Maria asked flatly.

'Yeah. I do,' he replied. 'And then when you have nothing, your time will be up. But at least you'll have had those months. That's more than Paul got, isn't it?'

Maria bit her upper lip. She needed to draw him out, find out who this guy was. 'Paul was lucky to have someone in his life who cared about him as much as you did.'

'Don't you *dare* say his name,' the man snapped, emotion causing his voice to rise sharply. 'Don't you *dare*.'

Maria nodded and squinted out of the window as she mentally worked it through. 'I have two brothers, as you probably know,' she offered, taking a punt. 'I imagine I'd feel the same way, if it had been one of mine.'

There was a short silence. 'Good try,' he replied. 'You'll receive a text shortly with the details of an offshore account. You have a week from today to make the first payment. One week,' he pressed. 'And if it's not there, I hand everything over.'

And with that, the call went dead.

TWENTY-NINE

Alex pulled up on his mother's drive and got out of the car, quickly hiding his frown and plastering on a smile when he saw the next-door neighbour waving at him through a gap in the hedges surrounding the property.

'Ooh, Alex, have you got a moment?' she called.

Alex suppressed a sigh and walked over. 'Of course. Everything alright, Beryl?'

Beryl had lived there for as long as he could remember and, for the last couple of decades, alone, after her husband had passed away. She'd always been a good neighbour, never once commenting on all the various comings and goings, or police visits, over the years. Even though she *had* to have been curious.

'Yes, it's all fine thank you, Alex,' she said in a thin voice. 'It's just there's a fence panel at the back that's come down in the wind and split. It's my responsibility of course, that side,' she added quickly. 'It's just, I wondered if you might know someone trustworthy I could call to fit a new one? I know so many people see an old girl like me in a big house like this and try to pull a fast one. One lady I know booked a man to do her drive and he just took the money and disappeared.' Her face was a mask of worry.

Alex nodded. 'Don't you worry about it. I'll get it sorted,' he told her reassuringly. 'I'll have one of my men pick up a panel and fit it for you today. Alright?'

'Oh, thank you,' Beryl replied. 'That would be marvellous. You'll tell them to pop me the bill?'

But Alex shook his head. 'Nah, I'll take care of it. It's no problem at all.'

'Oh no, I couldn't let you—' Beryl started to protest but Alex cut her off.

'No, I won't hear of you paying a penny,' he insisted, giving her a smile before he turned to walk towards the front door. 'We're neighbours, and it's really nothing. We've got to look after those around us, eh?' He let that hang in the air a moment before continuing. 'I've got to pop in now, but I'll catch you later.'

'OK,' she called back to him. 'Thanks again, Alex.'

Alex walked into the house and shut the door behind him, making a mental note to follow that up. It was a small enough gesture, but those were the ones that were always worth giving out. You look after the people around you, they'll look after you back. It was one of the first lessons his father had ever taught him and one that had proven true, time and again.

Hearing his sister's voice in the lounge, he made his way in there and found that she'd already gathered all of their closest men. This didn't particularly worry him – they had meetings like this all the time. What *did* worry him was the look on Danny's face. He stopped short of the coffee table and glanced around, his gaze coming to rest on his sister.

'What's happened?' he asked.

Maria sighed. 'Those photos of me blowing up the pub. Apparently, Malcolm wasn't our only problem.'

Alex's dark brows furrowed. 'What do you mean?'

'I got these through the letterbox this morning.' Maria gestured to a photo and a cheap black phone on the coffee table. Alex moved to take a closer look. 'Hand delivered. I called the number in the phone, and the guy who answered demanded I start paying him a hundred grand a month or he'll send the photos and the details of two witnesses to the pigs.'

Alex stared at her. 'What witnesses? Surely he's bluffing.'

But Maria shook her head. 'There were two homeless men nearby. Boys really. They saw it, and we paid them off. It was handled. But if they're dragged in, that'll be a different story.'

'Shit,' Alex muttered, rubbing his eyes with a groan. 'That's all we need. Who is he?'

'Well, he didn't exactly leave me a business card,' Maria said wryly. 'But my guess? It has to be the photographer Malcolm hired. He mentioned Malcolm and a deal they'd made. He also brought up Paul Walker. The photographer Antonio killed a few months back.'

Maria sat forward, pulling the sleeves of her light cream jumper over her hands in a subconsciously defensive gesture that didn't go unnoticed by Alex. It was one of her tells, for people who truly knew her. She was worried, he realised. Genuinely afraid.

'He got very emotional, on the phone,' Maria continued, in her cool, calm way. 'I think either they were family or lovers. Very close. More so than just a friend, I'd say.'

'So we go with that,' Alex said, turning to Danny. 'Pull together all the details we can on Walker's family. Hit his socials, go through close friends' accounts. See if he had an agent. If he did, put a call in pretending to be an old friend returning from a year abroad, say you want to talk to those closest to him, see if they know anything.'

Danny nodded curtly. 'Yes, boss.'

Alex turned back to Maria. 'The number?'

She shook her head. 'That was a fresh burner, which means his will be too. We can try it, but I doubt we'll get anywhere.'

Alex grimaced. 'How does he want you to pay?'

'Offshore account,' Maria replied. 'I've already looked. It's a company account. And the company is registered as owned by another company, which is owned by another. It's your typical chain that goes off into oblivion. He's been careful to leave this airtight.'

'No one's that good,' Alex told her. 'We'll figure it out, and we'll sort it. OK?'

Maria nodded, but she didn't look convinced. 'I think we need to pull together the first payment,' she said. 'Just in case.'

'I'm sure that—' he started to respond, but Maria shook her head.

'No, Alex. He's got us, well, *me*, by the balls. I think we need to be ready to comply. Even just to buy us some more time. Call Cat, see what we can pull and where from, at short notice.'

For a long moment, Alex just stared at her. But then he nodded. 'If that's what you want to do,' he agreed.

'It is,' she replied before turning her unreadable gaze to the window.

As he watched his sister, Alex's blood turned as cold as ice in his veins. Because he'd never seen her like this. Maria was always on top. She was always one step ahead. Always ready with the next plan to get what she needed or overcome a challenge. Never, in all their years working together had he seen her so spooked. So ready to give in to the demands of an enemy.

And that frightened him more than any enemy ever could.

THIRTY

Alex slammed his hand down on the horn as another car pulled out in front of him, gesturing at the other driver angrily as he just managed to stop himself from spilling the coffee in his hand.

'Fucking moron,' he muttered, taking a sip from the steaming takeaway cup before carefully placing it in the drinks holder. His phone rang, and Alex hit the green button on the centre console screen. 'What?' he barked. There was a pause, and he instantly let out a deflating breath, tempering his tone to a calmer level. 'What is it?'

'Er, whereabouts are ya?' Danny asked.

'Five minutes out. Why?' Alex replied, turning the corner as the next set of lights turned green.

'OK, I'll catch you when you get here,' Danny replied. He sounded worried.

Alex frowned. 'What is it?'

'Just... I'll show ya when you get here,' Danny repeated, clearly reluctant to share whatever it was on the phone, now he knew his boss was close.

Alex checked the road ahead. 'Two minutes.' He ended the call and sighed.

He needed to get out of this brooding funk he'd woken up in today. But that wasn't easy when he was juggling all the dilemmas they were currently up against. Maria's reaction to her blackmailer's demands had shaken him. Maria had always been the steadfast one. She never lost her cool and was always one step ahead. Always. But it seemed that had changed. Why was she suddenly so unsure of herself? Was this really the adversary she thought would beat her? She'd come up against bigger and bolder than him before. Hadn't she? As well as all the obvious fires they were fighting, Bianca had been unusually quiet too, which was never a good sign. And something was strangely off with Cat. He didn't know what to make of that at all.

It was at times like this that a part of him missed Antonio. Not that he wanted to bring his brother back. Antonio had leaped so far across the point of no return, it was a mere speck in the distance. And Alex could never forgive him for the awful things he had done. But, in some ways, the mischief his brother had caused in the years before that had been so much simpler to deal with. So much easier to unpick.

He pulled up at the front of the hotel and parked, a space outside conveniently becoming free as he arrived. Locking the door behind him as he walked across the path and in through the front door, Alex made his way into the lift and pressed his key card to the reader. A few seconds later, the doors reopened as he reached his floor, and he stepped out, surprised to see a group of his men standing in the hallway waiting for him.

'Boss,' Danny said in greeting, exchanging an uneasy look with one of the others.

'What is it?' Alex asked, his eyes moving quickly across the group, searching their faces.

'It's the printer,' Danny started before biting his bottom lip.

Alex strode past them towards the printing room, not waiting for further explanation. In the middle stood a huge, ancient machine they were careful to keep in tip-top condition, as it worked so much better than the newer, cheaper alternatives. He cast his eyes quickly over the metal beast, noting that it appeared in order. From the outside at least.

'What's wrong with it?' he demanded as he heard the men fall in behind him. 'Have you called Guy?'

Guy was the engineer who kept it in such good condition for them. The man they called if they ever came across a problem, knowing better than to try and fix it themselves.

'That ain't gonna help this time, boss,' Danny replied. 'Not unless he has the plates.'

'What?' Alex swivelled to face him, eyes flaring wide.

Danny nodded at the machine. 'Ain't no plates in it. They've gone.'

Alex's heart lurched. 'What do you mean, *gone?*' he demanded, turning back and reaching for the machine.

He opened it up and, sure enough, the spaces where the four metal plates should have been were empty. Alex's mouth fell slack, and he stared at it for a few seconds, as if doing so might make them reappear. Shock flooded through him, turning the blood in his veins to thin streams of ice as the implications of what this meant hit him. Someone had taken their plates. Without the plates, they couldn't print. If they couldn't print, they couldn't deliver the orders their clients were expecting. If they didn't deliver, they would lose credibility and cause their clients a significant amount of trouble. The knock-on effect continued, but he quickly stopped his racing thoughts. He couldn't let himself spiral into that right now. Right now, he had to think.

'What happened?' he asked, hearing how stupid the question was even as it left his lips. If they knew, they'd have told him already.

'We don't know,' Danny answered, shaking his head helplessly. 'It was all there when we locked up on Friday, and no one can get up here without a key card. I know you said even the staff can't get on this level, but I double-checked with them anyway. They looked at the 'ard records – nothing's been created that ain't ours.'

'Manual doors?' Alex checked. 'Windows?'

'All still chained and locked from the inside,' Danny confirmed.

Alex swallowed, feeling sick. He ran a hand back over his hair and turned in a small circle, thinking it through.

'What should we do, boss?' one of the other men asked.

Alex stared at the machine for a moment. 'Go home,' he said flatly. 'All of you go home. Except you, Danny. I want you to stay here, keep watch on the place.'

'Yes, boss,' Danny replied.

The others nodded and shuffled off.

Alex wiped a hand down his face, shaking his head. Whoever had done this knew they were hitting him where it would leave the most damage. There was no recovery from this. At least, not a quick one. Those plates were unique. Custom made, following a long and expensive trail of trials and errors that weren't up to scratch. It had taken years to get them to the standard they were now.

'The men who were here Friday,' Danny ventured, scratching his neck as he glanced back at the hallway. 'They've all been here a long time. They've all proven they're trustworthy.'

Alex's jaw formed a hard line as he turned to face him. 'Well, it seems one of them has decided to be a turncoat, mate..'

The thought settled like a cold stone in his stomach. Every

one of their men had been with them a long time. Were people they trusted with their innermost secrets. Secrets that could see them jailed for life, or even killed, if placed in the wrong hands.

'I don't know who or why yet, but we have a rat.' Alex held Danny's gaze, his expression darkening. 'And one way or another, we're gonna have to smoke that rat out.'

THIRTY-ONE

Monday morning came around all too quickly for Cat, as it always did, following a weekend of fun with Orla. Greg had dropped her back very early Saturday morning, clearly already sick of his only child, in a way only the most narcissistic of men could be, after just one night. He'd attempted to play the hero, harping on about the bedtime story he'd read her, as if he'd just taken her on a two-week trip to Disneyland. And when Orla had run in past Cat without even looking back to say goodbye to her father, he'd had the audacity to ask if he could come in for a coffee, stating that he really needed one after a whole night of hard parenting. Cat had promptly shut the door in his face and thanked God, for the millionth time, that she no longer had to deal with such an insufferable arse in her life.

She and Orla had spent the day making paper lanterns and watching *Frozen* on repeat, screeching out the songs together so loudly that Cat was sure they must have scared off all the cats in at least a two-mile radius. On Sunday, they'd played at the park and made cookies together, before a very long and bubbly bathtime and then bed. It was exactly the kind of weekend Cat loved best. Quality time with her beautiful girl and no one else around to spoil it.

So when she arrived at Sophia's house on Monday morning, after dropping Orla off to pre-school, she'd completely forgotten all about her Friday night escapades, following Bianca around London. And it was only when a stricken-looking Alex had burst into the kitchen, where she, Maria and Sophia were enjoying a nice morning coffee, that it all came back to her with a sickening, heart-lurching crash.

'Someone's taken the plates from the presses in the hotel,' he stated urgently.

'*What?*' Maria asked. 'What do you mean, *taken?*'

'I mean exactly what it sounds like, Maria,' Alex replied, sounding uncharacteristically irate. 'I mean *taken* as in they've been *taken*. As in, someone has gone in, removed them from both presses and left the building with them.'

Maria gasped, and her hands flew to her cheeks as they drained of colour. She shook her head. 'No. No, no, no, they *can't* have. That's...'

'Years of work,' Alex finished for her. 'I know.'

As they continued talking, Cat's heart began to thump uncomfortably in her chest. So *that* was what Bianca had been doing. She'd stolen the plates. And Cat knew what that meant to the Capellos. When Alex said it was years of work, she knew he wasn't exaggerating. He'd explained the painstaking lengths they'd gone to, to create exactly the right mould for the plates. All the runs they'd wasted, testing them out. It had taken thirteen tries to create a plate that gave them a result that looked genuine enough to pass as real money. His lucky thirteenth, he'd joked. And each of those plates, four in total, to run the front and back of the notes on each machine, was irreplaceable. They were absolutely unique. The rest of the machines or even just parts of them, should they need fixing, could be bought easily enough. But to replace the plates would mean to start the design process all over again.

What on earth was Bianca *doing* with them? Cat should have told Alex as soon as she'd sensed something wasn't right. She was kicking herself now, for not trusting her instincts. She should speak up, tell them both what she saw. Then again, Bianca was still Alex's wife. Cat didn't want the guilt of causing problems between them to lie on *her* shoulders. Even if it *was* Bianca's own fault. Whatever she did now, there was going to be fallout. Guilt flooded her, along with a twisting anxiety. She didn't want to be part of this at all. But she had to do something. Watching the siblings talk before her, Cat knew it was only a matter of minutes, if not seconds, before they asked her if she'd noticed anything strange on Friday. And then she'd either have to tell them or lie, neither of which sounded like a great option right now.

Maybe Bianca had a perfectly reasonable explanation for it all. Or maybe she didn't but just needed a stern push in the right direction to fix her mistake. Making her decision, Cat stood up and pretended to take a call.

'Hello? Yes, speaking... Oh! Of course, that's today... I'm so sorry. I'm on my way now.' She pretended to end the call and grabbed her bag. 'Sorry, I just have to nip out. I'll be back soon.'

Alex half-heartedly nodded her off, and Maria was too caught up in what she was saying to notice anything else, Sophia worriedly looking on from the sides.

Cat took the opportunity to hurry out of the house and into her car. It was time to nip this in the bud and sort it all out behind the scenes, before the firm, or Alex's marriage, took a hit they couldn't come back from.

THIRTY-TWO

Pulling up on Alex's drive, Cat was relieved to see that Bianca's car was still there. She wasn't out for the day yet. She might not even be up, from what Cat had heard of her usual daily routine. But as Cat got out and walked up to the front door, it opened, revealing a fully – if casually – dressed Bianca, with a mug of something hot in her hands.

Bianca immediately put on the friendly smile she'd been flashing Cat recently, though Cat now recognised it as fake. The realisation irritated and saddened her. Much as she'd not been desperate to be Bianca's friend or drinking buddy, she had been glad of the olive branch. She had hoped it was the start of better things to come. It was a true shame that it had turned out to be nothing more than a ruse.

'Alright, Cat?' Bianca greeted her. 'He's not 'ere, I'm afraid. Left about half hour ago.'

'I know,' Cat replied. 'I'm here to see you.'

'Oh! Well, ain't that nice?' Bianca gushed. 'Girls' coffee morning, eh? Just what the doctor ordered. Come on in. I'll get a pot on.'

Cat shook her head as she walked into the house. 'Cut the

crap, Bianca.' She turned to face her as Bianca shut the door. 'I know what you did.'

'*Excuse* me?' Bianca tried to look affronted, but Cat caught the calculating look behind it.

'I know you don't give a shit about being my friend,' Cat said, wrinkling her nose. 'I know that was all just a load of bull to get me out somewhere with my guard down, so that you could steal my card for the hotel. Spilling the water on me was a clever touch, I'll give you that. I was so distracted it didn't even cross my mind, the fact you had access to my bag.'

Bianca snorted and crossed her arms. 'I don't know what the hell you're on about, love. Seriously, what's got into you?' She gave Cat a pitying look. 'You seem really stressed, babe. But I ain't your enemy. I'm your friend. So why don't you come sit down and tell me all about it, eh?'

'I saw you, Bianca,' Cat said, ignoring the other woman's words. She narrowed her eyes. 'I saw you, Friday night.'

Bianca blinked and a touch of panic flitted across her face. 'What you on about?' she asked with a forced laugh. 'I didn't see you Friday. I was here, chilling all night.'

'No, you weren't,' Cat pushed back. 'You were at the hotel. You snuck in, after everyone had left for the week, stole the plates out of the machines, put them in your bag and then left. I watched you, Bianca. I was in my car outside. I saw you. I'd recognise those leopard-print trousers and red shoes anywhere.'

For a moment, Bianca's face contorted as she tried to look confused, then amused, then angry, until eventually she dropped the act altogether. Her expression darkened, and the old hatred she used to throw Cat's way glittered in her eyes.

'You saw me, did you?' she asked disdainfully. 'What were *you* doing there?'

'Dropping files off,' Cat replied. 'Which is why *I* have a key. I was just leaving, then there you were. I followed you too. To those flats. To whoever lives there.'

This seemed to spark an extra flare of interest in Bianca's eyes. '*Whoever* lives there?' She pulled back, appraising Cat for a moment. 'Who do you *think* lives there?'

'I have no idea,' Cat admitted. 'At first, I wondered if you were having an affair, but now, well...' She shook her head again. 'I assume it's probably whoever you've sold those plates to.'

Bianca let out a cold laugh. 'Ahh, Cat. You're a modern-day Poirot, aren't ya? Honestly, you're wasted here – you should set up your own little PI agency. Far, far, *far* away from here.'

The nasty glint was back in Bianca's eye, and Cat felt a cold shiver rake up her spine.

'Listen, Bianca,' she said, getting to her point. 'I haven't told them yet because I wanted to give you a chance to do that yourself. Or to get them back and put them back in the printers. I don't know. Either or. But one way or another, you need to pick one of those options. Because I can't hold on to this knowledge if you don't.'

'Oh, you're going to *tell on me*, are you?' Bianca mocked.

Anger flared up from the pit of Cat's stomach. 'This isn't a *game*, Bianca. This isn't a fucking playground, and trying to belittle the situation won't make it go away.' Her voice began to rise. 'You're Alex's *wife*. You should know, as well as any of us, how serious this is. And I doubt I need to tell you how it's going to go down for you when they *do* find out, so just get your *shit* together. Figure out how you want to deal with this and *do* it. Because I'm serious. I will *not* hide this if you don't.' Cat clamped her mouth shut and exhaled heavily through her nose as she regained her composure. 'I'm giving you a chance here. A chance to make sure this goes a better way for you. For *all* of you.'

Bianca's gaze bored into her, full of fire and fury and hatred, but after a few moments, the fire seemed to fade a little and she stepped back, her eyes narrowing. 'Fine,' she said, her tone much calmer than Cat had been expecting.

'Fine?' she queried.

'Fine,' Bianca repeated with a slow nod. 'I'll deal with it. Just... give me some time to see what I can do.'

'You have until tomorrow night,' Cat warned. 'Because I *won't* lie to them. I can avoid them until then, but that's it. You got that?'

'Loud and fucking clear,' Bianca replied. 'Now get out my fucking house, you pathetic simpering bitch.'

Cat's eyebrows shot up. There had been a time Bianca had scared her when she spoke like that. But that time had long since passed. '*Simpering?* That's the best you can come up with?' she asked flatly.

'Oh no. I could come up with much better, but that's what you are, ain't it?' Bianca said cruelly. 'You've been following my husband round like a little puppy ever since he hired you. Just waiting for the tiniest little scrap to be thrown your way. Scratching and whingeing and wagging your fluffy little tail, practically *begging* for his attention.'

Cat felt her cheeks warm but shook her head and forced a look of disgust. 'Do you *hear* yourself? Alex is my *boss*, Bianca. It's literally my *job* to be where he tells me to be and to do the work he tells me to do.' It was the truth. There was no denying that, no matter what else she felt. 'And yeah, I do count him as a friend too. Because he, and Sophia, and Maria were all there for me and Orla when we needed it most. That's all.' This was *mainly* the truth. Though it was clear they both knew that wasn't really all there was to her feelings. 'I would *never* go for another woman's husband after what mine did to me.' A full truth again. 'But maybe, if you're so worried about his head being turned by someone else—'

Bianca snorted, cutting her off. 'I ain't *worried*. Why would *I* be worried?'

But her defensive tone betrayed her, and Cat gave her a cold half-smile to let her know as much. 'If you are *so worried* about his head being turned,' she repeated, 'then maybe you need to start looking at *why*.'

Bianca's cheeks flooded crimson, and her eyes flashed with anger. 'Get the *fuck* out of my house.'

'Gladly,' Cat replied icily. She turned and opened the door. 'Tomorrow night, Bianca. You sort this by tomorrow night, or *I will*.'

She heard the intake of breath behind her as Bianca prepared to fling back another response. But with a flick of her wrist, before the other woman could utter a word, Cat slammed the door shut behind her.

THIRTY-THREE

With everything that was going on right now, the last thing Alex needed was to have to help his cousin out of a tricky fix. But Marco was family, and he'd been right when he'd said Alex was the only person he could come to for help with this. If he'd gone to the police, he'd likely have found his car lot petrol bombed. Or worse, his home. Because all that would have told Maloney was that Marco was scared. And bullies loved to hone in on those who were scared. And so, now, here Alex was. All geared up, with his men, ready to teach the guy a lesson. He only hoped that Seamus's information was correct, and this didn't escalate things instead.

Maloney had told Marco, after beating up his father, that he'd be back tonight to collect his money. That this should give him enough time to see sense. He'd demanded that Marco be there at seven sharp. After closing, so that they were alone. Of course, his hopes of being alone were about to be well and truly dashed, but luckily he didn't know that yet.

Alex checked his watch. It was seven on the dot. He peered out from his hiding place behind one of the cars and caught Danny's eye. Danny was crouched behind another of the cars, on the other side, similarly dressed to Alex, in all black. Alex couldn't see them from here, but four of his other men were hidden in various places around the lot. It wasn't ideal, hiding behind the cars like this, but they didn't have a lot of choice. Other than the toilets – which Alex really *didn't* feel like squeezing into with all five of his men for an extended period of time – the entire place was open plan with glass walls. Marco did have an office, but even that was surrounded by glass, only the bottom half frosted for privacy. Maloney would see the six of them hanging around in there from a mile off. Their saving grace was that, due to the early February sunsets, it was already pitch-black, leaving them ample darkness to melt into.

Headlights swept across the lot as a car pulled in, and Alex ducked further back, out of sight. He waited until he heard the engine stop and the lights flicked off, then listened to the sounds of the men getting out. One door opened and shut. Then a second and a third. *Three of them then*, he noted. That boded well. That gave him and his men the advantage of having two on one, as well as the element of surprise.

As the sounds of their mutterings and footsteps moved inside, Alex peeped around to look at Danny. He was already waiting with an expectant expression. Alex gave the signal and then let out a low whistle to tell the others to move too. Dark figures crept forward quickly, from all sides, crouching low as they ran together and then towards the glass front door. Alex moved to the front and paused to peer inside. The three men from the car were already in Marco's office, and one of them, the biggest one, was leaning over Marco's desk aggressively. Marco had to be able to see them by now, but he kept his eyes carefully trained on the angry man in front of him.

Alex opened the door, and they filed in, silently crossing the lot floor within seconds. The men were facing away from them as they approached, giving them time to pull out their weapons before announcing their presence. The others all held various blunt heavy items. Crowbars, bats, sledgehammers. But Alex pulled out a gun. It wasn't something he liked to carry around often, but they had no idea how armed these guys were, and he wasn't taking any chances. Faced with the rest, they might get brave and try to fight their way through, but with a gun that was an unlikely outcome.

Grasping the handle, Alex opened the door and strode in, puffing out his chest and glaring at the three men with his cousin as the others walked in and formed a semi-circle to face them.

'What the fuck is this?' the scruffy-looking man in the middle asked, in a thick Irish accent. He had to be Maloney.

'*This*,' Alex growled, 'is the welcome party you get when you step on my fucking toes.'

'And you are?' Maloney asked, pulling his head back and squinting at Alex with an unimpressed expression.

'Your worst fucking nightmare, mate,' Alex replied.

Maloney seemed to appraise Alex and his men for a few moments, while Maloney's companions – much younger men, Alex realised – kept glancing sideways at him, as though seeking instruction.

'I'm not your mate, mister,' he eventually replied. 'But you crack on wit' whatever you were here for. We were just leaving.'

Maloney tilted his head, indicating to the others to leave, but Alex stepped into his path, lifting the gun a little. Maloney's gaze flickered towards it and back up again. The man reeked of alcohol and stale smoke, and his greasy brown hair was a little too long, half covering his eyes. His stubble was more than a day old, his oversized T-shirt had coffee stains on, and his teeth were yellowed in a face that would be hard even for a mother to love. The other two weren't in much better shape. They looked every bit the community outcasts that Seamus had described.

'You ain't going anywhere, ya cunt,' Alex told him in a low, angry voice. ''Cause I want to talk to you.'

Maloney had the sense not to talk back this time. Instead, he jammed his hands into his pockets and watched Alex warily.

'Marco, you all good?' Alex asked, not taking his eyes off Maloney.

'I am now *you're* here,' Marco answered.

'Now, what was it you were telling me the other day?' Alex asked, staring Maloney down hard as he spoke to his cousin. 'That thing about Maloney here demanding you start paying him for his protection on this place?'

Maloney tutted and opened his palms to the sides. 'Demand? *No.* No, you've got it all wrong. It was simply an offer. That's all. Simply an explanation of our services, should they be of use.'

'Right.' Alex nodded, his expression serious. 'That makes sense. Don't it, boys?' He glanced round at them, cocking an eyebrow. Danny huffed out a humourless laugh and shook his head. 'Funny thing is though' – Alex turned his attention back to Maloney – 'offering a service don't usually come hand in hand with beating old men, does it?'

'I don't know what you're talking about,' Maloney answered.

As quick as a flash, Alex drew back the hand he held his gun in and smacked the heel of it hard across Maloney's head. The man stumbled sideways and fell, grasping his head with a cry. His cronies stepped back away from him, as if this slight distance between them might help them in some way.

'It's one thing trying to squirm out of your dues, Maloney, but it's quite another making out that my cousin's a liar,' Alex said, bending down and bellowing it in his face. He straightened up again. 'Now *get up.*'

Maloney looked at his hand, saw the blood from the wound Alex had just created and shook his head. 'You don't know what you've just done. Do you not know where I'm from?'

'I know exactly where you're from, mate. And from what I

hear, they won't give a monkey's what happens to you tonight,' Alex replied. 'Now, here's how this is gonna go. You have two choices. Either you can pay my cousin back for all the damage you did to his cars. And I estimate his trouble to have cost around the region of twenty grand. Pay him that, here and now, and I'll just do *you* over.' Alex gestured to his face with his gun. 'That part's to pay for the rest of it. Or *don't* pay the twenty grand, we do all *three* of you over. After which, you will *never* set foot in this place again. Not you, not your mates, not *anyone* connected to you. Because if you do, I'll burn your fucking caravan down in the middle of the night, with you inside it. And I mean anywhere. There is nowhere you can fucking move that I can't get to you. So...' Alex took a step back and appraised him. 'What's it gonna be?'

Maloney stared up at him with wide eyes now, panic flaring in them. 'I – I don't have twenty grand to hand that I can just *access*.'

Alex gave him a look of mock sympathy. 'Ahh, that's a shame for these two then, ain't it?'

He'd hoped this would be the case. Marco, he knew, had insurance, and now, any lingering loyalty these two might have had for Maloney would be nicely severed.

'Ah, come *on*, man,' one of them beseeched. 'Pay it!'

But Maloney steadfastly ignored him, closing his mouth tightly.

'I did tell you to get up, Maloney,' Alex reminded him. 'Make me ask again, you'll regret it.'

Gingerly, Maloney rose to his feet, shooting a murderous glance at Marco.

'Hey, don't you look at him like that. Don't you ever look at him again,' Alex warned. 'It's *me* you need to focus on.' He levelled a dark stare at the other man. 'And it's me you'll be begging to let you go.'

Alex gave Danny the nod, and his men jumped forward to

grab the other two as he grasped a handful of Maloney's dirty T-shirt. It wasn't hard shoving him back against the wall. The man was much smaller and lighter than Alex was, and with the gun still in his other hand, Maloney had clearly thought twice about trying to fight his fate. With the others already busy, Danny came over to join him and grabbed Maloney's arms, pinning them behind his back. Slipping the gun back into his pocket, Alex rolled up his sleeves.

'Let's see how you like being the helpless one, shall we?' he growled.

He pulled back his fist then punched Maloney hard in the stomach. The action caused him to double over as the air whooshed out of his lungs. Alex didn't waste any time coming back with the second punch to the man's face, and a sickening crunch sounded as his nose exploded. Blood splattered everywhere, and Maloney let out a blood-curdling cry.

'My nose!'

But Alex didn't stop there. He rained down punch after punch, breaking ribs and causing both eyes to begin swelling almost immediately. It took a matter of minutes to reduce the man to a bloody, blubbering wreck, begging for it to stop. The other two at least had the balls not to beg, Alex noted. As Maloney fell to his knees, his head hanging down with a sorrowful groan, Alex lifted his hand high up in the air and made a fist. Instantly, the beating stopped, and the only sounds that filled the room became those of weapons being put down.

'Get them out of here,' Alex ordered. 'But don't you fucking forget this day, Maloney. All of you. You stay away from here, or there'll be dire consequences. You don't cross a Capello and get away with it. No matter who you are. Remember that.'

He sniffed and wiped the sweat off his forehead with his arm. It had been a short, swift dole-out, but he'd given it his full effort, and now he was ready for a rest. He watched his men drag the others out and then hung back, turning to drop into the seat in front of his cousin's desk. Marco stood behind it, his expression hard and neutral, but Alex could see the colour had left his complexion.

'They won't bother you again,' Alex told him.

'Thank you,' Marco replied sincerely. 'That was... Well. Thank you. I can't tell you how much I appreciate it.'

'Bullies are the same everywhere you go. They're nothing but weak men trying to look like strong ones by pulling down everyone more vulnerable.' Alex reached out and straightened a pen, where it had rolled away from the neatly positioned stationery set on Marco's desk. 'All they ever need is a good slap and a valid threat.'

Marco nodded and took his own seat opposite Alex. He steepled his hands together and tapped them to his mouth for a moment, looking pensive. 'I was thinking, I really owe you now.'

Alex shook his head with a frown. 'You owe me nothing. You're family.'

'Well, I feel that I do, and I've been thinking of a way I can pay you back. Or *give* back then,' he corrected. 'Or maybe it's neither really. As it would benefit us both.' He ran a hand back through his jet-black hair.

Alex lifted one dark eyebrow in question, unsure where this could possibly be going.

'I was thinking,' Marco went on, 'now everything's out in the open between us, perhaps we could work together on something.'

Alex instantly shook his head. 'No. Marco, you don't—'

'Please,' Marco interrupted. 'Think about it. You must have cash to wash. Why not run it through here? We're a long-established business, so we're unlikely to get looked at too closely. And it could easily be done.'

'Why?' Alex asked. 'Why take that kind of risk?'

Marco swallowed. 'Because this place isn't making the money it used to. It's, *ugh*...' He rubbed his face tiredly. 'It's run at a loss more often than not, these last few months, and it's killing me. I need in. I need something. Run some cash through here, benefit from it and pay me something in the process. Please.'

Alex shook his head. 'This life, it ain't for you, cousin,' he said. 'Trust me. I'm doing you a favour, turning you down.'

Things were very different for Marco. He had a hard-earned family business that was honest and above board. He could go home every night knowing he was safe. Knowing there was no threat of losing everything he'd ever worked for if he made one wrong move. Knowing he didn't have to worry about the prospect of himself or his sister spending the rest of their lives in jail. Or worse, being killed by an enemy because he'd dropped a ball and hadn't managed to stay one step ahead. For Alex, this life was all he'd ever known. It was in his blood. There had never been any other option, and he was fine with that. But Alex also knew that were he in Marco's position, had this been his life instead, that freedom and peace wasn't something he'd give up so lightly.

Alex lifted himself up out of the chair. 'You'll turn things around here. This is just a rough patch.' He turned to leave.

'I *won't*,' Marco replied passionately. 'I've *tried*. It's not just a rough patch; it's the market. It's the two other lots that have opened up nearby who're owned by big groups and can afford to offer better deals.'

Alex sighed, feeling his pain, but continued. 'It's better this way. You're gonna have to trust me on that.'

'It's not. I'm a sinking ship, Alex,' Marco called after him. When Alex didn't respond, his tone quickly changed. 'Well, maybe I'll speak to Antonio then.'

This halted Alex in his tracks, and he cursed under his breath. He was *trying* to protect Marco from their way of life, but he couldn't let him run into his brother's waiting arms. Because Alex knew, without doubt, that Antonio would use

Marco without caution or care for his safety, then throw him to the wolves the moment they came sniffing around. While they all had to adopt an element of ruthlessness in their line of work, Antonio had always taken it to the next level.

'I don't know what's happened with you, but I know you're not working together right now,' Marco pushed. 'Maybe he'd appreciate a new laundry of this size.'

Alex turned and took a couple of steps back. 'For your own sake, *don't*,' he said strongly. 'Antonio is...' He scratched his cheek and glanced over his shoulder to check his men were still out of earshot. 'He's just not in a good place right now. He'd pull you under, Marco. If you value your freedom, you'll steer clear of my brother.'

Marco lifted his chin, holding Alex's gaze. 'It's you or him, Alex. But either way, I *need* this.'

Alex sighed and ran a hand down his face, stressed. 'It's a fucking terrible idea. For *you*, not for me. You aren't from this world. You don't know what it means to be in it. You don't understand the risks you're taking, and, honestly, I don't think you realise the level of loyalty that would be expected. What you'd have to do if the shit hit the fan.'

'That new girl of yours. Cat. She ain't from your world either, is she?' Marco countered. 'That much was pretty obvious just from meeting her.'

'That's different,' Alex replied.

'How?' Marco asked, holding his arms out to the sides before dropping them.

'When she asked to be part of all this, she'd already worked for us for a while. She knew who we were. She'd already stuck herself in the line of fire to protect us and had proven herself.'

'OK, so how do I prove myself?' Marco asked.

'It's not that simple,' Alex tried to explain.

'Well, I don't know what else to say,' Marco admitted. 'Take me or I offer myself to Antonio. Because I've got nowhere else to go.'

Alex gritted his teeth and looked up towards the heavens. He'd been wrong about tonight. That hadn't been the last thing he needed right now. *This* was. But what choice did he have? It seemed Marco was hell-bent on becoming a criminal, one way or another. At least with him, his cousin stood a chance of not screwing his entire life up completely.

'I'll talk to Maria, and we'll have a sit-down soon,' he said eventually. 'But that's all I'm promising.'

'Thank you,' Marco said quickly.

Alex shook his head and turned around to go and find his men. 'Don't thank me yet, cousin,' he called back grimly. 'Because whether you see it or not, this is the worst decision you're ever going to make.'

THIRTY-FOUR

Bianca hadn't got as far as she had in her life without knowing how to get herself out of a few bad situations, and she certainly wasn't giving up and rolling over now. Who the hell did Cat think she was? Prissy little bitch, turning up at the house and throwing her weight around like she was of any importance at all. She *wasn't* important. She was a damn nobody who should have kept her nose out of other people's business and her mouth shut. But here they now were, thanks to Cat's meddling, and it was time for Bianca to get creative.

Getting the plates back wasn't an option, even if she'd wanted to. Antonio hadn't exactly been overly grateful when she'd handed them to him. He'd just told her she was lucky she'd done as he'd asked in good time and then dismissed her, like she was some lackey. Which irked her greatly. Whatever was going on now, they were still family. And up until recently, they'd always got along pretty well. But now it was like he'd shut himself off from her, the same way he had the rest of the family. All bitter and drugged up and aggressive towards her, as if *she* were the enemy too. It was ridiculous. She might be toeing the line on the subject for the sake of her *own* position, but she'd never agreed with what they did to him. And it wasn't OK for him to treat her like this. Not that she was stupid enough to kick off about it though. Not when she knew exactly what he was capable of. So the chances of getting those plates back were zilch. He wouldn't give a damn how sticky her situation was.

She wasn't going to walk up to her husband and tell him what she'd done either. Because if she did tell the truth, if she explained that Antonio had made her do it, Alex would confront him, and then Antonio would out all her dirty little secrets. And if that happened, it was all over for her. Because it hadn't just been Antonio who'd messed with Cat's life. It had been *she* who'd told him the passcode to pick up Orla from preschool that day. And it had been *she* who'd followed Cat home to get her address and then suggested to Antonio that he set that fire in her building. She wouldn't even be able to lie if that came out because Antonio had made sure to save all their texts. She'd be screwed. And she'd be cast out without a second thought.

No, neither of those options would work for her. Which meant she had to go with a third option. One that dealt with Cat once and for all. And Bianca had already come up with a plan. Much as everyone seemed to be enamoured with the woman right now, she was still fairly new to the scene and, therefore, it wouldn't be too hard to undermine her trustworthiness. Bianca might not be the most popular member of the family at times, but she *was* family. Longstanding family. Who was going to take Cat's word against hers? Especially when Cat didn't have anything to come back at her with. Not really.

Bianca watched the weak rays of the winter morning sun creep into their kitchen and pulled her pink fluffy dressing gown a little tighter. She was sitting in the wing-backed armchair they'd stuck in some dead space opposite the window, not knowing what else to do with it, and she clasped a hot cup of coffee between her hands, her legs tucked up beneath her.

Usually, the thought of being up at this time of the morning was positively obscene to her. But today she needed to be here, before Alex roused. She needed the shock factor of him finding her down here, before him, to add to the validity of her claims. And, in truth, she hadn't found it that hard to be awake this early today. She'd barely slept all night, running through everything she was going to say to him. She'd rehearsed her story, over and over, and was now confident that she had this all sewn up perfectly.

The kitchen clock ticked over to seven o'clock on the dot and, like clockwork, Bianca heard the creaks and groans of Alex getting out of bed upstairs. She allowed herself a wry smile. He really was so predictable. Predictable and steady. It was something she'd always hated about him, finding unpredictability and impulsivity much more interesting and attractive in a person. Though she did have to grudgingly admit, it came with some advantages.

The creaking disappeared as he walked through to the bathroom, then reappeared briefly as he walked back in to dress. Eventually, a few minutes later, his footsteps sounded on the stairs. As Bianca heard him approach, she quickly schooled her expression into one of vulnerability and worry. Then she stared out of the window, glazing her eyes as if lost in thought, waiting for him to see her. Sure enough, he walked into the kitchen and halted, making a small sound of surprise.

'Bianca?' he asked, his voice lifting at the end, as if not sure he was really seeing her or if she was a hallucination.

Bianca blinked and turned to him, feigning surprise herself, pretending he'd pulled her out of her reverie. 'Oh. Alex. Morning, babe,' she said faintly.

He frowned, his expression instantly falling to one of confused concern. 'You alright? Are you ill?'

Bianca lifted one side of her mouth in a feeble half-smile. 'No. Not physically anyway...' She trailed off and waited.

Alex took the bait and stepped closer. 'What do you mean?'

Bianca pulled in a deep breath and then released it slowly and loudly, lowering her eyes as if she was ashamed. 'I couldn't sleep. Not after hearing what happened yesterday. Not after...' She clamped her mouth shut and shook her head.

Alex's frown deepened, and he dropped to his knees in front of her, tilting her chin up so that she was forced to look at him. 'Bianca, tell me what's wrong. I've never seen you like this. You're worrying me.'

It was true. He *had* never seen her like this. Because Bianca didn't do vulnerable. Bianca didn't do worry or shame or guilt, or any weak, pathetic emotion. She was as hard as they came, emotionally speaking. And if she hadn't known exactly how good she was at acting, she'd have labelled him a fool for falling for this shit now.

Bianca held his stare with wide, serious eyes. 'I should have told you when I saw her. I should have told you when I realised what she'd done.' She allowed her brows to pucker further. 'But I wanted to give her a chance. We've actually become *friends* lately and, yeah, OK, it was stupid and selfish of me to stay quiet. But I *really* wanted her to sort it out so that it could go away and nothing would change. It was good to finally have a friend within this family. You know? It's not like I'm popular with anyone else.' She cast her eyes down again, upping the misery in her expression.

'What are you talking about?' Alex asked, now sounding completely confused. Exactly as she'd planned.

Bianca squeezed her eyes shut for a moment and then opened them, moving her gaze up to his, full of sorrow. 'I saw her, Friday night. We were supposed to get drinks, but she said she had to go to the hotel first. Drop off some files. I wasn't far away, so I figured I'd just go meet her there and suggest we go straight off to this bar I know around the corner.' She bit her bottom lip. 'I pulled up just as she was walking in with the files, so I waited in my car. Obviously, I don't have access to the place,' she added pointedly. 'But then when she walked out...' Bianca trailed off and winced, as if she really didn't want to continue.

'Go on,' Alex urged, his expression tense.

'She didn't know I was there,' Bianca continued. 'But I saw something in her hands. I didn't really know what they were at the time, and when I got out of my car, she quickly put them in hers, shoving them under a jacket on her back seat. She seemed flustered. Annoyed that I'd surprised her.' Bianca adjusted her frown to one of confusion. 'Then yesterday when you told me about the plates going missing, it all clicked.' She shook her head. 'I confronted her, last night. I wanted to give her a chance to put it right herself. I told her to come clean or put them back. But she just got angry and refused, told me to keep quiet about it.'

'What are you saying?' Alex breathed, his face turning white.

Bianca lifted her chin and looked into his eyes. 'I'm saying that she took the plates, Alex. The thief you're looking for is Cat.'

THIRTY-FIVE

Bianca felt her heart race a little as she pottered around the kitchen, straightening things and wiping down the sides. Stage one of her plan was complete, and it had gone absolutely perfectly. Alex had gone quiet, looking almost ill as he'd processed the information she'd fed him, but he hadn't doubted her words for even a second. And *that* was how she was going to get out of this mess. She knew the hard bit was yet to come, but she was prepared for that too. In order to remain free from suspicion, she'd even been the one to suggest they invite Cat over this morning to explain herself.

Cat wouldn't know what had hit her when she got here. And when Cat realised what Bianca had done, and she attempted to turn the tables back on Bianca with the truth, she'd just look like she was trying to worm her way out of it. What proof did she have? She didn't even know whose apartment block Bianca had gone to. Her story would be vague and as the person defending herself it would all look like one big feeble lie. She'd be ousted from the firm in disgrace. And Lord knows what other punishment they'd mete out for this.

Bianca didn't give two hoots how bad it was either. As far as she was concerned, Cat had had something coming to her for a long time. And maybe, after she'd been dealt with and was no longer a part of any of their lives, Antonio would finally be allowed back home, the reason for his banishment gone. Bianca couldn't *wait* to tell him *that* news. And to let him know that it had been *she* who'd been responsible for his return. She'd finally be the hero in this story. Both at home with Alex, having revealed Cat as a thief, and with Antonio, for fixing the Capello family and becoming the unlikely glue that drew them all back together. Hell, she might even finally find some favour with Sophia, if she was lucky. Though this wasn't something she was counting on.

Alex now sat on the chair she'd vacated earlier to go and get dressed, looking ten years older than he had before she'd told him. It irritated her that he seemed so upset about it. He did seem pretty angry too, but in her opinion, his feelings should be that of pure rage, not mixed emotions like this. Cat was a nobody. A woman who'd wormed her way in with a sob story, had taken advantage of his whole family – especially when it came to that kid of hers – and who'd now betrayed them all by stealing from them. Or, at least, that's the version that *he* knew. So sadness shouldn't be coming into it at all.

Aware that she still had a way to go before this was all over though, Bianca was careful not to show her true feelings. Instead, she went with quiet sympathy, as though she completely understood. Indeed, the version of herself she'd created to carry out her plans with the plates was one who thought highly of Cat and was saddened at the betrayal by her friend. So she was careful to look a little saddened herself, as though bravely trying and failing to hide it.

'Do you want another coffee?' she asked Alex, walking over to him.

He waved his hand dismissively, his brooding gaze trained

on the garden outside. 'Nah. Thanks though.' He glanced round at her and gave her hand a quick squeeze.

Walking away, Bianca gave a little sigh. 'I still can't believe she did this. I mean, *why*? She wouldn't even tell me what she did with them.'

But Alex didn't answer.

As she rounded the kitchen island, there was a knock at the door, and her heart did a painful little flip. This was it. Cat was here. It was go time.

Alex rose from his chair and walked off to answer the door, and Bianca wiped her palms, which were suddenly very moist, on her jeans. She heard the door open and shut and the murmur of Cat's voice as she greeted Alex, who gave only a low grunt in response. They appeared a second later, and Bianca was thrilled to see that Cat's expression openly showed that she felt uneasy. *She* knew the reason for this was that Cat had been trying to avoid Alex until Bianca had fixed the problem, as she didn't want to have to lie. But after the version of events that Bianca had fed Alex, it just made her look very shifty.

'Cat, take a seat please,' Alex ordered.

Cat blinked, looking instantly alarmed at his low tone, her eyes flickering over to Bianca before moving back to Alex. 'Sure,' she replied, awkwardly tucking a lock of hair back behind her ear as she took a seat at the kitchen table.

Alex walked over to the breakfast bar and leaned back against it, facing her, rather than sitting with her at the table. 'I'm gonna cut to the chase. I know what you did. Bianca told me everything this morning.'

Cat blinked again, her gaze darting to Bianca and back, once more. '*Right?*' she said slowly. 'Well, that's good that you've talked.' She squeezed her gaze as she looked at him, as if trying to work something out.

Alex shook his head. 'That's all you've got to say?'

Cat frowned. 'I'm sorry?'

'You're *sorry*,' he repeated in a low, cool voice.

'*No*,' she replied. 'I just mean...' She trailed off. 'I'm sorry, what's happening right now? I'm confused.'

'Cut the crap, Cat,' Bianca interjected. 'I've told him everything. I've told him what you did. Now it's time to explain yourself.' She held Cat's gaze steadily and watched as the penny began to drop.

Cat's gaze sharpened and darted over to Alex. 'What does she mean?' she demanded. 'What does she mean what *I* did? What's she told you?'

'You're really going to drag this out?' Alex asked flatly. 'Fine. OK. Bianca told me about seeing you Friday night, taking the plates. So now I want to know what the fuck you think you were doing, *stealing* from us, after *all* we've done for you. I want to know what the fuck you've *done* with them. And most of all' – Alex stepped closer to Cat, his voice and expression equally as menacing – 'I want to know who the *fuck* you really work for.'

'Alex!' Cat exclaimed, shock bleaching her face of colour. 'Are you— What *is* this? *I* didn't take them; *Bianca* did! It was the other way round. I wouldn't *do* that! Alex, you have to believe me.'

Bianca scoffed. 'Yeah, good one, Cat. Trying to turn it round on me? I don't fucking think so, love. Why on earth would *I* steal them? Eh? I'm Alex's *wife*. I don't even work for the firm. I wouldn't have the first clue what was in there – if I could even get *in*! I don't have access to the hotel. So your attempt to twist it around falls a little flat there, don't it?'

Cat's mouth gaped open. 'You – you...' she stuttered, in complete shock.

'*I*,' Bianca said, stepping forward with her eyebrows raised, 'am loyal to my husband. Not to you just because we've had a few drinks and you told me to keep my mouth shut. Sorry, you're on your own, love.'

Cat's wide eyes narrowed at her, and hatred filled them as

the full extent of what Bianca was doing hit her. She began to shake her head, resolve setting into her expression. 'No. No, I'm not letting you do this.' She turned to Alex. 'It was me who saw Bianca, Alex. *Not* the other way around. I'd left for the night and was about to drive away when I saw her go in. I waited and watched because it seemed off, and when she came out, she had a bag filled with something I couldn't see. I followed her car to a block of flats and then I left. And I didn't say anything at the time because I thought I was being *ridiculous*. I thought I would sound crazy. But then yesterday when I heard about the plates, I knew that was what she'd taken, so I came here and confronted her, and told her to come clean with you or *I would*. And now, here she is, twisting it around on *me*, trying to get ahead of the game.'

Alex stared at her for a few seconds, his expression unreadable. 'Cat, Bianca can't get into the hotel. She's *never* been in there. She doesn't even know what equipment we keep there. But *you* do. And you have a key card. And you were there Friday night.' He shook his head. 'Honestly, Cat, I would never have thought this of you. Even having only known you a short time, I trusted you. But I knew something was up lately. You've been… off. You've been avoiding me, acting strangely.'

'No, Alex, listen…' Cat closed her eyes and dragged both hands down her face. 'I know what that must look like right now. But I promise you that was *nothing* to do with this. This wasn't *me*! I *caught her*. I – that stuff, me being preoccupied, that was – it was something else.'

'What?' Alex demanded.

'I – I can't explain,' Cat replied.

'Ugh, just stop,' Alex replied.

Bianca felt a flush of adrenaline course through her. What a delightfully helpful addition to the situation. She hadn't even known about Cat acting off, but it helped her case beautifully. She was *winning*.

'She *stole* my key, Alex,' Cat insisted, her eyes begging him to listen to her. 'Remember? I told you it went missing and that I *knew* I hadn't put it anywhere. It was *her*. She took it when I was in the bathroom at the bar, the day we went out for drinks.'

'How would I even *know* you had a key in there?' Bianca countered. 'And you were gone, like, two minutes. So your story is *what* exactly? That in the two minutes you were away from your bag, in a public place, that I went rifling through it on the off chance I might find something to help me steal from my own husband? *That's* what you're going with?'

Cat's cheeks burned crimson, and her eyes began darting worriedly between Bianca and Alex. 'Alex, *please*,' she begged. 'You have to listen to me.'

'I'm done listening. Now you better start answering my questions truthfully, Cat, or you're about to find out exactly why people don't cross me,' Alex said in a low, deadly voice.

His expression was murderous, and it was all Bianca could do not to squeal with delight as her plan came together utterly beautifully. Cat wouldn't be able to answer those questions. And when she didn't, it would make her look like she was covering for someone. And *that* was where the games would begin. Bianca briefly wondered what they'd do to her then moved her thoughts on to more important things. She didn't really care what they did to Cat. So long as the woman was out of their lives and she was in the clear, that was all that really mattered.

Tears filled Cat's eyes. 'I'm not lying to you, Alex,' she said strongly. 'I know it looks like I am, but that's only because I gave your *bitch* of a wife the chance to tell you herself, and she's had time to plot all this out. She is *framing* me.'

'You don't speak about her like that,' Alex snapped thunderously.

But Cat wasn't backing down. 'I most certainly *will* when she's setting me up like this.'

'What would she do with them, Cat?' He rounded on her. 'Come on, as you've got your story so fucking straight, what would she even do with them?'

'What would *I* do with them?' Cat cried back. 'And I don't *know* what she did exactly. My best guess is that she sold them, but I honestly couldn't tell you because I *didn't* follow her into that building. A choice I'm now *seriously* regretting. But, well...' Cat paused, as if something had occurred to her. 'I do have a picture of the building. And there'll be a time stamp on it. Why else would I take a picture of a random block of flats late on a Friday night, if my story isn't true?'

Bianca froze, ice zapping down her spine. *She had a picture? Oh, no, no, no, this was not good.* She noticed Alex was frowning at her suddenly, and realised her shock must be showing.

She snorted derisively, shaking her head. 'There could be any *number* of reasons why you've taken a photo of a random building,' she bluffed. 'She's wasting your time, Alex. Pictures don't mean anything.'

But he held a hand up to silence her, his dark gaze boring into hers. She shivered, seeing the flicker of doubt there. She'd fucked up. She should have been more careful not to react. Now he was suspicious. But if he saw that picture, she was done for. Because Cat might not know who that building belonged to, but Alex certainly did.

'Show me it,' Alex demanded, turning back to Cat.

'Why are you wasting time with this?' Bianca asked, now in full panic. She rounded the bar, hoping to intercept the phone, but as Cat passed it over, Alex quickly swiped it before she could reach. '*Alex. Hey!*' She stood in front of him, trying to draw his gaze away from the phone, but he looked past her to Cat.

'PIN?' he asked.

'Four-six-four-six,' she replied. 'In my photos, Friday night.'

He tapped in the PIN, and Bianca's heart lurched up into

her throat. 'Alex, what are you doing?' she asked, her mind jangling with alarm as she tried to work out a way to stop him. 'She's clearly *lying*. Just put the phone down and stop letting her distract you with this shit.'

The glare he levelled on her now made her stomach flip with fear. He wasn't buying it. She'd shown her fear, and he knew she was lying. It was too late, she realised, and suddenly she felt as though she was watching the events around her unfold from a distance. He knew. And the moment he reached that photo, any hope she had of getting out of this would be gone.

She watched as he found the photo app and scrolled back for a few seconds, and then he stilled, tapping on one single image. And as he looked back up into her eyes, she knew, in that second, that it was all over for her.

THIRTY-SIX

What most people didn't realise – or, perhaps, didn't understand the true extent of – was that no one needed to hire private investigators anymore. Or, at least, very rarely. Because ninety per cent of the time, people left a perfect map of their lives on the internet. Whether it was through social media, professional websites, advertisement of services, registered company details, it was all there for the world to find. So long as you knew where to look. So the moment he'd mentioned Paul Walker's name on the phone, Steven Moore had given himself away.

It had barely taken a day to pull together all the details of his life. He, himself, kept a rather low profile on social media. But Paul hadn't. And Steven was in far too many of Paul's posts, gushing about how much he loved the other man. They'd been dating for over a year after meeting on a shoot they'd both been hired for. Like Paul, Steven was a professional photographer, and a short search online had revealed he had a small studio in Shoreditch.

After keeping watch on the place for a couple of days, Maria's men had ascertained that he routinely closed the place at six p.m. on the dot and left via the back door to the small courtyard at the rear, which housed three parking spaces surrounded by tall, crumbling brick walls. He was always the last to go, the other two businesses that the spaces belonged to closing at five, and there was no CCTV coverage back there.

Maria was ninety-nine per cent sure that she'd found the right man. After all, she was looking for a professional photographer who was well established enough for a politician to hire, and one who had been very emotionally attached to Paul. Steven was both those things. But to be sure, she wanted to be there when they took him. To see his face when he caught sight of her. If he wasn't the one, he wouldn't react to seeing her face, other than maybe to smile politely or ask if she was lost. But if he was, it would be instantly obvious.

Maria's men placed themselves in the alley that ran up the side of the building into the courtyard at two minutes to six, set to stay out of sight until Maria was engaged in conversation with him. Maria was in the courtyard, just in front of Steven's car, facing away from the building. She listened as a door opened and shut behind her and as a jangle of keys indicated that it was being locked, then held her ground until she estimated him to be on his way towards her. He called out as he grew closer, and she smiled to herself.

'Hello? Can I help you?' he asked.

Maria turned around, her bright hazel eyes finding his and searching his face for his reaction. Sure enough, he stopped in his tracks, shock and panic widening his eyes. He took a step back and froze, reminding her of a rabbit in headlights.

'Hello, Steven,' she said in a low, silken voice as her men silently filed into the courtyard behind him.

Steven, either sensing that they were no longer alone or looking for a way out, glanced behind him and groaned. 'You can't, um, s-sorry, who are you?'

Maria laughed. 'It's a bit late for that, I'm afraid. You know exactly who I am. And I know exactly who *you* are. So do spare me the bullshit.' She walked forward, pushing her hands down into the pockets of her thick red woollen coat. 'We need to have a little chat. You can come quietly by choice, or Danny here can *help* you come quietly. Up to you.'

Steven licked his lips, and his eyes flickered around the group. 'I've put a failsafe in place,' he warned her. 'If I'm not here tomorrow morning, those files go to the police. I'm not stupid; I knew this could be a possibility. If you harm me in any way, or I disappear, you're *fucked*.'

Maria smiled at him again, causing him to blink and look confused. 'You'll be back,' she said simply. 'And completely unharmed. Unless, of course, you go with the Danny option. You might gain a few bruises that way, so I'd advise against it.'

Steven frowned warily. 'What's the catch? This feels like a trap. I mean, it's *obviously* a trap.'

Maria sighed and stepped towards him, her heeled boots tapping loudly on the cracked concrete ground. 'If I wanted to take you by force, I'd have done so already. I still can,' she reiterated. 'But I'm giving you the choice. I also give you my word that you *will* return in one piece, safe and sound. Either way though, the coming-with-us part isn't a choice.'

Steven looked around at them all again, fear and distrust written all over his face. Eventually, he huffed, his cheeks flushing red with annoyance. 'You'd better be telling the truth,' he replied. 'Because if not, it's *you* who'll regret it.'

Maria gestured to her men to come closer. 'Let's go. Hand Danny your keys please, Steven, and get in the back of your car.'

'*What?*' Steven asked, frowning.

'We're taking your car,' Maria confirmed. 'So, come on. Chop, chop.' Her smile dropped to a look of cold resolution as she turned to walk around to the front passenger side. 'We don't want to be late now. We have a long night ahead of us.'

THIRTY-SEVEN

Alex sat in the darkness, staring out across the smoky rooftops and snaking lines of traffic below. He'd helped himself to a large whisky upon entering this place and was now sipping it as he waited for what was to come. As he waited for Antonio.

He was still reeling from all that had come to light this morning. Reeling and furious. The only thing he'd known for sure, as Bianca had scrabbled to find any viable lie that made Cat look guilty, was that he wouldn't get any element of truth out of her. He felt sickened by what she'd done. Both for taking the plates and then for trying to frame Cat. Bianca knew who he was. The sort of consequences he'd have to mete out to Cat for a betrayal like that. But she hadn't cared.

He knew, without needing to ask, that this was all Antonio's idea. Nothing about this theft served Bianca in the slightest. What he *didn't* know was why his wife had gone along with it. Why she'd betrayed him. Was it for love? Were they having an affair? She had been talking about him in her sleep, after all. If not that, it had to be blackmail. But what could Antonio have over her that was so bad?

He felt awful that he hadn't trusted Cat. That he'd not

listened to her. Cat had more than proven her loyalty to them, and she'd become a good friend. But Bianca was his wife. The one person he should have been able to trust above anyone. And she'd played such a very convincing hand.

The sound of a key in the door jangled behind him, and he turned the chair to face it, placing his whisky down quietly on the side table next to him. Antonio walked in, thankfully alone, and shrugged off his jacket as he closed the door before switching the light on. He didn't see Alex for a moment as he hung his jacket straight and kicked off his shoes, but as he turned, he came to an abrupt halt, his dark eyes flicking down to the gun Alex was holding in his lap, before moving back up to his face.

A corner of his mouth jerked upwards wryly. 'Missed me too much, have ya?' he mocked. 'Come to visit?'

'Sit down,' Alex said in a low growl, gesturing towards one of the other chairs.

'Or what? You're gonna shoot me?' Antonio replied.

Alex's eyes grew flinty. 'I wouldn't test me,' he advised. 'Because this time I'm actually finding it a struggle *not* to pull the trigger.'

Antonio cocked his head to the side as he appraised Alex. After a moment, he nodded and moved to the chair Alex had indicated without another word, clearly realising his brother was serious. Resting back, he held his arms out to the side for a brief second before dropping them onto the arms of the chair, cocking an eyebrow at Alex.

'Now what?' he asked.

Alex watched him for a moment, suddenly feeling like he didn't know the man before him at all. Yet this was his brother. The person who'd been by his side for almost his entire life. They'd grown up together, lived together, fought together, taken over their father's business with Maria together. There had been a time when they'd known absolutely everything about each other. A time when they'd have died to protect each other. How had it all gone so wrong?

But, of course, Alex knew the answer to that question. It was down to Antonio's insatiable need to have whatever and whoever he wanted, no matter the cost. His inability to accept or live by even the most basic of boundaries. His inability to value human life that wasn't his own even slightly. Alex wondered then whether Antonio had *ever* truly loved his family. Or whether it had all been a game he played to reap the benefits of keeping them by his side. Because now, as his brother stared at him across the small space between them, he couldn't seem to find an ounce of humanity within his cold, dark eyes.

'Are you sleeping with her?' Alex asked, his tone devoid of any emotion. Anger simmered under the surface, but he refused to give his brother the satisfaction of seeing it.

The corner of Antonio's mouth hitched up again. 'Who? Bianca?' He chuckled. 'No,' he said firmly and shook his head. 'Wouldn't touch her with a barge pole.'

Alex narrowed his gaze but let the insult slide. He needed to stay on track. 'I don't believe you. Why else would she steal those plates for you?'

Antonio held his gaze, a smile playing on his lips that didn't reach his eyes. 'Because I told her if she didn't, I'd tell you all her dirty little secrets,' he said calmly. 'And they're a lot worse than a bit of fishing within the family.'

Alex frowned. He believed Antonio. For all his many faults, he wasn't one to come up with pointless lies. 'What secrets?' he asked, knowing full well it was exactly what Antonio *wanted* him to ask.

'Now *that's* the right question,' Antonio replied. 'I might as well tell you, now she's burned this bridge. But only if you're *sure* you want the answers. Once you know some things, you can't ever go back.'

Alex clenched his jaw. What could possibly be worse than

finding out Bianca was sleeping with his brother? 'I'm fucking sure, Antonio. Now spit it out.'

Antonio's eyes glittered with menace as that cold smile once more played on his lips. 'You cast me out of this family when you found out I'd taken Cat's kid as motivation for her to join me in that building.'

'And?' Alex asked flatly. It had been *far* more than just that, though that had been the final straw. But this wasn't the time to argue that point.

Antonio nodded. 'Who do you think it was that told me where her school was? Who do you think it was that sent me the password to pick her up? Do you really think I could have figured that all out on my own? I certainly didn't have the time to trail around after her and listen to her phone calls.'

Alex felt the blood drain from his face as he stared across at him. 'No,' he uttered, shaking his head. 'You're lying.'

He *had* to be, Alex told himself. Bianca was a lot of things, but she wasn't *that* evil. She wouldn't hand deliver a three-year-old girl into the hands of his brother. *Would she?*

'Ask her yourself,' Antonio offered. 'Watch her face when she finds out you know. I still have the messages.'

'Show me,' Alex snarled.

Antonio lifted his phone out of his pocket and tapped on the screen, then chucked it over to Alex. Alex caught it and turned it over, scrolling back through the messages until he saw what Antonio was referring to. His breath caught in his throat as he read what she'd sent him, and he felt bile rise up to the back of his throat.

'Go back further,' Antonio suggested in a low voice. 'See what else she came up with.'

Alex clamped his jaw tightly. 'Why don't you just fucking tell me?'

'Remember that fire in Cat's building?' Antonio asked.

'No. I *know* she didn't do that,' Alex replied firmly. 'I checked.'

'No, she didn't,' Antonio confirmed. '*I* did it. But it was Bianca's idea. And Bianca who got me that address too. You know, she really is *wasted*, out there partying all the time. She's actually really fucking ruthless. Maybe if you'd put her to work a few years ago, we could all have been reaping the benefits of that ruthlessness by now. You know...' His mouth curled upwards in a cruel smile. 'Instead of just me.'

Alex's calm disintegrated, and he launched himself across the space between them with a roar, grabbing Antonio by the neck. Antonio tried to twist sideways to get out of his brother's grip, but Alex was much stronger than him, and he clung on, squeezing harder. They landed on the floor with a thump, and Alex pulled back his other hand, bring the gun down hard on Antonio's face, twice in quick succession.

Blood spurted from Antonio's face as the blows split his lips and then his cheek, but instead of crying out, he began to laugh manically.

'What's the matter, Alex?' he cried. 'Don't like me playing with your toys?'

'*Fuck* you, Antonio,' Alex yelled, hatred pouring out of him as he stared at his younger brother's mocking face. 'Fuck you. *You* did this to yourself. *You* did this to *all of us*. You were my *brother*.'

'Hate to tell you, but I still *fucking am*,' Antonio yelled back, spittle flying from his bloodied mouth.

With a roar, Alex flung Antonio away from him, standing up and walking back to his seat, still seething. This time, he pointed the gun directly at Antonio as he crawled back up to his own seat. As he waited for Antonio to settle, Alex cursed himself. He shouldn't have done that. He knew he shouldn't have. He shouldn't have let Antonio see just how deeply this had all got to him, but he couldn't help it. Every time Alex saw his brother's face, it was like a stab to the heart. And to hear all of this new and awful information about Bianca on top of that – to know Antonio had collected and stored that information to use as a weapon against him like this... It was just too much.

'It's killed me, losing you, Antonio,' Alex admitted in a heavy voice. 'You think it was fucking easy? But you're a sinking fucking ship with its sails on fire and ten tonnes of gunpowder on board. We couldn't just keep going, keep letting you risk us all, every fucking day.' Alex wiped a hand down his face. 'We couldn't keep hiding those bodies and turning blind eyes to the fucked-up things you were doing. What did you expect?'

Antonio's dark eyes glittered with deep anger as he stared back across the room. '*Loyalty*,' he growled. 'Just like I always afforded you.'

Alex shook his head. This was a pointless conversation. And not the one he was here to have. He sniffed and straightened himself in his chair, trying to sort through all his racing thoughts. The one that stuck out was how utterly stupid he'd been, trusting Bianca. All this time that he'd made excuses for his nightmare of a wife. Picked her up off the floor, defended her to his family. All this time, he'd just thought her to be a bit broken. Lost. But she wasn't *lost*. She knew exactly where she was and had been playing him for a fool. Lying to him, stealing from him, hurting the very people he'd sworn to protect. He swallowed down the pain and the shame he now felt, unable to process it all. Unable to process what an *idiot* he'd been for all this time.

Seeing the dark amusement on Antonio's face, Alex stiffened, but he clamped down the violent reaction that begged to be set free. Because this wasn't the only reason Alex was here. There was still more to be discussed.

'Where are the plates?' Alex demanded.

Antonio just laughed. 'You really expect me to tell you?'

Alex simply lifted the gun and cocked it.

'You won't kill me. I'm your brother. Whether you like to be reminded of it or not,' Antonio taunted. 'Besides, do you really want the clean-up?'

Alex pointed the gun at Antonio's leg and hitched an eyebrow. 'Who said anything about killing you? And no, I'd leave you capable enough to clear it up yourself. Where are the fucking plates?'

Antonio's eyes darted around, and Alex could almost see the cogs turning as he tried to find a way to slither out of this. Then they narrowed with hatred as he came to the inevitable dead end.

'Fuck off, Alex,' Antonio said quietly. 'And maybe I'll think about having a sit-down with you about the p—'

But his words were cut short as an ear-splitting bang resounded through the room. Antonio jumped nearly out of his skin, his arms flying up in the air as he stared down at himself, doing a quick scan. Finding himself uninjured, he glared up at Alex.

'What the *fuck* you *playing* at?' he demanded.

Alex gestured to the hole in the chair beside Antonio's leg. 'Just reminding you what a good shot I am,' he growled. 'Now hand over the plates or I move the next one over a few inches. That was your one and only warning.'

The muscles in Antonio's jaw worked back and forth, and Alex waited for him to complete the internal war he was clearly having with himself. Handing them over was obviously the last thing Antonio wanted to do, now that he had them in his possession. But Alex wasn't playing, and he knew that this was clear to his brother.

Antonio's face contorted with rage and then settled as he struggled to control himself. 'They're in the den,' he muttered grudgingly. 'Filing cabinet.'

Alex nodded. The den was a hideout Antonio kept that was

off the books. A place they'd often used in the past to hold hot goods until the attention around them cooled.

'You'd better not be lying,' he said gruffly. But Alex already knew he wasn't. His self-preservation was too high a priority.

'There's one last thing you should know about your wife by the way,' Antonio said bitterly.

Alex narrowed his eyes and sighed, not sure he wanted to take this bait. What he'd learned tonight had already knocked everything out of him. 'What?' he asked reluctantly.

Antonio nodded to the side table next to Alex. 'In the drawer. Brown envelope.'

Alex clenched his teeth and then turned to open the drawer, pulling out the envelope he found there. He pulled out the photos within and then frowned down at them in horror. He'd thought the revelations of the evening couldn't possibly get any worse, but apparently he'd been wrong.

'I had her followed a few times. I had a suspicion she'd been touting it out,' Antonio explained. 'Turns out I was right. It wasn't *me* you should have been worried about, brother. It's everyone else in London she's been sleeping with.'

Each picture showed Bianca in a different outfit, in the arms of a different man. He closed his eyes, feeling himself deflate. How had he been so blind? She'd been making a fool of him all over town, for God knows how long. And what's more, Antonio had known. And instead of telling him, he'd simply kept the knowledge up his sleeve to use when it best suited him. Feeling his cheeks burn, Alex dropped his gaze, not wanting Antonio to see the hurt in them. Because he suddenly wasn't sure which betrayal was worse.

Carefully replacing the photos in the envelope, Alex put them back in the drawer and closed it without a word. Then, standing up, he uncocked the gun and placed it back in his inner jacket pocket. Staring at Antonio, he picked up his glass of whisky and downed it, in one, before heading to the door.

'Will you leave her?' Antonio called after him. When Alex didn't answer, he continued. 'If she's out, I need to know. It affects me as much as it does you, after all these years.'

Alex paused, breathing out heavily through his nose. His brother wasn't wrong. Much as he didn't want to answer him, much as he never wanted to speak to his brother again, at this point, his next decision *did* affect them all.

'She's out,' he said curtly, the disappointment of his failed marriage, as he said those words, stinging him deeply.

'And what will you do with her?' Antonio asked.

Alex swallowed, unable to answer that.

Being a part of, or attached to, a firm like theirs came with certain rules. It wasn't an office job that people could just quit. Once you were in, you were in for life. Your loyalty was demanded for life. There was no going back. There were certain circumstances where the rule could be bent a little. Like when they'd agreed to split the firm with Antonio, as they went their separate ways. He was blood born into the firm. And he hadn't betrayed them. They simply hadn't been able to work with him any longer, hadn't been able to get on board with his psychotic behaviour.

But Bianca wasn't blood. She wasn't protected the way he was. And she was an outsider who knew too much. By the unspoken laws of the underworld, after a betrayal like this, she couldn't simply be set free to move on with her life elsewhere. It was far too much of a risk. But how could he kill his own wife and ever look at himself in the mirror again?

'I'll deal with it,' he eventually replied through gritted teeth.

'And what does that *mean?*' Antonio pushed.

'I *said*, I'll *deal with it*,' Alex growled, walking out through the front door and slamming it shut behind him.

THIRTY-EIGHT

Bianca woke with a blinding headache, her eyes jumping to the LED display on the clock beside her. She'd only been out an hour or so. She must have drifted off, waiting for Alex to return home after he'd stormed out.

She tutted. That was *just* like him, waltzing off without letting her know where she stood. And she needed to know that now, more than ever. She needed to see him, face him, so she could work out how to pull herself out of this self-made mess. Should she pull out one of the carefully spun lies she'd crafted? Should she start crying and fall on her knees begging for mercy? Should she press home some guilt over what a terribly neglectful husband he'd been and hope he took pity on her? She had no idea which direction she needed to take, and that made her more anxious than she'd ever been in her life before.

She'd had a good cry earlier. Tears of self-pity and a few of sheer anger at that bitch, Cat, coming in here and ruining everything for her. She'd gnawed her nails and cried and paced, and eventually, as darkness fell, she'd opened a bottle of wine and taken it upstairs, trying to take the edge off her nerves while she waited. She'd known her husband would *have* to appear at some point. She hadn't meant to drop off though. Even if it was only for an hour.

A soft noise drew her attention to the other end of the room, and she quickly sat up, seeing Alex sitting there, watching her. He looked almost as awful as she felt, his shirt loose and his hair dishevelled, and her heart did an anxious flip as she saw the coldness behind his tired eyes.

'A-Alex,' she began, her voice trembling.

'*Don't*,' he told her. 'I've spoken to Antonio. I know everything.'

Her eyes dropped to the open canvas bag on the floor by her feet, and she let out a small sob as she saw the metallic gleam of the plates she'd stolen. Her hand flew to her mouth. If he'd been there, if he'd taken back the plates, Antonio would be furious with her. He'd have outed her secrets just to be vindictive. But how much had he shared? How much did Alex know?

'I – I – I can explain...' she stammered.

'No,' Alex replied. 'You can't.' He ran a hand down his face, the lines on his forehead etched deep as he looked at her. 'There's no coming back from this.'

Fear gripped her, and she began to shake as she contemplated what that meant. 'Please don't do this,' she begged. '*Please*.' She scrambled out of bed, ignoring the stabs at her temples, and dropped to the floor by his feet. 'Please, Alex. I'm sorry. I *know* I've done wrong. I know I've fucked up, and if I could take it back, I *would*.' Her tears coursed down her face. 'And – and I can change. I *know* I can. For us. For *you*. Please. Don't let her split this family any more than she has already.'

'*Cat?*' Alex repeated incredulously. 'Cat's not the problem, Bianca. *You* are.'

'None of this would have happened if she hadn't come along,' Bianca said vehemently, grasping his hand in both of hers. 'Before her, this family was *whole*. Now you've lost your *brother*. Now you're about to cast out your *wife*. *Look* at what she's *doing*, for God's sake.'

Alex shoved her hands off his with a look of disgust, his temper rising with his words. 'It's not Cat who's the problem,' he growled. 'She's simply the tool that's weeded out the poison in this family. Because that's what you *are*, Bianca. You are a *poison*. You have been sucking all the energy from this marriage and this home and my very soul for *years*. And I put up with it because you were my wife,' he hissed. 'I thought it was a phase. I thought you'd turn a corner, that it was all just something you had to work through. But it wasn't, was it? It was just your rotten core seeping out.' He shook his head. 'I never expected you to be perfect. In fact, I've never expected very much from you at *all*. But I *did* think that underneath, you were a decent person. I couldn't have been more wrong though, could I?'

'Alex!' Bianca drew back as though he'd slapped her across the face.

'The stealing and the lies, I could almost understand. You were being blackmailed, and you were just trying to get yourself out of it. But the rest...' He shook his head. 'How many were there, Bianca? How many faceless dicks did you fuck in clubs, while I was out working, or here waiting for you in an empty house, every night?'

What little colour had been left in Bianca's face now drained away. 'I – I don't know what you're talking about,' she said.

'Don't *lie to me!*' Alex roared. 'Do *not – fucking – lie.*'

Bianca scrambled backward as he seemed to expand with rage, as his eyes filled with murder.

'And as if all that wasn't bad enough,' he continued, standing up, fury radiating from him, 'you would have let an innocent woman and a three-year-old child *burn to death* – a way to die, by the way, that's slow and painful and terrifying – purely because you just took a dislike to her. For literally *no* other reason. No,' he corrected, 'not let. You *planned* it. You set the wheels in motion and made sure it was *carried out.*' He was bellowing at her now, and Bianca whimpered, crawling backward as he took a slow, deliberate step towards her. 'I can't even talk about what you did next,' he finished in a low, dangerous tone.

There was a short silence as he glared at her and Bianca tried to find the right words to say. The right lie to spin that could turn this around for her. But she couldn't.

'*Get up,*' he suddenly roared.

Bianca jumped nearly out of her skin and stood up, shaking. 'Alex, p-please,' she begged.

'Shut up,' he demanded. 'I don't want to hear another fucking word from you. You destroyed our marriage years ago, and *still* I held on. *Still* I fought for us. Fought for *you*. Like an *idiot.*'

'No – no, Alex...'

'I said shut up,' he yelled, his face dangerously close to hers now as she backed up against the wall. 'You don't get to speak anymore, Bianca. After all you've done, after all you've destroyed and poisoned and taken, you don't get to speak.'

Bianca swallowed and nodded, barely registering her head hitting the wall. She'd never seen Alex like this. So wild. So furious. He was looking at her like he was barely stopping himself from wrapping his hands around her throat and squeezing the life out of her. Maybe he was.

'You know what the rules are, don't you, Bianca?' Alex continued in a low growl. 'You know how it goes for wives of people like me, who betray their husbands and their firms.'

Bianca's throat suddenly constricted on its own, and she felt the blood drain from her face. 'No,' she whispered. 'You wouldn't. Alex, please. I-I'll do anything you ask. Please don't...'

'Don't what?' he asked. 'Don't kill you? Why not?' His dark eyes went cold, and Bianca's veins filled with ice. 'That's how it goes when a wife betrays someone like me. It's the law of this life. No one will question it. No one would ever find you. *No one* would fucking mourn you. And it's what you deserve.'

'P-Please,' she whimpered, tears streaming down her face now as fear overrode everything else. 'Please.'

There was a long, agonising silence as he stared at her, his eyes full of hatred. Then he suddenly took a half step back.

'I want you out of here,' Alex continued, his voice still deadly. 'I want you out of my house and out of my life – for good.'

Bianca blinked. *What was he saying?*

'I'm not going to kill you, Bianca. Not today at least.' He held her stare, a dark warning in his eyes. 'I've packed a bag for you. It's already outside in your car. You will leave tonight. You will drive to your sister's, and you'll stay there until you've sorted out somewhere else to live. Somewhere *far* from here, for your own good. Somewhere outside of London, where there's little chance of you bumping into anyone. At that point, you can send me your address and I'll send on the rest of your things.' His gaze moved coldly over her face. 'This is it now. We're done. You will not set foot in this house again. Nor my mother's, or anywhere else that belongs to us. And if you're wise, you'll never even come near the neighbourhood again. I'll push our divorce through quickly, and you will agree to whatever terms I put to you. To be clear, that will be half the value of this house. Not a penny more. And you're fucking lucky I'm giving you that after all you've done.' He clamped his jaw for a moment. 'What you do with your life after that point is of no interest to me. But you will change your name, and you will *never* talk about us. You will never talk about me, or this family or your life here. Because if you *do*, all bets are off. And I don't need to warn you what comes next.'

Bianca swallowed. 'You – you're letting me go?'

'I shouldn't,' he replied, holding her gaze. 'Not everyone's going to be happy about me doing it either.' He bit his upper lip. 'But out of respect for what we once had, a very, *very* long time ago, yes,' he replied. 'I'll let you go. Be warned though, Bianca, this is all you get. You talk, you reappear, you come up on a radar *anywhere* and you're gone. Do you understand me? You're already dead to me. So do yourself a favour and stay that way, so I don't have to fix it for real.'

Tears streamed down Bianca's face, and her heart was beating so hard in her chest she was sure it would burst through at any moment. This couldn't be happening. She couldn't be losing her entire life this way. Her access to nigh-on unlimited funds, her lavish home, her status, her notoriety through association with the Capellos. These were all the things that really mattered to her, and now Alex was taking them all away. This was never supposed to have happened.

'Alex...' she whimpered, reaching for him. Reaching for her golden ticket. For the comfortable ride she'd taken for granted one too many times.

'*Now*,' he roared. 'Get out of my house, Bianca, *now*. Before I change my fucking mind.'

Bianca quickly stood up, shaking, and turned, pausing only long enough to grab her phone before she took one last look at her bedroom and fled.

THIRTY-NINE

Maria watched the man who had been at the root of all her problems lately and wondered, idly, what she'd have done if she'd been in his situation. If the person she loved had been killed by someone like her brother. Would she have blackmailed them? Or would she have killed them? She'd probably have killed them. But then, that was the world she lived in. It was an eye for an eye. Survival of the most savage. The laws most people lived by didn't apply in her world. Or on this side of her world at least. And she hadn't become a lawyer, in her more public life, to dedicate herself to the rules of law either. She'd become a lawyer to help protect herself and those around her *from* them. And, of course, to provide herself with a flawless mask.

Danny passed her a flask of something hot, and she unscrewed the top to sniff the contents. Whatever it was, it was definitely Irish. She shook her head and handed it back.

'I'll pass,' she said. 'Need to keep a clear head.'

'You warm enough?' he asked.

She was actually bitterly cold, but she wasn't about to admit that weakness in front of her men, or the man who was currently barely visible at the bottom of a large hole in the ground, digging away at the bottom.

'I'm fine,' she replied, crossing her arms over her middle and tucking her hands underneath her armpits.

They were in the middle of a dense piece of woodland, a couple of hours outside of London, and the dark would have been all-consuming were it not a cloudless night with a full moon. She was sure she had to thank someone for that luck tonight, but considering what they were using it for, she was pretty certain it wasn't God.

Steven had pushed back at first when they'd told him to pick up the shovel and start digging, but after Danny told him in no uncertain terms what would happen if he didn't shut up and put up, he shakily picked it up and started doing as he was told. Maria's men all had their own shovels and had broken ground with him, all chipping in for the first few feet, but then they'd sat back in the semi-circle of camping chairs and left him to it. Maria now sat on the end in her own camping chair, half wishing she'd picked up a shovel herself. At least she'd be warmer. This was taking forever.

Standing up, she pushed her hands deep into her pockets and walked forward to the edge of the hole, sizing up the depth. Steven was around six foot, she gauged, and his head was now definitely below ground level.

'Stop digging and put the shovel down,' she ordered.

He looked up at her fearfully, all his earlier bravado gone. 'Please,' he whimpered. 'I get it. You could bury me if you wanted to. Please just – just let *this* be the lesson. I'll drop it. I swear. Just please don't kill you here tonight. I – I wasn't bluffing earlier,' he added, wetting his lips. 'There is a failsafe. This – this isn't a wise move for you.'

'I told you earlier, Steven,' Maria answered levelly, 'we aren't going to kill you. We just want to make sure that the photos you kept are returned to us, with *no* copies hidden away anywhere that could ever get out again.'

Steven nodded quickly. 'Yes. Yes, of course. Anything. You're right, this was stupid of me. Reckless and just very, very stupid. You have my word.'

Maria smiled, the action not warming her eyes. 'I'm afraid your word isn't enough. We need something a little more concrete than that.'

She turned and gave Danny the nod. He and the others stood up and walked over to the car, popping the boot. They'd stopped on the way over, blindfolding Steven and ignoring his questions as they picked up their cargo. Now her men carried it to a spot about three feet from the edge of the pit, using the old dustsheet they'd found in the back of Steven's car.

'Get out of the hole now, Steven,' Maria ordered.

He scrambled out, all too happy to be out of the hole he'd previously thought was to be his grave. But as he saw what awaited him above, he baulked and bent over double, immediately throwing up all over the ground.

Maria lifted an eyebrow and took a pointed step back. 'Do you recognise your friend, Steven?' she asked calmly, watching his face.

'Wh-What are you...' He retched again and turned away.

'Answer the question,' Maria demanded.

'Y-Y— We weren't friends,' Steven stammered breathlessly. 'But yes. I recognise him.'

Maria stared at Malcolm's grey, puffy face with detachment. He hadn't decomposed really at all. They'd been careful to keep him at a steady four degrees since he'd died. It was a little trick her father had once taught her. It slowed down deterioration of the body to almost zero for up to three months and would throw off the date of death in an autopsy later on. Ideal for situations where one needed to arrange a good alibi. If a body had been fully frozen, that was easily detected, but this exact temperature would keep a body suspended in whatever state it had been first chilled in for a while. This meant that Malcolm currently looked no more than a few hours gone. He definitely looked dead, but rigor mortis hadn't fully set in, and there was some definite fluid leakage, which was what Maria had been counting on when she'd come up with this idea.

'Push him into the hole,' Maria instructed.

Steven's eyes widened. 'Wh-*What?*' he asked, aghast.

'I said, push him into the hole,' Maria repeated.

There was a long silence as Steven floundered, his gaze darting from Malcolm's body to her, to her men and back again. Eventually, realising he didn't have much choice, he stumbled over to Malcolm's body. His bottom lip wobbled, and his body shook as he bent down and reached out. But then he sagged back, putting his head in his hands.

'I *can't,*' he cried.

Maria's expression hardened, and she stepped towards him. 'Push him in right now, or you take his place. And then once you've taken his place, he'll go in right on top of you.'

Steven began to cry, his entire body now shaking violently.

'The choice is yours, but you have about five seconds to decide.'

He didn't move, and she clicked her tongue. '*Five,*' she said pointedly.

'OK, OK!' He scrabbled forward and gingerly placed his hands on Malcolm's body, letting out a sound between a groan and a retch as he began to push him towards the edge.

'You might be better off rolling him, mate,' Danny offered. 'Less resistance.'

Steven attempted to do that but instantly dropped Malcolm back when he saw the wet stains seeping through at the back. Crying loudly now, he continued pushing, inch by inch, until he reached the side of the hole. Then, with one final shove, he sent Malcolm's body over the edge.

'Well done,' Maria said, no emotion in her voice. 'Now, come with me. You've done enough for tonight. You can sit in the car while the others fix the rest.'

Steven stood up and walked towards the car in a daze, Maria following behind him. Danny walked beside her as her other men picked up shovels and began to fill in the hole.

'Now, Steven.' Maria clicked her fingers to get his attention. 'We're going to go and get your copies of those photos after this, and then you're going to go home, get washed up and get on with your life,' she told him. 'You'll never mention this night, or us, to anyone else ever again. And we'll never bother you ever again. Everyone can go off and live happily ever after.'

'Except Malcolm,' Danny added.

'Except Malcolm,' Maria agreed. 'And if you ever get questioned about his disappearance, you'll need to forget all about what happened here tonight. Voluntary amnesia, let's call it. Because if you *don't*, and you decide to help point them in this direction, do you know what they'll find?' She paused. 'They'll find that.' She pointed at the grave. 'But they'll also find your DNA on Malcolm's body. They'll find it in the ground, on the shovel we're conveniently leaving in there. And then, when they seize and search your car, no matter how well you've scrubbed and bleached it, they'll find traces of Malcolm's bodily fluids in the boot. Then they'll start digging a bit deeper and find the professional connection between you. Do you see where I'm going here?'

Steven turned his gaze on her, misery mixing with bitter resentment in his face. 'Yeah, I think I got it.'

'Good.' Maria smiled. 'Then you'll also, I'm sure, have figured out that should I find out you're hiding a copy from me, or I hear you've been looking into us again, I'll happily point the police to this place myself. Have I made that part clear enough?'

'Crystal,' he muttered.

'Good.' She nodded. 'Good. Then I think we're just about done.'

Steven opened the back passenger door and slumped down in the seat, defeated, and Maria turned to walk back to the camping chairs. Danny fell in beside her, glancing back at the car over his shoulder.

'So, you're sure this is enough?' he asked. 'We're in the clear?'

Maria smiled, the first smile that had been genuine all night. 'We're in the clear, Danny. After tonight, there will be *no* more copies of us blowing up that pub popping up anywhere. All copies will have been destroyed, and it will be like it never happened. For now, at least, we're finally safe.'

FORTY

Antonio drove slowly through the streets around the run-down sink estate where he knew Bianca must be lying low. He'd had confirmation that Alex had, indeed, given her the boot and knew that her sister's flat was the only place she had left to go. Not that he'd really needed the confirmation of course. What else *could* Alex do, faced with all the information Antonio had given him, the night before? He'd had to admit, it had given him a very satisfying thrill, delivering all that devastating news. At one point, he'd thought Alex might even cry. But ever the square brick of control, he hadn't, much to Antonio's disappointment. It would have been the icing on the cake. But even without that, it had felt good. A bit of payback for all his brother had done to him, including the newly swollen face that would take weeks to heal. This had annoyed Antonio a lot more than he'd let on.

Now, though, there were more pressing matters to deal with. Like cleaning up the mess Alex had created with Bianca. Because from what he'd heard, Alex *hadn't* dealt with it. Alex had simply let her go. And that wouldn't do at all. This wasn't a simple case of divorce and move on. Bianca knew *everything* about them. She might not have worked in the firm, but she knew all their businesses, knew how much they brought in, half the places they hid and laundered their money. Because those were all things it was OK for a wife to know in their business. But a disgruntled *ex-wife* was an entirely different story. Her loyalty was no longer guaranteed. In fact, it was more likely to have turned a full one-eighty.

The truth was, in this business, partners weren't allowed to just come and go. In the early stages, sure. In the early stages, people like them still protected themselves and hid what they were doing from their other halves. But after years of marriage, of living and breathing this life, day in and day out, there was no exit option. Like the rest of them, beyond a certain point, the only way out was death. And that's why he was here tonight, scouring the streets like some young hoodlum looking for trouble. Because he needed to find *her*. He needed to do what Alex wasn't man enough to do.

He'd been rolling around for over an hour when Ben, one of his men who now sat in the passenger seat, let out a low whistle and pointed down the road. Sure enough, it was Bianca, coming out of the corner shop with something in her hands. She stood under the streetlight and fiddled with something. As he slowly drove closer, he saw it was a pack of cigarettes. She'd pulled one out and was now trying to light it. She didn't see him as he drew close, only looking up when he pulled up beside her and put the window down.

'Bad for your health, those,' he said, nodding to the packet.

Bianca blinked, startled. 'Antonio,' she muttered with surprise. She glanced back down the deserted street, moving uneasily from one foot to the other. 'What you doing here?'

The corner of his mouth hitched in a crooked half-smile that didn't reach his cold eyes. 'Get in the car, Bianca,' he said quietly, scratching his cheek.

She swallowed and glanced down the road again, as if

hoping someone else might appear. 'Why? Where we going?' she asked, her tone unnaturally bright.

Antonio stared at her, holding her gaze for a few seconds before answering. 'Get in the car,' he repeated quietly.

Bianca stared back at him, her eyes serious and wide, and she gave a very faint nod. For a moment, he thought this meant she was going to do as she was told, but then suddenly she turned and ran as fast as she could down the road behind him.

'Fuck's *sake*,' he muttered.

He swung the car around and followed her, surprised by how far she'd got already. Putting his foot on the accelerator, he sped up, covering the distance quickly. But as he pulled onto the kerb in front of her, attempting to block her way through, she darted down a side alley.

Antonio jumped out of the car, leaving it where it was, Ben hot on his heels as he raced after her. She disappeared at the other end, just as he entered the alley, and he bore down, putting as much power as he could into his legs. He *had* to get to her, and it *had* to be now. Now she knew he was after her, she'd hide. This could be his only chance.

He reached the end of the alley and turned into the internal square beyond, all four sides of it edged by tall tower blocks of flats. He ran forward and jerked to a halt, twisting his head one way and then the other as he searched for a sign of her. His face contorted, but he quickly hid his annoyance. She was here somewhere. She was hiding. She couldn't have got far, and if she was still running, he'd be able to hear the pound of her footsteps on the concrete. He held a hand out to Ben to indicate that he should stop too as he finally caught up, then pointed towards the other end of the square. Ben nodded and jogged silently away to search that end.

Turning round in a slow circle, Antonio narrowed his eyes. 'I know you're here, Bianca,' he said in a loud voice. 'I just want to talk.' His gaze flicked over the many alleys and doorways and stairwells leading to the balcony walkways of the other floors, one by one. 'I don't know why you ran. It's *me*, for God's sake. We're *family*.' He took a step nearer to one of the stairwells. It was where he'd hide, if it was him on the run with no time to choose somewhere better. 'I want to help you. I feel bad about telling Alex. For what it cost you. I just want to put things right.'

A noise caught his attention somewhere to his left. It sounded like an empty can falling over. Or being *kicked* over. Antonio narrowed his eyes and began to move in that direction.

* * *

Bianca covered her mouth as she almost let out a cry. How could she have been so *stupid*? She cringed as the can toppled down the step it had been standing on and rolled to a stop in the gutter. There was no way Antonio hadn't heard that.

'I know you don't want to be here,' Antonio called. 'Why don't you come back and stay at mine for a bit? I have a spare room.'

His voice was so much closer now, and Bianca could feel hot tears stinging her eyes. She knew why he was here. And she knew it was definitely *not* to help her. Unlike Alex, Antonio wouldn't hesitate to take her out of the equation. Because unlike Alex, Antonio had no real feelings. He had no soul. He was nothing but a cold, hard predator.

Pulling some courage from somewhere deep within, she eased herself up off the step, making sure to stay low behind the wall. She had to move. She had to get out of here before Antonio got hold of her. Because she knew, without a doubt, that if he managed to get his hands on her, in any way, she would not make it through to morning alive.

'Come on, Bianca,' he crooned.

Bianca's breath caught in her throat. He was practically behind the wall now. She began to shake. He would be here any second. She had to move. But to move, she had to run out into the open. If she ran up the stairs, she was dead. There was no way out up there. Which meant she had two options. Left or right. If she picked the correct side and ran at exactly the right time, she *might* just get out of here and across this courtyard without him seeing her. The wall around her was like three sides of a square, so there was enough to block his view if she could manage it. But if she chose the wrong side... No. She couldn't think about that. Not now. Not when her life was down to this one final last chance.

Earlier today, she'd been ready to give up hope. What was the point anymore, now that she had nothing? No money, no status, no easy ride. But suddenly she wanted to live. She desperately, wholeheartedly wanted to survive this. She *wouldn't* just roll over and die. Not without a fight.

Antonio's footsteps stopped behind the wall. 'Are you behind there, Bianca?'

She waited just one more painfully hard heartbeat and then, with her heart rising into her throat, and without daring to let herself think it through any further, Bianca picked a side and she ran.

EPILOGUE

The first few days after everything came out were tough on everyone. On the outside, Alex looked as steadfast as ever, as though he was taking it all on the chin. But those who really knew him knew it had crushed him, finding out all the ways his wife had betrayed him. Finding out all the ways she'd betrayed and hurt them *all*.

Cat had been thoroughly shocked and a little shaken after finding out that she'd been around the woman who'd orchestrated the fire and her daughter's kidnapping all this time without knowing. It had made her feel sick, realising she'd let Orla sit across the table from her at Sunday lunches and had gone for drinks with the woman, laughing over cocktails. Cat was angry, too, at how badly Bianca had treated Alex. Because he really was a good man. A *truly* good man. And she knew, better than most, how rare those were these days. Her own confusing feelings aside, he'd deserved so much better from his wife. He deserved so much better in general.

Maria was absolutely livid and, for once, was unable to contain it in her usual controlled manner. She was more furious than any of them had ever seen her. Frothing away like she'd been boiling quietly for some time and the lid had finally been thrown off, gas up to the max. She'd stormed over to Bianca's sister's in a red-hot rage, demanding to see Bianca, wanting to look her in the eye as she gave her what for. But Bianca hadn't been there. Her sister had worriedly explained that she'd only been there for one night and then had disappeared the very next evening, after nipping out to the corner shop for some cigarettes. Maria had threatened to come back every day until she found her, but although she did just that, Bianca didn't appear. She seemed to have vanished off the face of the earth.

The only person who seemed able to find a silver lining in the situation – furious as she was herself – was Sophia. She ranted and raved about all the things she'd do to Bianca if she ever got her hands on the girl, after what she'd done to her son, but then every now and then she'd smile and point out that it was a *good* thing all this had come out now. Because now he was free and had a chance to find a *decent* wife. A good girl who would treat him well and that Sophia could approve of. It didn't matter how many times Alex told her that he couldn't even contemplate that right now, she wasn't deterred in the slightest.

They finally put the plates back in the printing presses and, after some adjustment and test runs, had managed to get the operation up and running again, much to everyone's relief, Cat's especially.

She stared at the machine as it printed off a new sheet and then turned to Alex with a sheepish smile. 'I still feel awful for falling for that bloody toilet trick,' she admitted.

'Don't,' he told her, shaking his head. 'She's always been a master manipulator. If you hadn't been taken then, she'd have moved on to the next attempt. And the next, and the next, until she had what she wanted. It's what she's always done, in one way or another. Scammed and schemed her way through life.'

Cat looked up at him, noting the way his eyes turned down to the ground as he spoke of his soon-to-be-ex-wife. 'It's hard to lose someone you love,' she said quietly as they walked back out into the hallway.

He looked up at her, meeting her gaze. 'I didn't love Bianca,' he said tiredly. 'I mean, I did once. But that died a long time ago. I've actually *hated* her for a long time. And I felt *so guilty* for that. Because what kind of man hates his wife? The woman he's promised to love and care for forever?'

'Lots of men,' Cat said gently.

'Not good ones,' he replied. 'I felt like it was *me*. That *I* was causing us to not be so close anymore because maybe that hatred was coming through somehow. That I wasn't doing enough to hide it or change it.' He ran a hand back through his hair. 'But realising it wasn't that – realising she was out...' He trailed off and clamped his jaw. 'And then finding out she was that *evil*, that she could do what she did, I finally realised it was her. That it was out of my control. And that *should* free me, but I just feel so angry that I wasted all that time and effort. I feel like an idiot for not seeing it sooner.' He bit his bottom lip and looked away.

'I actually understand that completely,' Cat told him. 'When I found out about Greg's mistress – his *first* mistress – I felt like my whole life was just one big sham. And that I was the ignorant clown in the centre of it. My life being mocked and belittled by everyone around me.' She pushed her hair behind her ear, thinking back to how dark everything had felt during that time. 'I didn't love Greg either, at that point. But I didn't think I could ever shake off the damage he'd left behind. I did though,' she added with a small smile. 'It takes a bit of time, but you'll see. It'll fade. Like some horrible, big shitty bruise that eventually goes away.'

Alex grinned. 'I like that analogy. From now on, that's exactly how I'll think of her. As one big shitty bruise.'

'Who's one big shitty bruise?' Maria's voice came from behind as she entered the room. 'Bianca?'

'Actually, yes,' Cat replied with a laugh. 'How did you guess?'

'Well, you don't need Poirot for that one, darling,' Maria joked back. She looked at the freshly printed sheet as Alex picked it up to inspect, and smiled. 'All back to normal?'

'All back to normal,' he confirmed. 'No damage done, and with overtime this weekend, we should get back on track with the orders by next week.'

'Good.' Maria laced her arm through Cat's and turned towards the exit. 'In that case, I'm taking you both to a celebratory lunch.'

'Absolutely not,' Alex replied. '*I'll* take *you two*. It's my treat.' He smiled a light, genuine smile as he guided them both forward. 'And I won't take no for an answer.'

* * *

Halfway across London, Bianca stood in a shadowed doorway, staring at the building across the street with wide, haunted eyes. She was dishevelled and dirty, still wearing the same clothes she'd had on when she'd run from Antonio, several days before. By sheer luck, or a miracle, she wasn't sure which, she'd managed to time her run perfectly and had picked the right side. By the time he'd rounded the wall to where she'd been hiding, she'd already vanished. Or at least, she assumed that was how it went. He hadn't come after her.

She hadn't dared go back to her sister's or attempt to contact anyone who had any connection to the Capellos. And so she'd found herself alone. Alone and completely screwed. Her one saving grace was that she'd still had her purse on her, though she must have dropped her phone at some point. She'd had enough cash on her for a bed in a hostel the first two nights and some food to keep her going. She could have managed a third night there too, but a couple of the other guests had begun watching her, asking too many questions, so she'd left. It hadn't been worth the risk. If Antonio or one of his scouts found her, and she knew he *would* have them out looking, then she was as good as dead.

Now, though, she was out of money, out of friends and out of options. At least, all options except one. It was something she'd sworn she would never do. It was something that, if she did do it, was worse than all the other things she'd ever done combined. It was something she knew she could never come back from. But it was either this or give up on life altogether. And she wasn't ready to die today.

Pulling in a deep shuddering breath, Bianca braced herself and crossed the road, climbing the few steps to the front door and pushing it open with shaking fingers. Around her, she could hear the sounds of a buzzing office. Phones ringing, people talking somewhere behind closed doors. Almost in a trance, she walked up to the front desk and cleared her throat.

'Hiya, how can I help?' asked the young woman behind the desk.

Bianca wetted her lips. 'I need to speak to someone about giving evidence on the Capello crime family, in exchange for police protection. I'm Bianca Capello. Alex Capello's wife. And I'm ready to talk.'

A LETTER FROM EMMA TALLON

Hi everyone,

Thanks so much for reading this second instalment in the Capello crime family series. I had a lot of fun writing this one! As far as villains of the stories go, Bianca was a fantastically colourful one to write. I hope you enjoyed reading this story as much as I enjoyed writing it. If you'd like to sign up to hear about the next book in this series, please join my email list . Your details won't be shared, and you can unsubscribe at any time.

www.bookouture.com/emma-tallon

And if you'd like to follow me on socials, to keep up to date with all my book news and events, my links are on the next page.

If you enjoyed this book and could spare a couple of moments to leave a review on Amazon, it would be hugely appreciated. Reviews help authors like me more than you know, and after spending so many months writing and editing these books, it means a lot reading all your lovely comments. I love finding out your favourite parts and characters, and discovering what you're looking forward to finding out in the next one.

I hope you'll join me again on the next journey in the Capello family series. But for now, stay safe, stay happy and I wish you all the best!

With love,

Emma

        instagram.com/my.author.life
        facebook.com/EmmaTallonOffocial
        tiktok.com/@emmatallonauthor
        x.com/EmmaEsj

ACKNOWLEDGEMENTS

Firstly, I'd like to thank you, reader. Thank you for picking up my book and joining me on this journey – whether you've bought it or borrowed it from the library. Whether you're reading on Kindle or paperback, or listening on audio. Without you, I wouldn't be able to do something I love so much for a living, and I am eternally grateful to you for that.

Secondly, I want to thank my fantastic editor and friend, Helen Jenner. This is now the eighteenth book we've done together, and I feel so lucky to have the wonderful working partnership that we do. As we both know, these books wouldn't be what they are without you. We're two halves of a team, and I'm very grateful to have you in my life.

Lastly, I want to give a big shout-out to all the wonderful friends around me who've had my back when I've been juggling all sorts of crazy things. Who have spurred me on with their kindness, love, motivating words and unwavering belief in me. You know who you are, and I treasure you. Now and always.

PUBLISHING TEAM

Turning a manuscript into a book requires the efforts of many people. The publishing team at Bookouture would like to acknowledge everyone who contributed to this publication.

Commercial
Lauren Morrissette
Hannah Richmond
Imogen Allport

Cover design
The Brewster Project

Data and analysis
Mark Alder
Mohamed Bussuri

Editorial
Helen Jenner
Ria Clare

Copyeditor
Jon Appleton

Proofreader
Laura Kincaid

Marketing
Alex Crow
Melanie Price
Occy Carr
Cíara Rosney
Martyna Młynarska

Operations and distribution
Marina Valles
Joe Morris

Production
Hannah Snetsinger
Mandy Kullar
Nadia Michael
Charlotte Hegley

Publicity
Kim Nash
Noelle Holten
Jess Readett
Sarah Hardy

Rights and contracts
Peta Nightingale
Richard King
Saidah Graham

RAISING READERS
Books Build Bright Futures

Dear Reader,

We'd love your attention for one more page to tell you about the crisis in children's reading, and what we can all do.

Studies have shown that reading for fun is the **single biggest predictor of a child's future life chances** – more than family circumstance, parents' educational background or income. It improves academic results, mental health, wealth, communication skills, ambition and happiness.

The number of children reading for fun is in rapid decline. Young people have a lot of competition for their time, and a worryingly high number do not have a single book at home.

Hachette works extensively with schools, libraries and literacy charities, but here are some ways we can all raise more readers:

- Reading to children for just 10 minutes a day makes a difference
- Don't give up if children aren't regular readers – there will be books for them!

- Visit bookshops and libraries to get recommendations
- Encourage them to listen to audiobooks
- Support school libraries
- Give books as gifts

There's a lot more information about how to encourage children to read on our websites: **www.RaisingReaders.co.uk** and **www.JoinRaisingReaders.com**.

Thank you for reading.

www.ingramcontent.com/pod-product-compliance
Lightning Source LLC
LaVergne TN
LVHW041625060526
838200LV00040B/1440